WELCOME TO THE WORLD OF

Shallow Cove™

DARK DIMENSIONS

HUSH
THE MONSTER STALKER SERIES BOOK 3
JANUARY RAYNE

ALSO BY
January Rayne

Shallow Cove™ Dimensions
The Eternally Series:
Book 1: Eternally Hers
Book 2: Eternally Damned
Book 3: Carnival of Creeps
Book 4: Eternally Cursed
Book 5: Eternally Rare
Book 6: Eternally Lost

Shallow Cove™ Dark Dimensions
The Monster Stalker Series:
Book 1: Honeysuckles
Book 2: Snapdragons
Book 3: Hollyhocks

AUTHOR'S NOTE

PLEASE READ THIS BEFORE ENTERING THIS WEIRD BOOK

Heads up: Everything in this book is fiction. If you find it hard to believe that any of this would happen in real life, you're right. *Nothing about this story is believable.* My imagination went wild.

Content Warnings: This book contains abuse (when mmc was 18), stalking, dark themes, non-consent, S/A, somnophilia, forced breeding, pregnancy, and murder. Please refrain from reading if you are affected by these subjects. Mental health matters. You matter.

DEDICATION

Fuck him wild. Make his knees weak. Have him beg for more.

Mark your territory.

PROLOGUE

HOLLY

Before Creed (In Honeysuckles, Book One) was able to break everyone free

I'm dying.

I never thought those words would play through my mind so soon. I'm so young. I have so much life left to live, but I won't get to see it. The only thing I have right now is my imagination. I'm dreaming of the future I'll never have as I'm strapped to a cold table, my skin burning as if kerosene is being pumped through my veins.

"I had high hopes for you."

One of the doctors who kidnapped me from outside of the dance studio I own sits down on the edge of the tables. From here, I can see his glasses need cleaning. Smudges are all over the frames from his greasy fingers.

I told myself I would never give these doctors the satisfaction of seeing me cry or beg. They want my tears to add to their little data collection, and I refuse to let them have it.

"You are magnificent. Such a beautiful creature you've turned into." His fingers trace the horns protruding from my forehead. "These were created by the succubus DNA. Extraordinary."

A new feature I didn't have when I was human.

When I was human.

I never thought I'd hear those words from myself either.

"God, look at you." Glasses, as I call him, grips the horns with both hands, stroking them with fascination.

I can't reply. The group of doctors has covered my mouth with a disgusting leather strap, and by the taste of it, I'm not the only one they have used it on. They learned that because of the DNA splicing the doctors have done on me, my voice puts them in a trance and weakens them to my will.

I wish I had known that trick sooner.

Maybe then I wouldn't be on my deathbed. Maybe then, I'd be able to fight for myself.

I can smell his desire as he traces the ridges of my horns. The putrid scent lands on my over-sensitized tongue, and I can taste the bitterness of his greed.

"You're so stunning. It's a shame, really." He takes off the round frames he wears perched at the end of his nose, wipes the lenses with his shirt, then puts them back on. He smiles when he can see me again, showing me his cigarette-stained teeth.

I mumble behind the leather strap, "Fuck you" but it's barely audible.

"What a naughty mouth." With a sigh, he backhands me across the cheek. The slap echoes in the small enclosure of the room. "You need to remember who has the power here and it certainly is not you."

I don't whimper. I don't scream in pain as my cheek burns from the harsh force. Blood fills my mouth. Iron floods my taste buds. Anger slips down my throat as the hatred for my enemy fills me.

My eyes swim with tears, but I refuse to let one fall unless it's over his dead body. By then, they would be tears of happiness.

He looms over me, his nose nearly touching mine, and his hand wraps around my throat. "It's a good thing I can't remove the strap from your mouth or it's a hole I'd be desperate to fill."

His finger slides down my chest and the touch hurts, igniting the nerves that are already on fire to a scorching, uncomfortable blaze that brings searing pain. I bite the inside of my cheeks, refusing to make one singular noise that sounds like pain.

"You probably have another few hours before your heart gives out," he whispers, trailing his fingers under the curve of my breasts before gliding down my stomach. "You would have been a beautiful specimen, but your body is fighting the DNA too hard. You're rejecting all the gifts we are giving you. Why are you doing that? Why are you not accepting all the strengths, all the wonders, and all the power?"

"I don't care about power." The words are, once again, muffled by the strap. My wrists are bound. Each ankle is confined to the table. I have no chance to move or protect myself from this monster.

They might have turned me into a creature I don't recognize, but the real monsters here are the men who kidnapped me outside of my own business. The only thing I remember about my previous life was how I was a pole dancing instructor during the day and a bartender at night.

I loved seeing women build confidence in themselves and their bodies. I loved when my clients would come up to me with tears in their eyes saying how I saved their marriages. It wasn't because of pole dancing, and I'm sure that helped, but the confidence ignited a spark inside them again. A spark that had disappeared. I think a lot of people need to remember that. A spark might fizzle out, but it can always be reignited with a little effort.

The bartending was for a whole other reason. I loved being behind the bar, flirting, and eating up the desire men always gave me. Pouring drinks was an excellent way to make some extra cash. Who doesn't love to receive attention? If someone says they don't, I'd call them a liar. It always feels good to be appreciated in the right way and circumstances.

Don't get me wrong, I hated being cornered to give attention to a man. I'd give my energy and desire to who I fucking wanted, when I fucking wanted, and if any man had an issue with it, I had a baseball bat and a Glock behind the bar I wasn't afraid to use.

I miss that woman. The woman who would take no shit, stood up for herself, and wouldn't allow herself to be in a situation like this. Now, I miss the spark I seemed to ignite in others.

I feel absolutely nothing inside. My spark is gone. My will to live has died.

The abuse, the torture, and the pain, I can't handle any more of it. I wish my heart would stop beating. All I want is peace. I can't do this anymore. My bones are tired. They are beyond aching.

They have been broken more times than I can count. I've

been assaulted, used, pricked, and prodded. I've had my legs spread more than I have in my entire life. For pleasure, for pain, for curiosity to see what I look like between my thighs, and I'll never be able to scrub the doctors' heated looks from my mind.

I don't understand why they just won't kill me now. Instead, the fascination in the doctor's eyes as I die will be the last thing I ever see.

Glasses shakes his finger at me with a snort-like chuckle. "You say you don't like power—" he curls over me, hands on either side of my head as he grips the table, "—but I don't believe you. Everyone loves power, Holly. Everyone craves to be at the top." He wraps a strand of my hair around his finger and then brings it to his nose. The wretched man inhales until his eyes roll to the back of his head. "You smell so good. I've always loved your naturally sweet scent. Do you like your blue hair? Another wonderful addition that enhances your beauty. We haven't figured out if it's the chameleon or siren DNA, regardless, it is such a shame the world won't be able to experience you."

I lift from the table, fighting against the restraints, cursing him behind my silencer.

"Shh. Shh. I know. It isn't easy." He skims his knuckles down my cheek. "You won't die alone. I'll be here." The evil doctor stands, walking over to the sterile stainless-steel counter.

Picking up my file, Glasses opens it and clicks his pen, his beady eyes skimming the information of what they have done to me.

"I think you deserve to know who you are before you die, don't you? As you know, you are part succubus, meaning you can invade dreams and feed off sexual desire. You must feel mine for you." Glasses bites his lips, his eyes roaming down my very naked, very vulnerable body. "The things I would do to you. Maybe I will before you die so I know what those tentacles in that tight cunt are like."

"Fucking try it!" I don't know why I bother saying anything when the words can't be understood.

Licking his finger, Glasses flips the page. "It is also why you have light purple skin, but it also changes with your surroundings–thank the chameleon DNA. I would show you, but that would mean unstrapping you from the table, and we can't have that. This table is what stops you from using your abilities." My captor steps forward, squatting, caressing my feathers. "These gorgeous wings are from your harpy DNA. Did you know harpies are considered guardians of the underworld and some are even known to have the ability to predict the future? I'd be so curious if you had that gift, but you don't have enough time for that."

Glasses skims his fingers down my arm, caressing my ribcage. My stomach trembles with fear and disgust. The soft pad of his finger has bile daring to spew from my mouth as it trails down my thigh.

"Your scales come from the siren DNA. And these fins?" The man I hate more than anything in this world grabs a spray bottle and sprays water on my fins, so they don't dehydrate. "Also the siren, which is also where your voice comes from, but you know that already, don't you? You know, Franklin, your guard, still isn't right in the head after you used your voice on him last week? He's still mumbling in our hospital room about how much he needs you."

Good.

Shows him what happens when he touches someone without permission.

"Clever girl, aren't you? You don't even know how to control your powers, and yet, you figured out how to use them. It's magnificent. As if it is almost natural to you. Shame you aren't strong enough to handle what we give you."

The grotesque fingers drift to the inside of my leg, migrating up to my knee, then my thigh.

"Your tentacles are from the squid DNA. Remember when we forced you to orgasm, and you squirted black ink? Staining the sheets?" His desire is rancid as it fills the air, turning my stomach as if I'm scenting rotten milk. "So fucking beautiful. Perhaps, the next test subject will handle the same DNA injections, but nothing will take the place of Patient 013025." His thumb skims the lips of my pussy. "You."

He dips his hands below and my tentacles stretch from my hole, snake around his arm, suction to his wrist, and squeeze.

"Ah, fuck!" His scream of agony brings me more pleasure than I have felt in a long time.

"Fuck. You." I yell behind the strap, narrowing my eyes as I tighten the hold on him.

Sweat builds above his brows as he tries to yank himself from my grasp, but the tentacles add more pressure to his bones. I want him to feel what I have been feeling all these months, lying here, strapped and defenseless while they do whatever they fucking want to me.

I'm dying anyway. I need to make this worth it.

I give every ounce of strength I have left inside my will and snap his wrist. The sweet sound of his bone breaking is a song I could listen to on repeat. He cries in terror, but no one can hear him because this room is soundproof due to my entrancing voice.

They didn't want to take any chances.

I inhale a deep breath, exhausted from all the energy I've used, and struggle to catch my breath. With every wheeze, I can hear the fluid pop and crackle in my throat.

"You fucking bitch!" he screams, lifting his hand in the air. The bone is protruding out of the skin, and I can't hold my smile back. Even behind the leather strap, I know my joy can be seen.

It's the singular moment of happiness I've had since I've been here.

Blood drips down his forearm and the sharp point of his bone is the most beautiful part of him I have ever seen.

He stumbles backward and smacks against a tray of surgical tools that falls to the floor with loud clinks. Glasses bends down, holding his hand to his chest, and snags a scalpel.

"I'm glad you're dying. You're weak, pathetic, and a useless specimen. It's your fault for what happens to the next test subject. Remember that as you die."

I stare at him, inhaling as deeply as possible, but breathing is becoming too hard. I gasp again.

And again.

My vision blurs. My breathing begins to slow. I sink into the table as my body becomes weightless.

I know this feeling. I think... I think it may be peace.

Once the scalpel touches my skin so he can slice me from ear to ear to end my misery, I end myself.

I focus on the ceiling. The fluorescent lights no longer bother me as my sight becomes darker. Water stains pool in the corner of the tiled ceiling. Dust sticks to the lightbulbs. Every small detail becomes stark in the midst of death.

My life doesn't flash before my eyes as I can't remember the majority of it, but I do think of dancing, and the happiness it brought me fills my chest for one last time as my lungs exhale their very last breath.

"That's it. Die. Stop wasting my space so I can have room for real subjects," he whispers into my ear.

Even though they are the last words I hear, I can't help but smile with relief knowing my journey here is over. There's no more pain. My skin doesn't burn. I own myself again in death. My body is mine once more.

I'm free.

The ghost of me stands away, staring down at my limp body. It's the first time I've gotten to see myself.

The horns are bigger than what I thought. They are black and the very tips curl over my skull. I have a tail that is thin with a pointed tip that is wrapped around my leg. My hair is long and blue, which I don't mind at all. I like it.

I look down at my hands, flipping them over to analyze the purple skin. I'm a little in awe. I'm torn between liking what I see and what I could have been, and hating what they have made me become. Even my memory is altered. Who I used to be died the moment they kidnapped me.

I've lost myself. I don't know who I am anymore.

"Don't like what you see?"

I gasp and jump back, seeing a skeletal figure standing next to me. I take another step back to get as far away from him as possible. I just want to be left alone. Can't a woman die in peace?

"I'm not here to hurt you. I'm here to take you to your

next destination. Your soul doesn't belong here anymore."

I'm skeptical but any place has to be better than here. "Who are you?"

"Trovian. Also known as one of Death's Voids. I'm new. Recently promoted to soul reaping." He puffs out his chest with pride, and I lift a brow.

"Excuse me? What? I don't know what that means."

"I'll explain along the way. Unless you want to wait and see what they do with your body."

"I'd rather not know." I swallow, taking one last glance at my body as Glasses loosens the straps.

Trovian cuts off a piece of his shadow and wraps it around my shoulders to cover me. He holds out his hand, the bones long and slender while his palm is wide.

"Let's go home."

My eyes burn with the emotion I've been holding back for months. Am I finally able to mourn what has happened to me?

"Your life here is over, Holly. Take my hand and you'll never see these people again."

A tear finally falls, the warmth rolling down my cheek to remind me that my pain is justified. I take one last look at Glasses throwing my body over his shoulder to dump it somewhere, and as I stare longer at my physical form, I happen to like what I see.

Wherever I am going, I can learn more about myself there. I'll accept myself in time.

I slip my hand in Trovian's and his bones curl around my fingers. To my shock, it isn't uncomfortable, and it doesn't hurt.

He stares down at me with his black, empty eyes, and

smiles before snapping his fingers.

Instantly, I'm in another place I don't know. It's darker than usual. The sky is black with hints of red. The trees are dead, but right in front of me is a place called Purgatory Pins.

"Where are we?" I ask Trovian, not understanding my surroundings at all. A jolt of fear coils inside me, slithering like a snake.

I shiver, whipping my head left and right to see what else is around me. I'm doing my best not to panic. So much has happened in the last ten minutes, I'm still processing my own death. Now, I need to process this place.

"Purgatory," he explains casually. "It's where paranormals go when they die. Some go straight to Hell depending on their crimes. Most of the time, they come here."

"Paranormals," I echo him in disbelief. "Like vampires and werewolves?"

He eyes me, giving me a crooked grin. "Exactly, but there are so many more creatures than that. Like you, for example. You're now a paranormal creature but you know that already, don't you?"

I nod, tightening the cloak he made me around my shoulders. "Yes, I do know that."

"You don't seem bothered."

"I'm pretty good at adapting. I accepted my fate a long time ago. There's nothing I can do about it. Especially now, since I'm dead."

"You're dead but your afterlife is just beginning. You're about to have so much fun here. This place can be danger-ous and maybe you'll need to fight to survive, but I have a feeling you'll be okay. If anything, you seemed relieved to be here."

"After dealing with what I did, you'd welcome anything else."

His hand drops to my shoulder, squeezing it gently as a friend would do. "You'll be alright."

The front door swings open and another Void stands in the doorway, hands on his hips, and flames dance on his shoulders until they fade away.

The other skeletal creature points at Trovian and growls, "You."

"Fuck," Trovian curses with annoyance. "I'm so sorry about this."

"Trovian! You mother fucker. You stole her soul. That's my territory. The area you went to is under my jurisdiction. You could have picked any other place, but nooo, you had to pick mine." The angry Void vanishes and then appears right in front of us. "You did that on purpose." He pokes a finger at Trovian's chest.

"You weren't available. I had orders from Death."

"Death?" I ask.

"Our boss. One of the Four Horsemen," the new Void says. "Just because you got promoted doesn't mean you can pop into wherever you want. Unbelievable." He turns to me, grinning before reaching his hand out to me. "I'm Lorcan. And you are?"

"Holly." I shake his hand, trying to understand everything he just said about Death being real.

"What a pretty name. I hope Trovian escorted you here without any issue." Lorcan narrows his eyes at Trovian.

"Everything has been smooth sailing," I explain, a small magical hint in my voice. I cover my mouth. "I'm sorry. I don't know how to control certain abilities yet."

"It won't work on us anyway. Though, that voice will earn you some eeries while you're here," Trovian informs.

"Eeries are our money here. Coins," Locarn explains, holding up a coin as an example.

"Ah," I nod my head in understanding even though I'm not sure I understand anything right now. I'm wondering if this is a fever dream. What if I'm not dead and I'm still alive in the hands of those doctors?

"You'll be taken care of here. We will help you get on your feet. Want to explain what happened to you?" Trovian questions out of curiosity as we all begin walking to the front door.

I follow them because what else am I supposed to do? They are the only ones I know. Either risk my afterlife with them or without them and right now, I'm feeling a bit apprehensive about being on my own here.

Sighing, I reply, "Not really. Let's say I was in the wrong place at the wrong time. That's all there is to it."

"So you don't want to tell us how you were a human turned into a paranormal creature."

"Not really. I don't want to get into it. It's not like you have to tell anyone, right? You have other souls to snatch?"

"Well no, we don't have to tell anyone, but Death would like to know."

"I'd rather him not. He doesn't need to know. I was the only one in that building anyway. Nothing he can do."

"He can kill the guy who did this to you." Lorcan opens the front door for me, bows, and extends his arm to show me inside. "Ladies first."

I giggle for the first time in months, and it takes me by

surprise. I stand still, hoping happiness is something I find again along with my self-confidence.

"Thank you, Lorcan." I step over the threshold and stare down, noticing faces pressing against the floor. With every step, the faces scream and groan.

"Don't mind them. They are the souls trapped in Hell trying to get free," Trovian explains.

I stop at the bar, mouth agape as I take in Purgatory Pins, noticing all of the different paranormal creatures.

"Take a seat." Lorcan slides a chair out for me. "I'll get us all drinks and we will tell you everything we know."

Without saying a word, I sit down, watching different creatures have fun while they bowl. Everyone laughs and cheers when someone gets a strike. The horror of what happened to me is still there, playing on repeat in my head, but being around others like me is healing in its own way.

This will be good for me. If I learn there is a way out of Purgatory to have a second chance in the real world, I might try to escape.

For now, my soul is in a safe space.

At last.

CHAPTER ONE

HOLLY

I inhale a deep breath causing dirt to invade my mouth. Clawing at the worm-infested soil I'm buried in, I keep my eyes closed to protect them from the granules of earth. Wet gunk sticks under my nails as I fight my way free. My lungs begin to burn with the need to breathe, but I can't. The pressure to get free has me fighting harder until I punch through the surface.

There's a second where I don't move because I'm shocked. When I feel the cool air make the hair on my arms stand, I place my hand on the ground to use it as leverage to get out of my grave.

My head breaks free, and I spit out all the dirt in my mouth, audibly gasping for air. My other arm becomes free and I'm able to flatten both hands on the ground, dig my fingers into the dirt, and drag myself out of the hole.

"Finally," I rasp, rolling onto my back to catch my breath. The light escaping through the cloudy sky is enough for me.

I lie there for a minute to allow myself a chance to feel

my limbs, wiggle my toes, feel the warmth of my skin, and appreciate my second chance at life in the real world.

Purgatory wasn't so bad, but I knew I needed to escape. I deserved a second chance at life and now I know how to embrace my new self. When I learned there was a way to escape by slipping through a tear in time and space, I used my abilities to my advantage.

There was a couple in Purgatory who wanted to find a creature called the Avisseus. Apparently, this creature was the only one who could perform the tear in said time and space.

I followed the couple on their journey to find the Avisseus, using my chameleon ability to blend in with my surroundings. They never saw me. They never knew I was a step behind them.

And when they jumped through the tear, I did too, which is why I woke up in this grave.

This must be where the doctors buried me when I died in order for me to wake up here.

"I'm surprised they buried me in the first place," I mumble to myself as I stand, wiping the dirt from my body.

There's a part of me that wants to go to their facility to see if they are still there. I want to go on a rampage. I want to kill them all. I've dreamed of feeling the warmth of their blood on my hands, to hear them scream, to hear them beg, and to see them cry.

Just the thought has pleasure simmering inside me, a pleasure that has my tentacles slip free, curl up, and rub over my clit. There's nothing more I want than to make myself come at the thought of my tormentors dying.

What if I had them on their knees, bound, and gagged?

They would be sobbing for their freedom, and I'd be right in front of those doctors, legs spread, and getting myself off to their fear.

Yet there is a part of me that doesn't want to go back. I only want to move forward and try to live a normal life– the best I can while looking like this. Some force tells me to pick the second option,

"Speaking of..." I talk to myself as I twist and turn, trying to figure out where exactly I am. "I don't see the facility." My brows furrow together and the leaves under my feet cause me to slip as I spin around again.

I inhale, using my enhanced senses to see if I'm any- where near the place I was held. I don't smell the wretched body odor of Glasses or the other doctors. There's no death or fear hanging thick in the air like a poisonous fog wanting to suffocate me.

Wet earth hangs in the air instead. Along with the hint of smoke from a bonfire somewhere in the distance. There's also rushing water to my left that sounds like a river. I cross my arms over my chest, a chill hanging in the air as I begin walking. I don't know where I'm headed but staying here in the middle of the woods will kill me.

And I've come too fucking far to die now.

It isn't long before the river becomes louder. My feet squelch in the damp ground with every step, the mud push- ing between my toes.

Since I'm alone, I'm left with my own thoughts. There's a small amount of guilt eating away at me for leaving Purgato- ry Pins without saying goodbye to the friends I made there. I wouldn't have survived that place if it weren't for Lorcan and Trovian showing me the ropes.

It was home but there was a need pushing me to escape. Even now, my heart is being pulled in a direction I don't understand. This feeling is all-encompassing, though. The powerful emotion overwhelmed me to leave. I don't know why and I'm not sure where it will lead me.

This is my chance to start over and own my life. If anyone gets in my way of that, I will kill them and I will enjoy it.

I step out of the tree line and stop at the edge of the riverbank. The wind is cool causing goosebumps to arise on my skin. A light mist from the water crashing against the rocks manages to leave a light cold cast over my skin. I stand there for a moment, at peace, dragging my eyes from right to left to enjoy the view.

I'm so used to darkness and death that I had forgotten what it was like to breathe in beauty and life.

The sun isn't shining. It's cloudy with the promise of more rain. It's comforting. I used to love thunderstorms but after being in a room for months by myself, trapped with no windows, the thunder and lightning morphed into a villain for me.

"Where will you take me, River?" I ask the water as I follow it downstream.

I shiver, wishing I would have escaped Purgatory with clothes on, but I would have been unable to use my chameleon abilities to escape. The clothes do not change when I try to adapt to my environment. Only my skin does. It's inconvenient. It could be worse. I could still be in Purgatory feeding off the desire of random unmated creatures.

I inhale a deep breath and whatever I smell has every new instinct I have on high alert. I spread my wings, groaning as they stretch, and I shake them to release the built-up dirt. I haven't gotten used to the wings yet. Sometimes, I forget they are there. It was hard to accept so many changes all at once.

I haven't mastered the art of flying just yet.

The aroma of smoke and fire becomes stronger, but it isn't what has my beasts growling in my chest. The wave of need is so strong I have to rub the ache in my chest. Whatever the need is, I'll figure it out to calm the raging monsters living within me.

For now, I'm going to follow the scent of smoke because where there is fire, there is usually a person. That means food, clothes, money, and whatever else I can find.

My morals fucking died the day I did. I don't care what I have to do to survive. Even if it means killing someone, I will. I've endured too much. I can't live in a world where I look like a damn cosplay character. In order to get ahead, I need money.

I crouch and give myself a small pep talk, "You can do this. You're in control now." Taking a deep, shaky breath, I launch myself into the air.

The strong gusts of wind sweep under me, rocking me from side to side. "Oh, shit!" I drop a few feet, the ground too close for comfort, and at the last second, I straighten out my wings.

I miss the rocks beneath me by inches as I curve up into the clouded sky. I smile feeling the wind on my face. Flying brings so much freedom and a sense of peace that not many could ever feel.

I'm soaring over the tall trees, getting a view of the vast mountain ranges. The world seems never-ending from up here. Endless miles of sky that the harpy inside me wants to explore.

I flip to my back, taking a quick glance at the feathers of my wings swaying from the wind. I spread my arms and allow myself to freefall again. I close my eyes, not wanting to see how fast I fall but wanting to feel how fast gravity sucks me into its trap.

As I descend through the sky, the ends of my hair sting my cheeks, and the strands dance in all directions. Most likely becoming a tangled mess, but I don't care. Nothing is better than this. There isn't a feeling in the world that could ever compare to the freedom of being in control of my own body and my destiny.

I'm about to spread my wings to fly when images of a man smiling and laughing slam into my mind.

A man I have never seen before.

A complete stranger.

A handsome stranger.

I remember Glasses saying something about being able to see the future due to my harpy DNA. I thought he was speculating or curious, just drawing assumptions about what I could and could not do like he always did.

Another image of this man I've never seen before barrels into me and the force of him jolts my eyes open. My heart punches into my sternum from how much I find myself wanting him.

I gasp when another picture of him floods my mind, and this time, he is shirtless. He wipes his forehead with his arm, his body shining in sweat. He is wearing an old stained, backward baseball cap. His muscles flex as he reaches above to tighten a bolt under a car. Those defined, hard-working muscles tighten with every motion, showing off every defined line.

I want him.

I want to feed off his desire. More than that, I want to claim him. I'm not sure what that entails but it's the only word bouncing around in my head right now.

Claim.

Own.

This man is mine. From the tips of his shaggy chocolate brown hair to the freckles across his cheeks and nose, to every divot and valley that showcases his muscles, everything belongs to me.

My beasts push against my bones wanting free so we can find him and make him ours. The tentacles slip from my pussy, reaching for him to feed from his desire, to drink his come, and I begin to throb with need everywhere.

My skin begins to feel similar to how it did when I was strapped to the table. Only this time, instead of burning pain, there's explosive desire. Even the wind grazing my skin has me slipping my hand between my legs.

"Mate," one of my creatures whispers into my mind.

The word echoes in the cavity of my body, my blood yearning to bind itself to him, my fangs aching to sink into his flesh, and my hole pulsates with the need to be filled by his cock.

Would he be thick like I crave? Not too long, I hope. I find giant cocks overrated because they hurt. I don't want to feel pain when I fuck.

Yet I find myself wanting to inflict it. Maybe my mate will like a little pain with his pleasure.

If I'm lucky.

This stranger possesses my mind again, yet this time, it's

as if I'm lying next to him, face to face, and I'm able to see the gold flecks in his light brown eyes. They are big, wide, and wonderous. His lashes are dark and long and have the right amount of curl.

Immediately, I see the innocence in them, the kindness, and then he smiles as he laughs.

He has dimples.

Goddamn it, I'm a sucker for dimples.

I can't wait to dip my tongue into them. I want to lick every inch of this man's body so every cell inside me memorizes his flavor.

My tentacles curl up, inserting themselves in my pussy, fucking me like I crave. I wish it were him filling me, stretching me, causing me to gasp and moan. I rub my clit in hard, quick circles, imagining him asleep as I climb on top of him.

I'll invade his dreams, morphing them into wet, needy, unholy thoughts until he is hard. He'll leak precome and my cunt will be there to drink every last drop of him.

I've fed from dozens of creatures in Purgatory but now I don't want anyone else except the man who is taking over my mind. My throat becomes dry needing his come to coat my taste buds and quench my thirst.

Another image bombards me just as I moan to the clouds, completely forgetting where I'm at, and it's him again. This time, he's wearing a shirt—pity—that says Snapdragons Garage, and right under it is his name.

Fitz.

It suits him. He grins at someone. Someone who isn't me and a murderous rage builds inside me.

What is he thinking, smiling at anyone and everyone? So much killing to do.

That smile belongs to me.

His happiness is mine.

And anyone who gets in the way of that will meet the wrath that has been building in my blood for months.

"Fitz—" I gasp his name as an orgasm sweeps over my body. My muscles tense and my wings flatten behind my back which has me cascading to the ground quicker. The river is becoming too close too fast. I'm riding out my orgasm still, my wings refusing to cooperate.

I can't help it. Just the thought of Fitz feels so good. I'll happily risk my life every day if it means getting to see him—even if he only lives in my mind.

The river is roaring so loud, the water rushing with angry waves eager to swallow me, and my wings spread out just in time.

I flip to my stomach to get the wind under me and drag my fingers along the surface of the river.

The warmth of hope envelopes me. I'm not too sure what to do with it. Hope is dangerous. I didn't have any when I was locked away in the facility or even in Purgatory because is living there really living when you're surrounded by death?

There is only one question I have when it comes to Fitz—will he accept me?

A loud bellow of a laugh slips from me and if it weren't for the crashing river, I know it would reverberate off the trees.

I don't fucking care if he doesn't accept me. I don't care if he hates me. I don't care if the man outright rejects me.

I'll make him love me. He'll learn to love me in time. He'll know that I'm meant for him, that I'm the only one who can love, own, and fuck him like his delicious body craves.

The scent of burning wood yanks me from my Fitz daydream which I'm not happy about. I growl under my breath with a slight sneer, turning right to follow the smoke.

I dislike being interrupted while I'm thinking of my mate.

I rear my wings up and then down, slicing them through the air to gain more speed. I'm furious and it is barely contained.

It's another side effect of the DNA experiments. I'm short-tempered, more possessive, hungrier, and stronger. The longer I'm in my physical form, the more I feel the primal instincts making themselves at home in my molecules.

My humanity is shrinking to be a thing of the past.

And the more I imagine Fitz's face, the angrier I become because all I want to do is dream of that face. I want to lie on the ground, my wings spread out to their full span, and let the blades of grass tickle the feathers as the sun beams down on my naked body while I imagine Fitz in every position.

A stalk of smoke billows from the middle of the forest, drifting over the treetops to meld into the sky. Narrowing my eyes, I swoop down, landing on the closest branch I can without giving myself away.

My tail wraps around the trunk to keep me steady and I lean forward to get a better view.

It's a woman.

Now, I'm more annoyed because no other woman is allowed to come between me and Fitz. Not even the dreams of him. Whatever my harpy DNA is telling me, I'm listening, and all I know is that man belongs to me.

The bitch below adds another log to the fire before standing and heading to the dull yellow van. She opens the back doors, revealing a small bed. She must live out of it.

My lips curl as a wicked plan begins to grow.

I jump down from the tree, landing firmly on my feet, and tuck my wings back. I take a step forward, the pine needles crunching under my toes, and the woman spins around.

She gasps, startled when she sees me before she doubles over in a laughing fit.

"Oh my God, you scared the hell out of me," she says, holding a hand to her chest. "What are you doing out here in cosplay gear? You look amazing, by the way. Are you getting into character? For what? Is this a character you made yourself?"

I take another step forward, out of the shadows the trees create. "Something like that," I reply, tapping the tips of my talons against each other before I show them to her with a big smile. "You like?" I lift my lips so she can see my fangs.

"You look so realistic. Wow. You must have worked so hard on those wings. May I?" She reaches for them to touch.

I growl, turning away. "No, you may not."

The audacity.

The only person I want touching me is Fitz.

Quicker than she can blink, I wrap my hand around her throat. My touch alone has her falling limp, a lust-struck light appearing in her eyes.

She'd let me do anything to her if I wanted.

"Do you want me?" I ask her, as I bring my lips close to hers.

Her desire smells like wilderness and rain.

I don't like it. My hunger for desire disappears now that I have scented her. None of my beasts want this camper, not even the succubus that thrives off the desire of others wants her. Even when the scientists would bring me men and women to feed from, none of my beasts were picky.

Except for now.

The only taste I have, the only craving torturing my body, is for Fitz.

"Yes," she moans, reaching for me again.

I snap her neck before she can blink. Unwrapping my hand from her slender throat, her body falls to the ground.

"Too bad. That's for interrupting my fucking thoughts." I squat down, tucking her blonde hair behind her ear as her lifeless eyes stare back at me. "Only one person can have me. You understand, don't you?"

I don't feel bad for killing her. The old me would have, but I've noticed all my give-a-damns died when I became a monster.

"You were pretty." I bend down and kiss her cheek before whispering, "But you are so much prettier dead."

My fingers drag across her cheek and that's when I see the light purple flesh of mine morphs into her skin tone. Curious, I grab her arm so hard the bone breaks, and her features take over my body.

"Woah," I whisper, turning my hands over to see how I've changed.

My nails are shorter. The light purple skin is gone. I look down, noticing my breasts are hers. Everything is hers. I rush to the van and rip the side mirror off, needing to see my reflection.

My horns are gone.

The bright orange glow of my eyes are now baby blue. Instead of long blue hair with a shaved side, I have wavy blonde hair. Inspecting my mouth, even my teeth are dull.

The longer I stare at myself, the more uncomfortable I become. I can sense my beasts inside me, roaring and clashing together to be freed.

"How do I change back?" I ask myself, touching my cheek as a slight panic plucks at my heart.

I focus on my form, wishing for it to return, and my eyes widen as I watch the change happen in real-time. The light purple skin returns, the blonde is overcome with blue, and in the next instant, I'm looking at myself again.

"Can I change back into her?" My curiosity has always known no bounds. I focus on her features, and they return with no issue.

I can change into her whenever I want. If I want.

Not liking the human appearance, I bring my new form back and stay in it. Being around other humans one day, my trick to change or blend into my surroundings will come in handy, but right now, it is best if I stay in the body that can protect me best.

"What do you have in here?" I ask her dead body, the only reply is the crackling of the fire. Walking to the back of the van where the doors are open, I claw through the pink curtains she has on the windows. "Cute," I tell her. "Not my favorite color, though."

Her suitcase is open on the small twin bed. I come across a cute white crop top that has black leather strings laced from the middle of the chest to the base of the neck.

"I like this too. I'm taking it. You don't mind, right? It's not like you need it anymore." I tug it on over my head and come across a brand-new pack of unopened underwear. "Oh, smart woman. I'm using these, okay?" I rip the bag open, the plain white panties spilling free.

"Again, not my style, but better than being completely naked, right?" I say to myself, curling my lips in disapproval as I hold up the basic panties.

A pair of jean shorts with pink daisies sewn on the pockets have me rolling my eyes but they will have to do.

"Out of all the people I had to come across, why did the universe send me you?" I grumble, wishing my victim had a little more taste in her clothing.

I rip a hole in the back for my tail, slip them on, tug my tail through the hole, and button them.

"How do I look? What do you think?" I give her a little spin. "Why thank you. I think it's cute too. What was that?" I pretend she is talking to me. "It looks better on me than you?" I place my hand on my chest. "You're too sweet."

I jump in the van, my horns grinding across the ceiling, and my head rings from the sound of metal tearing.

"What else do you have in here?" I hum, ignoring the photos of herself with a few friends and the canned food sitting on the floorboard.

My feet kick something under her raised bed. I bend down, moving the curtain of blue that falls in my face, and see three big black duffle bags.

"Well, well, well, what do we have here?" I pull one out, unzip it, and rip the flap open to see more money than I have ever seen before. "What the fuck did you do to get this money? I mean, lucky for me, but—" I take a stack of hundreds out, feathering my thumb through the ends. "—This is so much."

I freeze when I hear voices in the distance. Two men. I shift my eyes to the photos again, the urgency of my situation clicking into place.

"You weren't alone," I whisper, angling my head so I can hear her friends better.

"There are three bags and three of us. Each of us should take a bag and disappear or we all stick together. A million each. That's not a bad job," one of them says.

"When should we plan another robbery? Which bank? I want to go bigger."

"No. We aren't ready for that. We need to really think the plan through. The bigger the bank, the bigger their security, and because of you we almost got caught."

I sit on the bed, shaking my finger at my new friend. "Tsk, tsk, young lady. Your father would be so disappointed in you." I grab the handles of the back doors. "I guess you won't really have to tell him. I did you a favor. Thanks for the clothes, bestie. It's been fun."

I carefully close the doors, so her friends don't hear them in the distance.

"It's time to get a move on." I stuff the money in the bag, shove it under the bed, and climb into the driver's seat.

The van is an old Volkswagen. The seats are worn leather with a few tears. The steering wheel is faded where she kept her hands and there is a peace sign sticker in the corner of the rearview mirror.

"It's as if all this was waiting just for me." The engine sputters, eventually turning over, and I push the gear into drive.

The tires spin on the dirt, no doubt covering the dead girl with soil.

"At least she's buried. I'm spreading the kindness that was given to me." I smile and chuckle, flipping my hair over my shoulders, and then following the small natural road through the forest.

My wings are scrunched since the van is too small for them. They will have to manage. There's no way I'm leaving this van with all this money. I could fly, following the pull of my soul, but having a car will also help me blend in.

Rolling down the windows, I inhale the fresh air when a scent that has my body warming again hits me out of nowhere. The tug at my heart is stronger too. I listen to what the world is telling me.

Follow the scent.

Follow the pull.

And that's where Fitz will be.

I flip the radio on to a rock station, my mind wandering to my human memories, and how few I really have now. There aren't a lot of details I can remember. Only the jobs. Only how they made me feel.

Yet no actual memories. Those are gone. That's hard to come to terms with but that's okay. I'll make new memories with Fitz. He's my purpose now.

I might not be what he is expecting, but I'll be everything he had no idea he wanted.

"Fuck, I need you," I groan as his scent becomes stronger the closer I get to him. The impatience of not being close enough to him where I can see him has me pressing my foot on the gas.

I surpass the speed limit. A few hours of driving feels like centuries. My panties are soaked with Fitz's scent being so strong and his handsome face in my memories. He's consumed me, and I don't even know him.

I don't need to. He's my mate. That's enough for me. I don't know what it means but I trust my beasts and they want no one else but him. That has to mean something.

The sign to town appears, and I squeal because Fitz's aroma fills the van as if he is sitting in the passenger seat.

I'm so lost in thought that when a loud pop comes from the right side and the van lowers in that direction, I lose control.

"Ah, fuck! Oh, shit. Oh, shit!" I scream, turning the wheel left, then right, then left again. The good tires squeal. The scent of burnt rubber drifts through the vents causing me to curl my nose and it ruins Fitz's delicious aroma.

If I could shred this van to pieces for revenge, I would.

I finally come to a stop at the edge of the road, gasping for breath before giggling. Running my fingers through my hair, I groan, wanting that reckless experience to happen again.

"That adrenaline," I moan, arching my back to rock against the seat. I only need a little friction on my clit. It won't take long. Being so close to Fitz, his smell, the near-death experience, killing someone, I'm so close to orgasming.

One. Little. Touch.

It won't hurt anyone.

Else.

A red tow truck with 'Snapdragons Garage' in big white font across the side drives by. I take a peek into the driver's side mirror, watching the red taillights appear as the vehicle slows. The truck turns around, and I inhale a sharp breath when I see Fitz in the driver's seat.

His baseball cap is backward. The ends of his hair curl from under it above his ears.

He opens the truck door, climbs out, and begins walking

over to me.

A pleased growl rumbles in my chest as I look him up and down. He is taller than what my visions teased me with.

Fuck, he looks so good. He's wearing the Snapdragons Garage shirt. His chest is broad, tightening the material of the simple shirt. His pants are tight in the right places and those long legs deserve to be sat on while I fuck him.

Shit.

My eyes catch the mirror.

I look like me. I change into the woman I killed, my features fading away just in time as he bends down, placing his forearms on the door.

My heart skips—no—it stops beating.

With him this close, my mouth waters, my fangs tingle, my tentacles move inside me, and controlling this form is too difficult. I can't have him here.

"Hi, there. I can change that tire for you if you need." He leans on the car, his arms above his head as he places them on the roof.

There are plenty of things I need, but none of them are this fucking tire.

My vision tunnels to his biceps. The sleeves tighten around the muscles. A bead of sweat lingers on his neck. I can hear the small droplet moving ever so slowly until it soaks into the collar of his shirt.

I should have licked it when I had the chance.

My entire body begins to tremble with nerves and the need to throw him on the ground, unzip his pants, pull his cock free, and ride him right here and now. I don't care who sees.

Let them witness. Let everyone see him being claimed.

I stare down at my hand, my eyes widening when the purple skin comes through. I can't hold this form for much longer. Not when all I can think about is laying him across the hood and fucking him raw.

His desire hits me next, and it has my eyes rolling to the back of my head. My panties become wetter somehow. My nipples tighten under the white crop top and his lust for me becomes even heavier.

It fills the small space of the van. The air is so thick with him that I can taste it on my tongue and the succubus growls wanting more than just his scent.

I want his flavor.

I want to lick his sweat and drink his come.

My swallow is loud as I try to control myself. I take a few deep breaths, knowing I can't do anything in broad daylight to Fitz. I'm too close to town. And as much as this form is appealing to humans, I refuse to take my mate in any other form but my own.

He clears his throat. "I'm, uh, I'm Fitz." He holds out his hand. "New to town? I really don't mind changing your tire. It won't take long. I'll get you back on the road safely. If you're worried about getting hurt or taken advantage of, I'm not that kind of man. I really am trying to help you, Miss. I'd hate for something to happen to you."

Funny he should say that... when I'm the bad thing that's about to happen to him.

I smile at him, sliding my hand into his, and bite my lip to keep from groaning out loud. His calloused hands are rough. I bet they would feel good drifting down my body.

"I'm Holly."

"Holly? Is it, really? You know what? My favorite flowers

are hollyhocks. What a coincidence, right? Do you like flow-ers? You know what," he chuckles, hanging his head. "Sorry about that. I tend to get a little chatty and ask questions. I'll leave you alone. If you need anything, the shop is just two miles up the road from here. I really hope you do need something, though, Holly."

"Is that so?" My tone is flirtatious and sultry. "Why is that, Fitz?"

He grins, the same one I saw in my mind. His dimples are better in person, deep and pronounced. He is clean-shaven which allows me to see how the straight beautiful teeth, full pink lips, and all those freckles I'm already obsessed with.

His phone rings, interrupting our moment. Now, I want to kill the person who called him.

"I have to take this. It's work, but maybe I'll see you around, Holly." He gives me one last look before walking to his truck, answering the person who dared to ruin our first moment together.

Oh, you have no idea how much you'll be seeing me, Doe Eyes.

CHAPTER TWO

FITZ

That was wild.

I blow out a breath when I park the tow truck behind the shop. My heart won't stop racing. A nervous sweat breaks out over my entire body, and I have to wipe my forehead, so the warm salty liquid doesn't drip into my eyes.

I'm not sure who she was, why she is here, or if she is only visiting. One thing I do know is that I have to see that woman again. Even my palms are sweaty. Something about her calls to me. There was a uniqueness about her I can't quite put my finger on.

One moment, I swear her eyes were blue, then the next they were glowing orange. In the blink of an eye, she had horns protruding from her forehead, then they were gone. One minute she had blue hair and the next it was blonde.

I think my mind is playing tricks on me because even though I'm drawn to her like I've never been drawn to another woman in my life, I'm slightly disappointed. She is normal.

I don't want normal

Groaning, I rub my hands down my face. "Snap out of it, Fitz. You know that will never happen." My head thuds against the headrest as I stare out of the windshield.

I want a monster.

I don't want a regular human woman. After finding Rhett and meeting Creed, I want what their mates have.

I want to be someone's fated mate.

Rhett and Creed are monster DNA experiments. Rhett is my best friend and when he went missing, a part of me died. He is my brother. When I found him and he showed himself to me, his true self, I didn't fucking care what he looked like—I was just glad he was alive.

I hated what happened to him, what was done to him, the abuse, the torment, and I hate that he can't show the world who he is without humans casting judgment. He gets to hide in plain sight since our friend Caden knows a witch who casts a spell on the rain, tricking everyone into thinking Rhett and Creed are normal.

I'm not sure why the rain won't work on me. Maybe it's because I'm so open-minded? Or accepting. I'm not sure. Rhett seems to think it's because I must have a mate out there somewhere. The spell didn't work on Demi or Mickey, Creed and Rhett's human mates.

All I can do is hope that is the truth because I want to be mated. I want to belong to someone to the point where my soul is lost in theirs. I want my soul to be so intertwined that if they died, I'd die.

I know Rhett is just giving me hope about having a mate, but so far, only Rhett and Creed have made their way into this town. What are the chances there is a monster DNA experiment who is a woman?

And why would she even want me when she could have anyone?

I try to think about why I want what Demi and Mickey have with Rhett and Creed. I tap the steering wheel as my mind wanders and the only thing I can think of is the happiness that always shines from the two women when I see them. It's different from ordinary human couples.

I want to be so loved that my partner is obsessed with me. I want that deeply—fiercely. And while I've dated before, I've never loved or have had anyone love me to the point of madness.

That's what I want. More than anything, I want madness.

A knock at the window startles me. I roll it down and hold a hand to my chest. "Damn, Rhett. Warn a guy. You just scared ten years off my life."

His reptilian eyes harden and narrow. "Don't say that. You know I don't like it when you talk about your lifespan. Even if it's a joke."

"What about your lifespan? You need someone to shorten it? I'll do it," Creed shouts from the office.

For some reason, Rhett hired him for security. Creed has to follow one rule.

Do not scare the customers away.

He broke that rule the first day so now we keep him in the office to watch the security tapes.

"Fuck you, Creed," I shout out of my window.

"Not on my deathbed," he sneers, slamming the office window closed.

I give Rhett an exasperated expression. "He is a pain in the ass."

"Yeah, but he is our pain in the ass. He wouldn't actually

kill you."

"Yes, he would. You and I both know it."

"Okay, but he'd regret it after."

I toss my head back and chuckle, opening the driver's side door to get out finally. "No, he wouldn't. It's fine. I'm not here for him anyway." I slap Rhett's shoulder, the crocodile gargoyle skin causes a zing of pain to shoot up my arm. "Mother fucker! Holy shit." I grab onto my hand, holding my breath as I walk around to shake off the pain. "I always forget about the stone."

I kick a random bucket, and it slams against a junker of a car that's been sitting in the same spot for far too long. We use it for parts when we need to.

"Feel better?" Rhett asks.

"Kind of. I'm fine."

"You don't seem fine." Rhett crosses his arms and tucks his wings behind his back. "Actually—" he inhales, and I take a step away.

I lift a finger. "Don't you use that on me. You know the rules. No using your abilities to see if something is wrong. That was wild of you, Rhett. You know better."

With his vampire speed, he is directly in front of me, sniffing the air in front of me.

"Nothing is wrong. Your heart is racing. You smell like a woman. What happened while you went to get gas in the truck?"

I hook my fingers in my belt loops and rock on the heels of my boots. "Nothing." I check my watch, noticing it's close to the next appointment time. "I need to go. I have an oil change and a tire rotation coming in ten minutes." I start walking away but he snags the back of my shirt and yanks me, sending me flying through the air.

I land on my back, the air is knocked out of my lungs, and I cough. "Was that really necessary?" I groan.

"Sorry," he frowns, walking over with his hand extended. "Sometimes my strength gets ahead of me."

I slap my hand into his and stand, dusting off my jeans. "It's alright, but if you really want to know, there was a girl who had a flat tire on the side of the road. I tried to help her, but she declined. I didn't want to hover since she was alone. I didn't want to make her uncomfortable."

He grins, showing his fangs. "You're a good man, Fitz. You're going to get your happy ending one day, you know that, right?"

I shuck off my hat and scratch my head before putting it back on. I look away from my best friend with a shrug of my shoulder. "I don't think this universe has what I'm looking for, Rhett."

"It does. I refuse to lose my best fucking friend to old age while I stay like this forever. I won't allow it."

"Rhett, you can't force something like that."

"Yes I can!" he roars so loud, the rage has his eyes flipping a bright red. He turns away, shaking his head as if that will get rid of the crimson flooding his irises. His nostrils flare as he takes a calming breath. "I can. I will. It's why I don't like you joking around about your life. Every year you get older, you're closer to death, and I'm frozen like this."

"Okay?" I grab his shoulders. "Rhett, I'm okay with that. I'm okay living the rest of my life like this. I'm happy. If I die, then I'll die happy knowing I had a good life."

"That isn't good enough."

"It has to be," I tell him, "You have to face it, Rhett. I'm only human."

"I'll figure out a way. I need to go," he sneers, spinning around, and heads back inside the shop.

I sigh, tilting my head back to stare up at the grey sky. My phone rings in my pocket and I dig it out to see who is calling. I don't typically ignore my sister's call but right now, I don't feel like talking.

My head is a mess. I'm worried about Rhett, my fragile human life, and the woman I met not ten minutes ago won't leave my mind. I'm not in the headspace to talk.

"Hey, stop figuring out the shapes of the clouds. They don't look like fucking clowns or puppies. They are just water droplets and ice crystals. Nothing else. Your appointment is here. We have a business to run." Creed narrows his eyes at me from the window he somehow managed to open without me hearing, then slams it shut.

Yeah, I have no doubt he would kill me in my sleep. Luckily, I'm off limits because of Rhett.

"Grump," I mumble under my breath.

He knocks on the window. "I heard that," he shouts, his voice muffled from the closed window.

I smile at him, giving Creed a friendly wave and he lowers the blinds, so he doesn't have to look at me.

"I'll win him over one day. I have no doubt," I say positively to myself, smile, and head into the garage just in time to see my appointment pull in.

I wave her in, and she rolls down her window. "Hey, Fitz! How are you?" she asks, a bright genuine smile on her face, and I know she is interested. She bats her eyelashes, roaming her sights up and down my body with a small bite of her bottom lip.

I wish I was interested but this woman doesn't even pique my interest. Holly is the one running through my mind.

If I were a normal man wanting a normal woman, I'd ask her out, but I'd rather live in my delusions than settle for what I'm supposed to.

I might need to get my head checked because my mind was playing tricks on me when I looked at Holly because that can't be right. I saw a monster. I saw horns. I don't know if I'm that far gone or if I'm too wishful with what I want, but I wasn't interested in the blonde woman in the driver's seat. I am obsessed with what I thought I saw.

Light purple skin. Horns. Fangs.

Fuck yes, those fangs. I can't stop imagining them sinking into my throat or my cock.

I turn my body away so Ms. Livingston can't see my cock hardening in my jeans. I don't want her to think my arousal is for her. Not that she isn't a pretty woman, she is, but my body and mind do not want a normal woman. That's just how it is.

"I'm doing alright, Ms. Livingston. Loving that I get to have my coffee any time I want. Can't get any better than that, am I right?" I flash a friendly smile.

She blushes, waving her hand at me as she lightly scoffs. "Oh, please, Fitz. Call me Lily. Ms. Livingston is my mother."

Discomfort swirls in my gut. I don't want to call her Lily because then she might think I'm interested. I need to keep it professional. Damn it, why do I do this to myself all the time? My insides twist into knots during these types of situations because I really hate hurting people.

I feel deeply. I care too much about everyone and everything before myself. I'd hate it if Ms. Livingston thought she wasn't good enough for me when that is not the case at all.

"Sorry, Ms. Livingston. Don't take it personally. I'm at work and I like to keep things professional here. I hope you understand."

She smiles and it reaches her eyes that crinkle on the sides, showing she is a few years older than me.

Whew. I'm glad.

I don't tend to do well when someone is upset with me. I spiral and want to do everything I can to make their happiness return. Then, I become annoying. It's a vicious cycle I'm trying to break.

"Oh, I understand completely. You're so professional, Fitz. I really like that about you."

Well, that backfired.

I smile, opening the door for her to get out so I can drive her car into the bay. "No problem. Why don't you go to Demi's Diner for some coffee while I get this car to the highest of standards?"

Ms. Livingston grins and holds out her hand for me to take to help her out. Internally, I groan, and guilt tightens my stomach for a brief moment when her palm slides against mine.

Panic slips up my throat. Sweat beads on the back of my neck. The odd feeling of dishonesty overwhelms me as if I'm cheating on my partner, but I don't have one. The image of Holly comes into my mind which is outrageous because I don't know that woman.

But goddamn, I sure do want to.

"I'll make sure to call when the car is done," I inform, slipping my hand free as I grab the doorframe.

"Not a problem. I look forward to it." She hikes her over-sized purse up her shoulders, spins around on her heels, and sashays away by putting an extra sway into her hips.

An eerie force drapes over me as I get in the car. I pause and get out, placing my foot on the ground while I take a quick look around. The wind blows cool air promising winter and snow.

My eyes water from the quick chill and I rub them on my shirt sleeve before studying the area. I know I'm being watched. The only way I know how to explain it is a slight weight on my chest that resembles anxiety and curiosity.

"Everything alright, Fitz?" Rhett pops his head out of bay one while wiping his oil-drenched hands on a stained rag.

I nod, taking one more look around down the road, then the other direction, but all I see are patrons coming in and out of the quaint shops around us. No one is watching me.

I'm paranoid for no reason. I need to relax.

"I'm fine. I just thought I saw someone I knew. That's all."

"You're lying to me, but I'll let it slide since we are at work." He narrows his eyes at me. "You'll tell me later when I help you move the rest of your stuff into your new house."

I frown when I see the less-than-enthusiastic expression on his face. When I came to Rhett a month ago saying I found the perfect house for me, he seemed taken aback and surprised. He didn't want me to move out and to be fair, I didn't want to either.

But Mickey and Rhett are starting a family. They deserve their space, their privacy, and time with their children. I know he understands. We have had a great time living to-gether.

"I'm only across the lake, Rhett. You could swim to me. I

could swim to you." I sit down in the driver's seat and finally pull the car forward onto the lift.

He leans on a support beam and crosses his arms. "Yeah, but you know it won't be the same."

"You and Mickey are about to have two kids running around the house. You need the space. Isn't she due any day now? That will be wild even with me around. It's best that I have my own house, and you know it."

He runs his fingers through his long blonde hair before tossing it into a messy bun. I still can't get over his features. Reptilian eyes, stone skin, crocodile scales, fangs, and sure he appears to be scary but all I still see is my best friend.

He grins when he thinks about Mickey. "Yeah, she's due next week. We weren't sure how long the pregnancy would be because–well–" He roams his hand down his body to finish his sentence. "And we are curious if every pregnancy will be like this or if each pregnancy will be different based on my beasts? We aren't sure. I'm so excited. I never thought I'd have this chance, you know? Not when I'm like this. I got lucky. Unlike some of the other people that were in that facility." His tone changes from happiness to borderline guilt.

I slap him on the shoulder and give him a reassuring squeeze. "Don't feel bad for surviving, Rhett. Don't go down that road."

"You could have stayed in the house, you know. We have room and the kids would love their Uncle Fitz there."

"You and I both know it's best that I got my own place. You're having twins. Whenever you need me, I'm there. Even when you don't need me, I'm there. I'm always here, Rhett. I'm not going anywhere."

"So fucking cute. Why don't you two kiss now?" Creed

sneers at us before going inside and slamming the door.

"Why is he so fucking grumpy?"

"Eh, don't mind him. He is due to see Demi in an hour. His mood will be better then."

I press the button on the lift that raises the car so I can get under it and change the oil. "He hates everyone but her. Hell, I think he might tolerate you. I wouldn't even go as far as to say he likes me."

"No, he likes me. He tolerates Mr. Pete."

"What's that make me?"

"Someone he tolerates," Rhett tosses his head back and chuckles, his laugh echoing in the garage.

"Great. I'll need to sleep with one eye open."

"You're fine. You're my friend. He isn't going to touch you."

"Okay, but if I end up being skinned and my body chopped into pieces, you better fccl really guilty."

"I wouldn't let that happen, Fitz. He's a monster, but I am too. We have a mutual respect for boundaries. He is just ornery."

I stand under the car and immediately notice that Ms. Livingston needs new tires. Her tread is too low, and it won't pass inspection. I begin with the oil first, twisting the valve so it can drain.

"You could move into the house next to me. It's for sale. I know you guys just finished that renovation. I don't expect you to move when you have your home the way you want it."

"Yeah, sorry, Fitz. Mickey is proud of that house and what she's done to it. She healed herself there. I won't be the man to take that away from her."

"I know and I'm glad you are. Stop acting like I'm moving back home, okay? I'm going to be here at work, going to come over for dinner, going to go to the bar to have a beer with you. None of that will change."

He leans in and whispers, "But who is going to watch Grey's Anatomy with me?" Rhett glances around to make sure no one can hear him. "You know how much I love that show. We are only on season four."

"We will have regular Grey's Anatomy nights. I can't miss it either."

The familiar sparkle returns in his eye. "Great. I was worried about that. Wouldn't want to watch it without you."

We tried watching the show with Creed but anytime any character did anything he'd say, "Kill them. Slit their throat. Kill them too for being annoying. Why are they on the show? Dead. Kill them." Eventually, he got mad and walked out the door.

We've been watching it without him ever since.

Rhett pulls me in for a quick hug, patting me on the back, and he sniffs me which is then followed by a growl.

"Who is that? I know you told me you met a woman but something about the scent is off. Maybe it isn't her I'm smelling."

I pluck the middle of my shirt and bring it to my nose. "What? I'm not wearing cologne."

"It isn't cologne." He buries his nose in my chest, dragging it back and forth as he sniffs.

I lift my hands. "Okay, Rhett? Sniffing me like this is a little weird."

He stops, realizing what he is doing, and takes a step back. "Sorry. I can't place the scent. My beasts are grumbling about it. Maybe it's your laundry detergent."

I shrug my shoulder. "I don't know. Nothing has changed. Maybe I brushed up against something you don't like? The girl I saw, we barely had an interaction. It can't be her. Sorry, man."

"It's okay–" his phone rings and he slides it from his pocket. "It's Mickey. I have to take this."

"Hope everything is okay. I'll be here. Tell her I said hello."

"How's my Brave Little Flower?" he answers with a smile but quickly his enthusiasm fades.

My brows lift as I replace the oil filter. Mickey is a great woman. I don't know a lot about her past life but what I do know is abuse had a heavy hand. That knowledge kills me when I think about it. No man should ever treat a woman that way. I'm glad that bastard is dead, or I'd want to kill him too.

"What do you mean you can't get up?" Rhett asks, spiraling into anxiety. He begins to pace back and forth. He puts the phone on speaker and immediately a loud sob startles me, and I drop the wrench in my hand.

It lands hard on my foot, and I curse, hop on one leg, and then smack my head against a tire.

"Fucking shit. God–stupid fucking–son-of-a-bitch–mother fuck–" I hop to the bench that is against the wall to take a break. My head is throbbing, and I can't feel my big toe.

"I'm hungry! I want ice cream with pickles and peanut butter, but I can't get out of bed. I need to pee." She sobs even harder, small sniffles coming through the line with every breath she takes.

"I'm on my way, okay? I'll get you whatever you want. I'll

stop and get the ice cream."

"Really?" she asks, her sobs slowing, and I smile.

I want that so badly. I want to love someone so much that I can hear the smile in their voice when I can't see them.

Rhett and Creed are lucky bastards.

He hangs up the phone and runs into the office to grab his keys before coming back outside. "I have to go. Mickey needs me. I might need to take this week off. She's struggling, and I can't have her struggle. We could shut down the shop? I don't want you here alone."

My head swims from the smack it got from the tire, and yet, I manage to stand. "Go. I have the shop. I can move appointments around or cancel the non-urgent ones. Go to Mickey. Start your paternity leave early. I'll hold the fort down."

"Does that mean I have to be here with him?" Creed's voice comes from the shadows.

Rhett rubs his temples.

"I'll be fine without him. He can go."

Please, for the love of all things, fucking go.

"Great. I'll be stalking my mate." He leaves. Without a goodbye. Without looking back, he crosses the street to get to the diner.

"I'm sorry, Fitz. You're sure you're okay?"

"Keep me updated on Mickey."

"I will. Thanks, Fitz. You're the best."

I give a small wave as he climbs into his truck and speeds away.

Pushing through the dull headache, I begin working on Ms. Livingston's car again. While I work, I think back to when I was so in love that I'd drop anything for my partner. I can't think of one moment.

I've never been in love. I've dated, sure. I've had sex. But love?

Never. I guess even for me, it's too wild of a thought.

I'm starting to think someone like me won't get to experience love. I'm too much for people. I'm always going out of my way. I'm a big people pleaser. Love isn't meant for people who allow themselves to be taken advantage of like I do.

I'll sit back, watch my friends be in love, grow families, and dream of a life that's so far out of reach—it might as well be a fantasy.

Good thing I'm such a good dreamer. At least at night, I can have everything I want when I close my eyes.

CHAPTER THREE

HOLLY

Who the hell is that fucking bitch touching my mate?

My hands tighten around the steering wheel until it creeks from my strength. I crack my neck and try to take a deep calming breath.

It doesn't work.

I only feel more murderous.

I'm parked in front of an ice cream shop that gives me the perfect view of Snapdragons Garage. Fitz is gorgeous. I can understand why that woman wants to put her hands all over him.

She'll never get to. She'll never get to experience him like I'm going to. I'll own his laughs, smile, orgasms, and every other aspect of his life. No one is allowed to take what isn't theirs.

Didn't her parents ever teach her that? Perhaps, she needs a reminder of basic manners.

I growl under my breath, watching her smile, and toss her long hair over her shoulder. She twists it around her finger, flirting with my mate.

She must have a death wish. Why else would she be so careless with her life?

A third of the steering wheel breaks off. I sneer, tossing it in the backseat.

"Now she owes me a new steering wheel," I mutter, wishing my eyes could throw sharpened daggers at the woman who is flirting with my Fitz.

His doe eyes belong locked on me. I want to see them widen when he is about to come. He won't look so sweet and innocent when he is screaming my name with his cock buried deep inside me.

She'll never get the chance.

"Call me Lily," I mock with a curl of my lip.

I've heard every second of their conversation because of my newly enhanced abilities.

"Lily," I repeat her name. "He better not like those flowers."

Straightening my spine as I watch her walk away, she turns around to sneak one last look at Fitz. He isn't paying any attention to her, but he is looking around.

"Do you feel my gaze, Doe Eyes? You sense me, don't you?" I blow hot air onto the window, then kiss it, Fitz's figure blurs from the condensation. "It's okay, you won't miss her. She can't give you what I can. She can't love you like I can," I groan, licking the kiss I just left.

I roll down the window needing some fresh air. Inhaling, Lily's scent hits me harder than the scientists ever did.

Her desire for him makes me furious. So, I'm going to kill her and feast on her regret.

Because she will. She'll wish she never spoke to Fitz by

the time I'm done with her.

I roll the window up, hating her stench that lingers in the air. The condensation where I declared my love for Fitz is ruined in streaks, reminding me of the tears Lily will shed.

Pushing the gear shift into drive, I slam my foot on the gas and cut in front of a car. A horn blares at me which causes me to slip my attention to the rearview mirror to see a man behind the wheel gesturing with his hands.

He's clearly angry.

Rolling down the window, I flip my middle finger in the air. "Better count this day as your luckiest or I would slit your throat to match the damage I'd do to your tires, asshole."

He speeds around me, matching my pace, and he rolls down the passenger side window.

"You crazy fucking bitch!" he shouts, teasing me with danger as he jerks the car in my lane.

I don't move like he expects me to. The front left side of his bumper hits the side of my door. I only wave my hand at him.

"Fuck you," he yells, his dark furry brows pinching together to create one.

I drop my disguise, allowing my real self to show, and I flash my fangs. He screams, drifting the car to another lane.

"No, fuck you! You desperate, sad, pathetic man." I point in front of him. "Watch out."

He finally looks out the windshield and screams at the top of his lungs before a semi hits him head-on. He wasn't wearing his seat belt. His body flies out of the windshield, directly into the silver grill of the truck.

I'm able to smell his blood and his death. I tug on the

chains attached to my nipple rings and moan, my panties becoming soaked with need. The only man who can sate the craving is Fitz.

Needing to play along because a terrible accident has just occurred, I pull over into Demi's Diner parking lot in a hurry. Lily is standing in the grass, covering her mouth from watching the accident occur.

Cloaking myself in disguise, I open the door and step out of the van. The parking lot is paved, so dark that if I spilled her blood, it would have the appearance of a water puddle.

"Terrible thing that happened." Pushing the hypnotic tone of my siren in every word.

"I know. And it happened so fast. Are you okay? He was in the wrong following you like that. If you need a witness, I have your back. Us women need to stick together, right?"

I side-eye her, not liking how supportive and nice she is. If I were human, I would have been all about girl power, but now? It's survival of the fittest. I'm better on my own.

Trusting people always comes with strings attached. She might be supportive today, but the moment I tell her Fitz is mine, she'd turn her back on me so fast.

And I don't stab from the back.

Taking risks with my fated mate isn't an option so long as Lily is alive.

"It wasn't me. It was someone else he was road raging with," I say, adding a whimsical sound to my statement.

She turns to me, eyes glassy with a wide smile. "You're right. I got you confused with someone else. I'm sorry." Her voice is distant, proving my abilities should work on her.

"You know what you should do, Lily? Because you're such a girl's girl," I grin, pushing her hair behind her shoulders.

Her desire for me heightens. She leans in, wanting what she can never have.

"You should go walk into the road and have a car hit you. It would be such a tragic accident. Maybe you were that angry man's mistress. You saw what happened to him and—" I place a hand to my chest, feigning sorrow, "—you couldn't take living life without him."

She nods, her eyes watering with tears. "I did love him, didn't I? It was so sad watching the accident. Do you think he thought of me?"

I beg to run my claws through her hair, watching the car catch fire with his body hanging halfway out of the windshield. "Probably not," I reply, turning her to face me.

A tear drips down her cheek. "No?"

"I bet wherever he is, he is thinking of you now. Don't you want to join him?"

Lily begins to sway. "I do. I do want to be with him, but..." She licks her lips.

I sneer with impatience through tight teeth. "But what?"

"Fitz. I think I know someone by that name."

"You do. He's mine, though. Taken." I bite, wishing I could twist her neck and leave her limp body for all to see.

I have to be smarter than that right now. We are in public. Cops are around. Too many witnesses to prove my actions.

"Oh," she frowns. "I didn't know. It doesn't matter. The love of my life just died."

"That's right," I croon, sliding my hand away from her hair to grip the back of her neck. Tucking the strands behind her ear, I bring my lips close, so the full effect of my voice can finally get her to obey. "He needs you now. Go to him, Lily."

"I'm scared."

"Oh, you shouldn't be. Death is quick. You won't feel a thing."

I lean away, grinning and then masking my happiness when Lily tilts her head back to stare at me. Tears run down her cheeks in fast drops and her bottom lip trembles.

Ugh, so many tears. Why? Just fucking go walk in traffic already.

Without saying another word, she sniffles and begins to walk out of the parking lot in her trance. I can't hide my happiness. I didn't need to lift a finger for this to happen.

If taking what I want means leaving death in my wake, then so be it.

"Lily?"

She spins around with hope in her eyes. "I don't have to go?"

"You still do, but I want to let you know—" I lean over to whisper in her ear again "—If I can't have him, then no one fucking can. If I can't have him, I will burn this world to nothing along with everyone in it. I will gladly sit back and watch violence swallow the universe whole while my heart continues to beat for a man who has imprisoned himself in my blood. I do not care if you die. I do not care about your tears." I dig my talons into her flesh until she gasps. "I will be the murderer of all souls if it means I get to keep the one I want." I shove her away from me, getting sick of her scent.

Her aroma makes me sick. "Now, go on. I'm tired of knowing I have to breathe the same air as the woman who craved my mate's touch."

Lily nods in a daze, turns around, and heads to the busy traffic. There's only one lane open due to the accident. A firetruck is flying down the road, speeding to get to the scene in time in hopes of saving a life.

"You should hurry. That firetruck is the perfect vehicle. When you see the love of your life again, wherever it may be, send him my regards, okay? Tell him I said, 'Who's the fucking bitch now?'"

"Bye! It was nice meeting you."

"I hate you and just want you to die, Lily. Please—" I gesture to the road. "I don't have all day."

Finally, she inches closer to the main street. Vehicles of all shapes and sizes pull off to the side of the road to make room for the firetruck.

I tuck my hands in my pocket, waiting, watching, and Lily walks towards the firetruck before stopping in the middle of the road.

"Lady! Lady! Get out of the street. You're going to get yourself killed!" someone yells from their car window.

"Get out of the road!" another yells to try and help.

Their help is pointless. It's too late. See, if people truly cared, someone would get out of their car to help her, but that means risking their lives too. Not many would put a life before their own, not like me, not like what I'd do for Fitz.

I'd die for him.

Would anyone else do the same? No. Humans are selfish bloodthirsty creatures. I'm only doing what so many would do if they were in my shoes.

The firetruck honks its horn to get her to move but it's too late. The hard smack of her body hits the front, her bones breaking from the force. I can hear every snap from here. Her body flies through the air, landing a good fifteen feet away from the impact before skidding further down the road.

When she finally comes to a stop, her body is contorted in ways no one could survive. Blood pools around her. Her bones protrude out of her limbs. A rib pierces her chest. Her head is bashed in, bits of her brain scattered along the quaint hometown road where nothing bad ever happens.

Until I arrived.

Now, she won't be able to think or dream of my mate.

"Oh my God!" A voice from behind me has me schooling my features.

This is all so exhausting. I'm annoyed. Why can't I celebrate death in peace?

"This is terrible. Did you see what happened?" the woman with bright pink hair asks, staring at the wreckage.

"I did. That man lost control of his car and died, and I think she knew him? She walked right in front of traffic. Maybe she didn't want to be without him." There's something different about her scent.

It's wild and a claim has been put on her. I'm not sure by whom. Maybe the guy who owns Snapdragons Garage. I noticed he was a monster too.

"That's so sad. How terrible. You saw it happen?"

"I did. It was brutal." And fucking amazing.

Let's do it again!

"Oh my God, you must be in shock. Do you want a coffee? On the house. You're a witness so I can get Jake, the Sheriff, here to ask you some questions just to get it out of the way."

"I appreciate that, but I have an appointment actually.

With the traffic, I need to get going. Maybe another time I can take you up on your offer?" I don't know if I trust her, but she smells trustworthy. If she is mated to someone like me, she has to be.

I'll keep an eye on her.

"Of course. When you come by, ask for Demi." She holds out her hand.

I shake the small dainty palm, careful not to break it with my strength. "I'm Holly."

"It's nice to meet you. I'm sorry you had to see such a terrible accident today."

I'm ready to see more.

"Thank you. I'll be alright." Because I'm going to follow Fitz to his house and make myself at home. "It was nice meeting you too, Demi. I'm sure we will see each other again since I just moved to town."

She smiles and it irks me how much her happiness doesn't bother me.

"Well, welcome. We are so happy to have you. I hope you have a good rest of your day."

I climb into my van and reverse out of the parking spot. I pull out onto the road, passing Lily's body before she is covered with a tarp.

I've put my mark on this town. They have no idea what is coming for them if I don't have Fitz. It's a dangerous world out here.

So much violence. So much anger. So much revenge.

Every single ounce has been placed inside me and I'm ready to distribute every last drop of it until Fitz is in my arms and accepting of my love.

He will love me.

I don't care what I need to do to make that happen. His love is the only emotion that will balance me.

And I'll stop at nothing to get it.

FITZ

"No, I just pulled into the driveway, Rhett. I'm exhausted. I'll worry about getting the rest of my things tomorrow, okay?" I rub my eyes from how exhausted I am, hoping it helps me keep from falling asleep mid-conversation.

"Alright, if you're sure," Rhett says, clicking his tongue. "Are you okay? You sound more than exhausted."

I blow out a breath, leaning back in my seat as I stare at the front door of my new home. It's a large wooden door that is arched at the top with an iron handle. It was the first thing I saw that made me fall in love with this house.

"I'm okay. It's been a wild day. I was stuck in traffic for a while due to the accident."

A long pause occurs from his end. "And you had just talked to Ms. Livingston too. Are you okay? She's been a client of ours since the beginning. She was always supportive."

I scoff internally and immediately feel guilty about it. She only wanted to flirt with me, but I suppose business is business, right?

"Yeah, I just find it odd that she would walk straight into oncoming traffic like that. She seemed fine when I talked to her, Rhett. Hell, she has been wanting to go out with me for ages. I don't think she was seeing anyone like everyone is saying."

"Well, I hate to say this, but we really didn't know her that well, Fitz. She could have been seeing him, and in the moment of pain, she followed the path where she thought she'd find peace."

I shake my head but keep my mouth shut. I know in my gut that Ms. Livingston didn't know the man who died. According to the rumors spreading around town like wildfire, he was an out-of-town businessman just passing through.

How the hell would Ms. Livingston know him?

"I guess we will never know what happened." The same feeling I had in the parking lot overcomes me again.

The hairs on the back of my neck stand up, goosebumps tickling the surface of my skin. I glance out the window, darting my gaze through the darkness, but see nothing.

"Listen, I'm going to go. I need to shower and get some sleep. I'm barely able to function," I tell Rhett a small lie. I know I won't be able to sleep for another few hours, but he probably knows that too. It always takes me ages to fall asleep.

"No problem. If you need anything, you know me and Mickey are here for you, right?"

"Damn, I didn't even ask how she is doing. Is she alright?" I rub my temples, exhaling the all-too-familiar guilt slowly.

"Fitz, she is fine. Miserable. I don't blame her one bit. I'd tell you if she weren't. Thanks for asking. You're a good friend. Get some rest."

"Will do." I open the driver's side door, stepping out into the chill of the night. I'm about to hang up the phone when Rhett's voice has me bringing my cell back to my ear. "What was that?"

"Sorry. Quick question and then I'll let you go."

"Shoot," I tell him, flipping through the keys until I find the one that opens the front door.

"You're really okay with the shop?"

I grin, shaking my head. "Always so worried. I have rescheduled all non-urgent appointments. I'm only taking the ones that need to be seen immediately. I won't be okay if you don't let me go to bed."

He chuckles. "Alright. Have a good night."

"Night, Rhett." I hang up the phone and sag against the side of the truck. I'm bone fucking tired.

Grunting, I stretch to reach the door and close it. Tilting my head back, I stare up at the night sky, getting lost in the endless vast of stars. It's a moonless night which has the canopy of darkness somehow seem bigger as it stretches across for all eternity.

My phone rings again and I groan, "Come on, people. Can't a guy get a break?" My sister's name flashes across the screen. Another roll of guilt hits my stomach.

Ever since I moved away, I haven't been talking to her as much as I used to. It isn't because I don't miss her. My new life has just been busy.

It isn't right. I need to be a better big brother.

"Hey, Sis," I manage to answer, pouring every ounce of energy I have left for the day into those two simple words.

"Hey, Fitsgerald. About time I get to hear your voice. It's been too long."

I grimace when she calls me that. Fitz is only a nickname, shortened so I didn't sound like a grandfather.

It's a name passed down to every man in the family and It's a tradition that I would happily break.

"Sorry. It's been busy here opening up shop. I can't talk for long. I just got home and I'm so tired. Can I call you tomorrow?"

"Yes, I only called to make sure you were alive and well."

"I'm alive," I state, walking to my mailbox at the end of the driveway.

I haven't checked the mail in days. It's one of my worst habits. Nothing good is ever in the mail anyway unless I bought something online. If I get one more damn postcard about the pizza place in town, I'm never going to eat pizza again.

"But not well?" Her voice lowers to concern and a slight whisper.

"I'm well. I promise." Headlights coming down the street have me turn around. The beams are too bright and force me to turn away. "I love you, okay? I promise I'll call tomorrow when I get some sleep. It's not a good time. Give my nephew a hug for me."

"I love you too and I will. Talk at you later." She hangs up and I press the button on the side of my phone to turn the damn thing off. I officially no longer want to talk to anyone.

I flip through my mail. "Junk. Junk. Junk."

"Do you always talk to yourself or is this just a bad habit, Fitz?"

I look up from my gigantic pile of trash when a familiar voice captures my attention. My breath catches in my throat. My heart suddenly finds a different rhythm. My tongue forgets how to form words. The mail drops from my hands and the sound of it slapping against the pavement pulls me from my stupor.

"Holly? What—What are you doing h-here?" I stammer, wanting to kick myself for not sounding more put-together and smooth.

She smiles and I swear, I see fangs. I rub my eyes again and the long sharp cuspids are gone.

I really do need sleep if I'm hallucinating physical traits of monsters.

A man wants what he wants.

She bends down at the same time I do to gather my mail. Our hands touch, and a wild bolt sparks my fingertips and travels through my veins. Her touch alone gives me the bolt of energy I need.

I'm more awake than I was this morning.

"Sorry," she giggles, handing me a stack of mail.

"Don't worry about it. I'm glad to see you."

"Are you?"

I grin, running my oil-stained fingers through my hair. "I am. It's been one Hell of a day. It's good to see a friendly face."

"How do you know I'm friendly? I could be stalking you."

I lick my lips, wondering if that would really be so bad. "I think I'd live."

A flash of horns protrudes from her forehead but the moment she turns to look at the house next door, they are gone.

"Well, I'm sorry to disappoint, but—" she points to the house next door. "I just bought this house, so I'm your new neighbor. I guess I'll be bringing your mail to you, so it doesn't get so... piled up."

I tuck the thick stack of envelopes under my arms. "You're my new neighbor?"

"I am." Her long hair morphs from blonde to blue but just as quickly as the teal color is there, it's gone. "What a pleasant surprise to know I have such a handsome neighbor."

Heat fills my cheeks. I know I'm blushing. I've always been a bit bashful when it comes to women I like.

"I don't know about all that but if you need help moving in just let me know."

She closes the distance between us, locking eyes with me, before squatting ever so slowly. Holly is so close that her chin grazes my stomach. Then, my half-hard cock pressing against my zipper.

I gasp, and our eyes lock onto one another before she stands up again.

"You forgot a piece." She holds up another envelope that has a thirty-percent off sticker on it.

I swallow, unable to get my thoughts under control because all I see is her on her knees, sucking my cock.

"Have a good night, Fitz. I can't wait to see more of you." She backs away and if I'm not mistaken, she checks me out from top to bottom with a bite of her lip.

"Have a good morning. I mean day. I mean—" Kill me now. "—I mean night. Have a good night. Sleep well. Have sweet dreams." I wave at the most intriguing woman I've ever seen in my entire life.

"I'll be dreaming of you, so I doubt any of them will be sweet, Fitz." She blows me a kiss before unlocking her door and disappearing inside.

I'm finally able to let out a breath. "Holy shit." I toss the mail down on the ground and spin on my heel. Bending over, I rest my hands on my knees and chuckle, curious as to why I'm so out of breath as if I've run five miles.

Holly seems to suck the air out of the space she invades. My space. My head feels light, yet my body is wound so tight. I bet the only way to relax would be to feel her hands on me.

I bend down, again, to get my mail, and whistle as I walk to my own front door. My thoughts clouded with Holly. I almost feel like I've had one too many beers. I'm going to blame it on the long, odd day instead of seeing Holly and learning she is my neighbor.

How am I going to be able to act normal when I see her outside? What if she knocks and needs a cup of sugar one day?

"Get a fucking grip, Fitz," I tell myself as I fumble with the damn lock I need to replace. "Come on." I wiggle the key, kick the door, pull it towards me, and finally the damn thing opens. "Well, that needs to be fixed." I toss my keys on the small handmade coffee table sitting against the wall to the right.

Feels good to be home even if I'm alone. I sit on the stool I keep next to the front entrance and unlace my boots before kicking them to the side. Stretching my leg out, I kick the door closed, then reach for the deadbolt to lock it.

My head thuds against the wall as I take a moment to myself and appreciate the silence. With hooded eyes, I study my new space. Even though I have a sectional couch, a large flat-screen TV, a recliner, and a small wet bar to the right near the kitchen, the house is empty.

I hope that changes one day. The sound of silence is haunting. It's heavy, suffocating, and a stark reminder of how this house is not a home just yet. Love doesn't fill it.

Yet.

It seems the more I want an all-consuming love, the more unrealistic it becomes.

I groan as I force myself to my feet. My knees pop from the ripe old age of thirty-nine. Unbuttoning my pants, I head toward the staircase to go up to my bedroom. As I climb, I take a moment to look at the photos I have framed on the greyish-green painted wall.

From photos of me and my sister playing in the mud, to my high school graduation, to the first day of working at Rhett's Garage, to a picture of him and me in front of Snapdragons.

It's wild that I'm one of the few that can see him. It's a shame no one will be able to see how extraordinary he is because they will feel threatened. I hate it for him.

My hand follows up the industrial rail. The metal is a rusted dark brown. More my style than the old, chipped oak that was left behind. I've even put gorgeous metal beams across the ceiling to tie it in.

This house only needed a few tweaks. What sold me was the view of the lake. I can see why Mickey loves the water so much. It's so relaxing.

I kick my bedroom door open, the bathroom so close I can nearly feel the hot shower searing my back. I turn the knob that controls the new low-hanging lights installed, giving the room a faint glow instead of a bright light.

Shucking off my shirt, I toss it in the hamper, unzip my pants, and kick them off to the side.

I'll pick them up later.

Sliding the door open to the bathroom, I take a moment

to appreciate the upgrades the previous owners did. The tile consists of small dark green hexagons with black grout. The double vanity holds two copper sinks and a large antique mirror with a copper frame hangs on the wall above. The toilet is to the left but it's the shower and tub that I'm obsessed with.

Both the shower and tub are enclosed in the same space surrounded by frosted glass. The green hexagon tiles continue through the stall. The soaking tub can hold three of me while the showerhead is gigantic and hangs from the ceiling. There is a touchscreen inside that controls the temperature, a heated towel rack, and can frost the glass more or less.

I don't care about that since I'm the only one who lives here.

Snagging the black handle, I open the stall door and press a button on the touch screen that turns the shower on. Then, I press the aromatherapy button, and as soon as it begins to steam, lavender fills the air.

I inhale as deeply as I can, the stress from the day easing away. The spray of hot water soaks my hair as I step under it, allowing the water to wash away all the sweat, oil, and grease.

First, I wash my body with a loofah and scrub every inch of my skin. The second step is to scrub my fingers, getting the gunk from under my blunt fingernails. Like always, I wash my hair by squirting the shampoo directly on my head and continue scrubbing until the water runs from grey to clear.

Now, I stand there, enjoying the hot water and relaxing my tight muscles. I press a hand against the wall, my shaggy hair falling into my eyes. I brush it out of the way, hanging my head as the pressure from the spray massages the back of my neck.

Closing my eyes, my mind is occupied with Holly.

Not the human version of her, the monster my mind keeps conjuring. Groaning, I lean my head against my bicep, imagining I'm wrapping my hands around her horns as I thrust into her, using them as leverage to fuck her as hard as I can.

I have a feeling she'd love that.

"Fuck." I grip my thick cock, stroking it to the thought of fucking the monster who belongs to me.

Her blue hair is bright, draped across the black silk of the pillow.

She screams my name, "Fitz. More. Harder."

And I give it to her, giving her more with every fucking thrust.

"You like that. You love my fat cock. You love being stretched and used."

She growls at me, flashing her fangs with a promise of violence before flipping me onto my back.

"I'll show you what it's like to be stretched and used, Fitz." Something long and slick slips into my ass, pressing against a spot I've never explored before.

"Oh, fuck, Holly. That feels so good. Don't stop. Keep doing that." In my mind, it feels so good, but I don't know if I'd ever dare to actually do it.

Wings spread out of her back, the tips pinning my wrists above my head. Her tongue shifts from normal to a tentacle and she tests the suction by licking up my stomach. Small circular dots appear, similar to a hickey. The small mark makes me feel claimed like she has stamped ownership on me.

"You're all mine, Fitz. This body. This cock." Her tentacles wrap around my dick, giving it a teasing squeeze.

I whimper.

"I want your come, Good Boy. I want it so bad. You know I can't live without it." She slides her tight cunt down on my shaft and my fucking toes curl against the tile. Holly rocks back and forth. "Give it to me. Fill me. I want every drop. Be a good boy and breed me."

The praise has come shooting from my cock, my orgasm wracking through my body and causing my knees to go weak.

"Holly, oh, fuck, Holly. Take every drop. It's yours. Every fucking drop of me," I moan so loud, thankful I'm by myself.

Just as I tilt my head back, I swear a shadow moves from the corner of my eye. My chest rises and falls as I try to catch my breath from the best orgasm I've ever had.

"Hello?" I call out, licking the water from my lip.

There's no way someone could be here. It's only me.

I wash the evidence of my dirty thoughts down the drain, press the button on the screen to shut the water off, and snag a warm towel from the rack.

"Just imagining things," I mumble to myself while I dry off and another shadow captures my attention.

I laugh when I see my own shadow cast on the floor.

"Idiot. You need to sleep." I ignore the paranoia telling me someone is in my house.

I wipe the condensation from the mirror, staring at my reflection as I brush my teeth. My hair curls at the end just above my eyes and I make a mental note to get a haircut. I debate on shaving but damn it, I don't feel like it, so I decide to leave the stubble just to crawl into bed a few minutes earlier.

Spitting the toothpaste in the sink, I rinse my mouth out, and straighten, catching a glimpse of Holly in the mirror.

"What the fuck!" I spin around, but she isn't there.

It's just the wall.

I'm relieved and disappointed.

"Fucking Hell, Fitz. Get a grip. Your imagination is running wild. Calm the hell down." I flip the bathroom light off and crawl into bed, covering myself with the comforter.

It isn't long before my body becomes light, my mind becomes quiet, and my eyes close to finally get some rest.

I swear I feel someone watching me but I'm so tired, I don't care. Maybe my house is haunted.

"Make yourself at home," I grumble with my eyes still shut, fluffing my pillow.

"Don't worry, I will."

I chuckle at my own thoughts. It's official.

I've lost my mind.

CHAPTER FIVE

HOLLY

I only had the privilege of hearing him scream my name and watching his shadow behind the frosted glass while he stroked his cock. I got to see his shadow pick up a bottle and squirt shampoo onto his head—odd—but that isn't what is important.

I didn't get to see his face pinch with pleasure. I didn't get to witness his body finding relief from the thoughts of me. I didn't get to see his come paint the wall. I didn't get to see his cock tense and flex.

And I'm very fucking pissed off about it.

He shouldn't have to count on himself. He has me to make him feel good. My poor little Doe Eyes, so wound up by the thoughts of me.

I step out from the wall, unveiling my true self. My skin changes from the color of the wall and floor to light purple. I stretch my wings, rolling my lips together to swallow the moan trying to escape.

I'll need to find time to fly soon. I've been a busy girl

following and watching him. Let's not forget killing for him—well— for me. I haven't made time to take care of myself.

It's time I change that.

"Such a handsome man," I whisper in the dark, tilting my head as if he is the most fascinating creature I've ever seen asleep. "You deserve to be protected, Doe Eyes. You're all too sweet for this world." I tiptoe around the bed, pausing when the floorboards groan under my weight.

Fitz adjusts in his sleep, flipping to his side and the blanket slips to his hips. My mouth waters, my fangs descend, and I roam my gaze over every square inch of his torso. He is sun-kissed with a dusting of hair on his chest that is sprinkled down his abs. A thin, groomed happy trail leads below the blanket, and I want to see what it is hiding.

I can still scent his orgasm hanging in the air. Such a waste for it to have gone down the shower drain when I'm aching to feel the warmth of his come inside me.

"We can't let that happen again, Doe Eyes," I whisper, careful not to wake him. "You don't mind, do you?" I kneel on the floor, uncaring that it is uncomfortable, then crawl my way to his side of the bed. "I crave you. I'm so hungry."

I reach for him, running my fingers through his thick head of hair. He grumbles before a small smile curls his lips.

"My good boy needs attention. How long has it been since you've been touched, Fitz? How long has it been since you've been the center of someone's universe?" Daring to move my hand, I hold my breath, needing to touch his skin in some way.

My eyes water with need as an unfamiliar emotion tries to swallow me whole. A slight tremble has my hand become unsteady. Knowing I'm so close to my mate is an overwhelming sensation.

It's as if the love I am capable of has exploded beyond a level I can't understand. If my love were a star, it would burn slowly, so Fitz could have it for all eternity.

I release a nervous breath when the warmth of his cheek sinks into my palm.

"I'll take care of you," I say to him, leaning down to appreciate every freckle dashed across his nose. "You are mine now. I protect what is mine." Wanting more now that I'm so close, his lips are their own galaxy, beaconing for me to explore.

And who would I be if I didn't give in to such temptation?

Usually, it is me feeding from the desire of others, but my desire seems to be a constant flame being fueled by gasoline when I'm around him.

"You need to alleviate me." I cup his jaw, my lips so close to his, that I can feel the soft puffs of breath grazing my mouth.

Unable to control myself any longer, I press our lips together. The kiss is soft with barely any pressure, so he doesn't wake up, but still, the delicate clouds give and form to my own.

I lose control.

I begin kissing him harder, wanting him to kiss me back. I open my mouth, slipping my tongue across his bottom lip.

"Give me more, Doe Eyes. Let me taste your tongue," I beg of him.

His heartbeat changes, the steady usual pace becomes faster. His eyes blink slowly, fighting sleep, and I push myself from the bed to the wall, blending in with my environment so he can't see me.

Fitz sits up fast, flipping on the lamp sitting on the nightstand. "Hello?" He scrubs his eyes with his large hands which I imagine would engulf me in all the right ways. "Is someone there?" His fingers press against his lips, confusion pinching his eyebrows.

I move from the side of his bed to the bottom, staying close to the wall so he can't see me. He looks so fucking good half asleep. The brown strands of his hair stand up in every direction. He seems to be fighting sleep and reality as he scans his room.

I'm here, Doe Eyes. You aren't alone.

The blanket is just covering his cock. I can see the lighter part of his thighs that don't get enough sun, and they look so soft, so smooth. His abs flex and his bicep casts its own shadow on the blanket as he lifts his arm to reach behind his back to scratch his shoulder.

My tentacles slip free from me, stretching out in need for him. They drip with arousal fluid. I won't be able to wait for him. I'm going to have to invade his dreams to get what I fucking want.

"Get your shit together, Fitz," he says to himself, flipping the switch on the lamp to turn the light off.

He lies back down, one hand over his head, the other lying on his stomach, and I stand there in admiration while I witness the gift of him falling asleep. Only when his breaths are quiet and even, do I step out of the shadows.

I flap my wings until I'm barely off the ground, inching my way over his sleeping form. I hover above him, appreciating the defined line of his jaw. I bring my mouth to his ear and say the words that allow me to enter his mind.

"Let me give you the sweetest dreams." The statement is

delicate and soft, my succubus dying to get inside his head.

I want to force him to dream of me. I'm going to bombard him every night. Soon, he'll be so in love with our dreams, all he will want to do is sleep so he can see me.

His body relaxes even further and his eyes open, clouding with a light purple hue now that I'm in his mind.

"Let me see what you're dreaming about." I kiss his lips again, lowering my body onto his. I don't have to worry about him waking up as long as I'm in his mind. "Show me, Doe Eyes. Be a good boy for me. Let me in," I call out to his soul. "Where are you? What are you wanting? What can I make come true for you?" I lick his earlobe before sucking it into my mouth.

I sit up, straddling his lap, grinning from ear to ear when his dream includes me. I don't cloak myself. I reveal who I really am. This is a dream, after all. Anything is possible.

We're standing on the side of the road where we met. His dream is sweet, replaying the moment we first met.

"Mmm, but I want so much more, Doe Eyes." I open the van door and slip out of the driver's seat.

"You are fucking beautiful," he says loud and clear, but under the influence of my power. "I've always wanted someone like you." He grips my horns in the dream and in real time, his hands barely move.

He drags me toward him, kissing me with a ferocious vigor that I would not expect from him. He's so kind and sweet. His eyes seem to light up in a way when he talks to someone who isn't seen anymore.

Right now, his light brown eyes are ink-filled pools. The pupils are blown with lust, leaving no room for the golden flecks of his irises to show. In the dream, he slams his lips down on mine, and I can't help but take advantage of it in real-time.

He is laid out for the taking and what kind of monster would I be if I didn't take advantage?

Sliding my hand up his chest, I tweak his nipple along the way until I palm the side of his neck, kissing him as if I've been waiting my entire life for his lips on mine.

I suppose I have in a way.

Our tongues slip together as the kiss deepens. In the dream, Fitz slams me against the car and strokes my horns.

I can feel that. I can feel the callouses of his hard-working hands sliding up every ridge. I whimper into his mouth, and he groans in return. I wish he could move. Invading dreams is different for all men. Some can move and even act out every motion while others are still.

At least Fitz can speak and kiss me. His kiss alone is an experience I needed if I ever died, then I would live in death in ecstasy.

He pushes me down to my knees in his dream and I break our kiss, dragging my lips across his jaw.

In the next dream, I'll control his thoughts, but this one was already set up just how I wanted it.

"Fuck. Oh God, you feel so fucking good. What are you going to do to me? Don't make me wait."

I silence him with my tail, slipping the tip between his lips. He moans, sucking and nibbling, stroking it with his tongue, and it has a direct line to my tentacles. They become crazed, each sucker dripping with my arousal, drenching his sheets.

My tongue shifts into a thicker tentacle, suction cupping to the side of his neck to leave a mark. He arches his back off the bed and yet in the dream he slams his hand on the roof of the van, his self-control spiraling.

I lick down his chest, kissing his left and right pec before sucking his nipple into my mouth. I tug on the chains attached to my nipple piercings, wishing it was his hands that were controlling how much pleasure I felt.

I can't risk it.

Even if he saw me outside of his dreams, he would be saying something completely different. He may say he has always wanted me, but that's the succubus power controlling his mind. He is emanating desire, and my body is soaking it up, feeding me like a king would his queen.

I have to have him while I can.

He's the reason for my existence. I was created to be his and his alone.

I rake my fingers down his chest, dipping my tongue into his belly button, and he tosses his head back in his dream. What I love about manipulating thoughts is I can do whatever I want. I don't have to unbutton his jeans or lower his zipper. If I imagine him naked, he'll be naked.

When I get to the edge of the sheet covering what I so desperately want to see, my fangs scrape across his hip bone, and he hisses.

"Be a good boy, Fitz. You're going to give me your come. I can't live without it. I need to taste it. I need you bound to me. Can you do that for me?"

"I'll give you whatever you fucking want. Please, don't stop."

I rip the blanket from his body, uncovering what I've been wanting to see since the moment I met him.

"Oh, Fitz," I gasp, palming his thick weight in my hand.

"You're perfect." He isn't too long. I'd say he is more on the average side, but he is thick. I wrap one hand around the rock-solid length and my fingers don't touch. I can't wait for my tentacles to wrap around him, my cunt stretching as he pushes inside me, claiming me as his mate.

There's a vein traveling the impressive girth. I swirl my tentacled tongue around it, the appendage waving, the suckers moving and massaging him before I suck him into my mouth.

His grip tightens on my horns the moment I suck the wide crown into my mouth, tracing the outline with my tongue. His knees tremble in our escape together by the van, but even in this bed, a slight tremor vibrates his body.

A sardonic grin takes over my face knowing I have such an intense effect on him.

"My own monster," he gasps when I take him to the back of my throat. "Fuck, that thought alone will make me come."

"Not yet," I tell him, licking the bead of precome from the slit. "I don't want you to spill down my throat. I need you to breed me, Fitz. Are you going to fill me to the brim? Are you going to make sure you claim my womb?"

He rips me from his cock, pulls me to my feet by my horns, and grabs my shorts. Fitz rips the button free, the zipper breaking. My wild mate tugs the shorts down, letting me know loud and clear what he wants.

"Such a naughty boy. You can't wait, can you? Only good boys get to come."

"I'm the best fucking boy. I'll be your good boy. I need you so much. I need to feel you."

I ignore him, continuing to suck his hard cock. The tip is a light dusty red. His entire length is filled with so much blood, that it almost looks like he is in pain.

"Such an impressive cock, Fitz. I can't believe you've been hiding this. I wanted to so badly get on my knees for you by the van. I would have too. You just say when and where, and my mouth is yours to use."

I cup him between his legs, rolling his orbs in my palm. His sack is pulled tight, the filled orbs dying to release. I kiss them, suck one into my mouth, then the other, wishing I had all the time in the world to have my way with him.

But he'll wake for work in a few hours and there's so much I want to do.

I drag myself up his body, my tight beaded nipples scrape over the dips of his abdomen. His breathing is quick and shallow. He fists the sheets under him, twisting them so hard his knuckles turn white.

"Relax, My Sweet Doe." I grab his hand and kiss his strained knuckles. "I'm going to take such good care of you." I kneel over his lap, staring down to watch my tentacles wrap around his cock.

His mouth drops open, his eyes shine a brighter purple as the dream changes, and I have him flat on his back in the van. I'm projecting into his mind what I'm doing to him in real-time. I don't want him to dream of anything else right now but our first time together.

I might not be able to have him in the day, but he is all mine when the darkness falls. He won't ever be allowed to be with anyone else. His loneliness will be cured, and he'll have no idea why.

Maybe one day I'll tell him, and he'll figure out a way to forgive me.

His forgiveness can be earned when he remembers my

love and want for him.

"Holly," he croaks, slapping his hand on the inside wall of the van. "Fuck. Oh my God—" his eyes round when he sees the tentacles massaging his cock, up and down, twisting and turning, the suckers moving at their own rate. "You have to stop. You have to. I can't hold back. I'm going to—I'm going to—" White streams erupt from his cock, splashing against my pussy. The wild white ropes drench my tentacles, and I can taste the saltiness of his come on my tongue as if I've licked him clean.

His entire body jerks when the tentacles continue to stroke him. Sweat drips from his temples. He is falling apart and the only person who can catch him wants to enjoy the tumble through the unknown. To taste his fear, the nerves, and the panic.

But then I'd just wrap him in my arms and take care of him forever because he is mine. He's fucking mine. I'll stop at nothing and no one to get to him. If anyone dared to take him from me, I'll kill them. I'll murder everyone on this planet in cold fucking blood if it means he would live a happier life.

He has a monster now and there is nothing in this world that matters more than his life.

"I. Need. More." Spit flies from his mouth while trying to speak through clenched teeth. The tendons in his neck are tensed and there is a red flush to his cheeks. "Please, I need it."

"Such a good pretty boy when you beg," I croon, curling over him while I continue my assault on his shaft.

"I love being your good boy." He licks his lips and those big round eyes blink at me through long lashes.

Staring down at him in his dream and real life has me wishing he could truly see me. His eyes are the innocence I miss from when I was human. I don't feel that anymore. All I have is rage for everyone except Fitz and this need to claim and protect him with my life.

While I don't feel those human emotions the same any longer, I'm reminded of them when I look him in his eyes, giving me a glimpse of what a good soul is.

"I would kill for you, Doe Eyes." I press my forehead against his, tracing his jaw. "I have killed for you." His cock jerks wrapped in my grip. "You like that, don't you? You love being the center of my attention. You love that someone would go that far for you."

He nods, stretching his neck to try to kiss me. "I do. I want you to consume me until I can't live without you. You're my reminder to breathe."

My tentacles part, giving me access to his cock, and I slide myself over the wide thick tip. I rip my crop top off over my head in the dream, and his eyes widen when he sees my nipple rings attached to chains.

He tugs them softly and I hiss, loving the pain.

"Yes, Fitz. Just like that." My wings spread of their own volition as I lose myself in our fantasy. I barely have one toe in reality, wanting to be with the man who can see me for me.

The crown of his cock rubs against my clit with every slow rock I give him. "Such a big cock, Fitz. Anyone ever told you that?" My talons grow to a dangerous length at the thought of him fucking another woman.

I'd need names. I wouldn't be able to live in a world knowing there are other women who know what it feels like to have their pussy stretched by Fitz.

No, no, that wouldn't be allowed to happen.

"No," he grunts, biting his top lip as he watches my tentacles slip between his thighs. "Everyone said I was always on the shorter side."

I wrap my hand around his throat at the same time a tentacle plays with his hole. "By morning, you'll leave a list on your nightstand of the women who said that to you. Okay?"

His eyes are glassy, and a single tear rolls down his cheek when I press a tentacle inside, pressing against his prostate.

Fitz shouts as more come spurts from him.

"Answer me," I demand, rolling a tentacle over his prostate.

"Y-ye-yes," he stammers.

I gasp when I sink down onto the first inch of his cock. I take my time with him, slowly swallowing him. "This cock was made for me. So fucking thick, Fitz. God, you're taking my breath." Those other women were stupid to think his cock was anything less than perfect. I get to ride him for the rest of our lives and there is no way I'll get used to the stretch of him filling me.

Slapping his chest, I dig my nails into his pecs riding him hard and fast. I don't want to waste any more time. "You feel so good. I wish you could see me using you, Doe Eyes. I wish you could see how much I love your cock. I can't wait to claim you for all to see. You're mine." I lean back, slapping my hand on his knee while rolling my hips. "This is mine. Mine to taste and fuck. Mine to care for. No other pussy could take you like this." I have suckers on the inside too, massaging every inch of him, length and width.

In the dream, he begins fucking me from the bottom. His hips slightly moving in real-time from his wicked intentions happening in our heads.

"Fitz." I run my hands through my hair and tilt my head back, increasing my pace. My clit slides across him with every thrust. "You make me so wet. Do you hear it? Do you hear how much you drive me crazy?" I fuck him harder, wanting nothing more than to ram my horns into his bedframe.

"You're so fucking tight. I love those tentacles. Fucking—" his groan is so loud, I'm curious if the neighbors across the lake heard it. "You're going to make me come, Holly. I need to pull out. If you don't—" I cover his mouth with my hand, my whimpers becoming louder and faster the closer I get to orgasm.

Nothing will stop me from drinking in his come.

My wings stretched as wide as they possibly could, breaking one of the dangling light bulbs. The headboard smacks against the wall and I claw his pecs as the biggest orgasm I've ever had convulses my muscles.

I tense, moaning his name for all to hear, "Fitz. Oh, fuck. Yes, oh, good boy making me come." Black ink squirts from me making the space between us an absolute mess.

"Holly! Damn it. No," he groans, his cock flexing as streams of warm come fill me. "Didn't want it to end." His eyes roll to the back of his head in pleasure.

The ink spills between us from my orgasm, my claim officially finding its own pattern to mark him forever. I'll need a few more nights with him for the pattern to grow to its full potential. Only when the marking is finally visible, is the mating complete.

I bend down, kissing him, realizing our time together is almost over.

"Please, don't go," he says between kisses, tucking a piece of blue hair behind my ear, and that gesture alone, has me feeling like a fragile woman in the hands of a strong man.

I've never felt that before.

"I'll be where you can see," I tell him with a smile, wishing I didn't have to go, but he'll wake soon now that the dream is over.

"What's that mean?"

"Everywhere you'll be, I'll be, Doe Eyes. I'm your monster mate. You won't go anywhere without me." I slip from his cock, my tentacles rolling together to create a plug so his come doesn't leak out, and stare down at the mess I've made on him.

Onyx drips down my thighs, proof of my orgasm. I dash to the bathroom, and I still don't feel sated after I claimed him. I need something else. I need my scent on him every day.

Remembering how he washed his hair, I open the stall to the shower and snag his shampoo. Twisting off the top, I sniff the liquid when I notice it is dark. "What..." I read the label and grin.

This couldn't be more perfect for my plan. Fitz has detoxifying charcoal shampoo which is dark grey. I'm going to take advantage of this and anything else I can put my ink into. I press the open bottle against my thigh, catching the excess drops.

Twisting the top on, I give the bottle a good shake and leave it in the same spot on the shelf. Walking back into the bedroom, I stare at my beautiful mate.

"Holly," he whispers in his sleep.

My heart tugs towards him. I want nothing more than to crawl into bed and have him hold me. I could.

But I won't.

Before I go, I snag one of his work shirts from the laundry bin and slip it over my head. His scent surrounds me, easing the tension of my beasts. I don't like or want to leave him.

I have to.

I sink into the shadows, blend into my surroundings, and watch him.

If watching him were all I had to do, my life would be fulfilled.

CHAPTER SIX

FITZ

The jarring sound of my alarm going off wakes me with a start. I sit up as I gasp for breath. My head feels a bit cloudy. My heart is racing. I turn, glaring at my alarm when a low aching throb begins to pulse in my temple.

I snag the alarm, rip the plug from the socket, then throw it across the room. It smashes against the wall; the loud obnoxious beeping slows until it finally stops.

Dead.

I've been known to be a really kind guy. I've given the shirt off my back before. I've bought coffee for people I don't know. I've donated. I've built homes for others that aren't as fortunate as I am. I've gotten calls in the early morning from friends who need help or a ride.

I'm there.

But I am not a morning person. I hate mornings.

It's wild to me that people have to get up early for work. Whoever made that rule deserves a punch in the face.

I'm more of a noon to eight kind of guy. It's why Rhett

lets me work behind the desk for a few hours when I get there. I'm not a fully functioning human being until my second cup of coffee. I buy alarm clocks in bulk because I end up breaking more than three a week.

I tried the alarm on my phone twice and that was two times more than I wanted to dish out funds for a phone. It's cheaper to buy alarm clocks.

Rubbing my eyes with the palm of my hands, I yawn, stretching my arms above my head. My shoulders pop and I groan, cracking my neck next. I inhale, smelling the brew of my coffee lingering in the air from the kitchen.

I love automatic programming.

Snagging the edge of the blanket, I rip it off and swing my legs over the edge of the bed. As I stretch my back, I cock my head to the side when I see one of my lightbulbs is broken.

"When the hell did I do that?" My voice is raspy with sleep and my mind still isn't clear enough for me to remember how I did that.

I sidestep the broken glass on the floor, stumbling my way into the bathroom. My hand slaps the wall searching for the light switch. Once, twice, finally, I find it and flip it on. I wince from the light.

I close my eyes while I brush my teeth, needing a few more seconds of shut-eye. I don't bother to rinse my mouth out when I'm done. I'll do it in the shower.

Some people might find this odd, but I sit down while I use the restroom, so piss doesn't get everywhere. It's gross to me. If I stand to do my business, splashes of urine and water go everywhere. Gross.

And I wipe.

Because why would shaking it be enough? I don't want to walk around with piss dribbling out of my dick. I'd rather just deal with it when I'm going.

Call me crazy, but I rather like that my bathroom and I don't reek of piss.

Finally, I make my way to the shower. I'm still half asleep and can't walk in a straight line. Why is waking up so hard? I don't even see which button I press to turn the shower on, but whatever I hit, it worked. The hot shower spray is instant, and I slip under the spray, closing my eyes to relax and enjoy the warmth.

As the water runs down my body, the dream I had last night comes back to me in pieces.

It was a dream with Holly.

Wild.

I tilt my head back, the water running down my face like tears, and the image of her on top of me in her van has my cock hardening. I readjust my stance, a slight ache in my ass for some reason.

Pausing, I think back to everything I did yesterday, but I can't think of one thing that would hurt me there.

Maybe I played with myself in my sleep from the wet dream I had. I wouldn't be surprised. That was the hottest fucking thing that has ever entered my mind. When her tentacles gripped around my cock, milking me, massaging me, I lost it. Her horns felt so good in my hands. Her wings were silky smooth.

And her nipple rings?

"Fucking hell," I groan.

I have no time to enjoy all these replays. I need to get going. The shop opens in two hours and there's plenty I have to do.

Snagging my shampoo, which my sister got me, or I wouldn't use this fancy shit, I squirt it onto my head, then lather. I wash it free, loving how the light coming through the window reflects the different colors in the grey bubbles. There is almost an iridescent sheen, reminding me of what happens when light meets oil.

Next, I scrub my body.

And that's when I notice it.

There are thick black lines on my cock, veining out where my pubic hair is, and one of the very tips swirls up and stops at my mid-hip bone.

"What the fuck is that? What is that?" I shout, using my loofah to scrub the spot.

I rinse the bubbles off and it's still there.

"This is wild. What the fuck happened to me? What is this? Is this a joke?" And then it hits me. "That mother fuck-er." I bet he broke into my house in ghost form and played a sick joke with a permanent marker.

I never thought I'd sleep through another man drawing on my dick, which now that I think of it, I know he wouldn't do. I don't know another option, though. How did this mark just appear out of nowhere? This wasn't here yesterday.

I don't bother washing off the suds from my body. I run out of the shower, water dripping from my body onto the floors. I slip, catching myself on the corner of the vanity.

"This can't be real. This isn't real," I mutter in panic, snagging a towel off the rack.

There is no condensation on the mirror because the bathroom door is open. Only a little at the very top since heat rises.

"Holy fucking shit!" I shout at the top of my lungs, staring at my dick's reflection.

It's still there.

I scrub my skin with the towel. "Come on. Come on. This isn't funny. I swear to God, I'm going to kill Rhett. I'm going to kill him." He'll probably kill me first before I have a chance to charge but at least I tried.

This mark isn't coming off.

I toss the towel on the floor and stare at my reflection again. I comb my fingers through my hair, taking a deep breath as I try to calm down.

"Wild. Fucking wild." I tug on the roots of my hair. "There's no other way to explain it and there has to be an explanation as to why I suddenly have a tattoo on my fucking cock." I yell at my dick, wondering how it got itself in this position.

How I got myself into this position.

With angry steps, I stomp my way to the bedroom, snatching my phone from the nightstand. I don't care how early it is. Rhett is going to hear from me.

I click his name in my phone and press call, placing him on speaker. Five rings sound before he finally answers.

"Do you know what time it is?" He yawns. "Everything alright? You never call this early."

"No. Everything is not alright, Rhett. I need you to be honest with me. Do not lie."

"Fitz, what's going on?" My best friend sounds more serious, the sleepy tone of his voice replaced with concern in an instant.

"Did you shift into your ghost, break into my house, and draw something on my dick?"

Silence falls between us before a loud laugh has me tugging the phone away because the speaker crackles.

While he laughs, I open the nightstand drawer, pull out a pen and paper, and start writing the names of all the girls who thought my cock was too short. I have no idea why. I just know I need to. The satisfying rip of the page from the pad can't even be heard over my best friend's laughter.

I slap the note on the nightstand, trying to figure out along with everything else why I needed to do that.

"Rhett, I'm serious. This isn't funny. I can't get it off. I've scrubbed it until the skin is raw. I just need to know if you did it."

His laughter dies and he becomes more serious. "It won't come off? At all? Not even a little?"

"No. Nothing. I'm worried, man. I need to go to the doctor to make sure everything is okay. I don't have any clients coming in today. Their cars are at the shop already. I'll get to the garage, but I'll be a few hours late. I just wanted to let you know."

"Listen, I don't know what is going on, but I wouldn't break into your house when I have a very pregnant wife who is about to give birth to twins. I wouldn't leave her alone at night. And I love you like a brother, but I'm not drawing on your dick."

I'm not sure why I release a long breath of relief. I knew in my heart he wouldn't do that to me but since it wasn't Rhett, I'm at a loss.

"I don't know, man. It's wild. Maybe I did it. A lightbulb is broken too, the one hanging near the wall by my bed."

"Maybe. Don't worry about the shop. It will be fine for the day. Take care of yourself and keep me updated."

I nod, forgetting he can't see me. "Yeah, I will."

"I'm sure it's nothing. Okay? Don't borrow worry when you don't have all the facts."

"Yeah, yeah–" I clear my throat. "Okay, go back to sleep. I'll let you know when I have updates." I hang up the phone, my heart thudding in my chest with fear.

I can't help but spiral and think of the worst. What if I have that flesh-eating disease? On my dick? That's a stupid thought. It wouldn't look like this... would it? I don't know.

My body is still damp when I throw on sweatpants, a T-shirt, and a hoodie. I don't even bother with my coffee. Nothing is going to slow me down from getting to the doctor. I slide my phone into my pocket, then run down the steps so fast, that I miss the last stair, and run right into the front door.

"I hate mornings," I grumble, pushing myself away from the door.

My jaw aches. My cheek is red from the hit but the only thing that would stop me from getting to the doctor is if I died. I grab my keys from the coffee table, slip on my boots without tying the laces, and I'm out the damn door.

It's a chilly morning with fog heavy in the air, rolling in from the lake. It's quiet. Peaceful.

Unlike me, right now.

Morning dew sticks to the blades of grass. The green is slowly fading to brown from the chill swooping in and preparing for winter.

I press my forehead against the window of my truck. It's cool and a bit slick from condensation but it feels good. I take big deep breaths. I'm blowing this out of proportion. Everything is fine. I'm acting like this for no reason other than the fact it's morning and the mark caught me by surprise.

Other than that, I had a great night. Hell, I had the best night of sleep I have ever had. If I think about Holly scraping her nails down my chest, the light purple hue of her skin, and her horns protruding out of her forehead, the panic is gone and replaced with desire.

Holy shit.

I've made up a monster in my head because I want her so badly.

"Stupid. Stupid. Stupid." I thud my forehead against the window, unlock the door, and jump in the driver's seat.

It only takes a second for me to peel out of the driveway, take a peek at Holly's house, and drive away. The further I get from home, the more my stomach twists. My mind is consumed by this image of Holly that I've created. It isn't fair to her. I'm completely changing her image to suit what I crave.

I have to stay away from her. It's the only way these thoughts will end. Damn it, I love all the thoughts, though. She's so fucking beautiful. She is prettier than a sunset by the lake. All the shades of red, oranges, yellows, and purples hold no flame to her.

The monster, that is. I don't have feelings for human Holly.

"You're a damn wreck, Fitz." I peek in the rearview mirror and point at myself. "Get your shit together." I slap my cheek to give me a sharp wake-up call.

What's sad is I can't even say this isn't like me. I've always liked the unusual. I've always appreciated someone's quirks. The little gestures and odd things that make them, them.

I know I say the word 'wild' too much, but it's such a

perfect thing to say to pretty much anything.

Someone had a baby? That's wild.

Someone die? That's wild.

Someone dreams of a monster fucking them with tentacles? Also, wild.

I pass the gorgeous mountains as I drive down Main Street. The town looks deserted. There isn't a person in sight. The fog creeping gives an eerie appearance as if the entire town has been abandoned.

I pass Demi's Diner. The bright pink neon sign is on. It's the one place anyone can go any time of day for peace and a nice cup of coffee. Maybe I'll go there after I see the doctor.

If I'm feeling lucky, maybe Demi can add a little something extra to the cup to help my mind ease.

A few minutes longer of following the same road, the urgent care comes up on the right. Putting on my blinker, I turn into the empty parking lot, but I know they are open. They always open at six in the morning.

I grip the steering wheel before pressing my forehead against it, trying to calm my racing heart. I'm trying to think about what happened last night. Did I have too much to drink? I don't think I drank but it's the only explanation I have for not remembering a damn thing that could explain this mark.

Unless...

I pinch the bridge of my nose, knowing the thought that just entered my mind is impossible.

What if I do have my own monster?

"You're losing your fucking mind. That's too wild of a thought. Rhett and Creed would know if there's a monster in town. Think logically, Fitz." Blowing out a breath, I turn off the truck, grab the door handle, and open it. "You can do this." I step out onto the empty parking lot, and there it is again, that fucking feeling I have of someone watching me.

I rub my temples, wondering if I just need some sleep. My thoughts keep spiraling. Do I need therapy? Is something actually wrong with me?

My boots thud against the pavement with every determined stride. The undone laces drag on the pavement, tempting me to trip over myself. If I do, fuck it, I'm already at urgent care.

What's a blow to the face after noticing an odd mark on my dick? This day couldn't possibly get any worse.

I run smack into the automatic sliding glass doors.

That is the second time I've hit my face in a thirty-minute period and I'm starting to get annoyed at doors.

Stepping away, I rub the side of my cheek, and then the doors open. I clench my fists, wanting nothing more than to punch the glass but knowing my luck today, I'd break my hand.

Entering through the doors, I wipe my boots on the very used cheap rug. The soles squeak on the tile floor, the bright fluorescents gleaming off the freshly polished white squares. The waiting room is quiet with only dozens of empty blue cushioned chairs.

A few TVs play different shows in every corner and there is a small play area for children on the left side of the room.

A sterile hospital scent hits my nose. I swallow so loud, that the person behind the desk looks up at me, smiling.

His name tag says Archie.

"Well, good morning. I didn't even hear you come in. How can I help you?" He grins so earnestly that it is hard not to remain a grouch.

"I need to see a doctor."

He snickers, typing on the keyboard. "Of course you do, silly. It's why you're here. Have you been here before?"

"I have been. You have all my information. My name is—" I hate saying my full name. "Fitsgerald Wallsworth the Third," I mutter.

"Wallsworth? Like the candy canes?" His eyes widen in shock.

"Yeah, listen, I'm not really part of that side of the family. So if you could not say anything, that would be great."

He zips his lips and throws away the key. "Your secret is safe with me. Those are the best candy canes though. I am so curious what they do to them."

"They infused the wrapper with the tiniest bit of rosemary so when you open it, you get a burst of the aroma. It makes you feel like you're actually experiencing Christmas. That's the secret. Can I see a doctor now please?"

He blinks at me in shock. "Um, yeah. Yes. What's going on so I can let the doctor know?"

"I have a questionable mark."

"She will be with you in just one moment, okay Mr. Wallsworth?"

I give him a tight smile, tapping my fingers on the front desk before turning around and taking a seat.

I don't like talking about my family history. That's something I keep close to my chest. I had a falling out with my family when I was eighteen. My parents and my grandparents disowned my sister for getting pregnant at sixteen with my nephew.

I chose her.

Luckily, I had been entitled to the small trust fund I had set up by my grandparents since I turned eighteen. I left home with her and never looked back. She never got her trust fund, so I gave her most of mine. I have enough to live how I need to live and so does she.

As far as our family, they are dead to us along with those damn Wallsworth Candy Canes.

I won't be a part of a family that is full of that much hate. To disown your daughter when she needs her family most is an unforgivable act. If my parents ever knocked on my door after all these years, I would slam it in their faces.

As far as I'm concerned, my last name is just a name and holds no meaning. I'm Fitz, the mechanic. I never want to be confused with Fitz, the heir to Wallsworth Candy Canes.

That part of my life is dead to me.

"Fitsgerald?" A nurse pops her head out of the door before swinging it wide open.

I stand, raising my hand to let her know it's me. Who else would it be? I'm the only one here.

"How are you doing?" I ask as I slip by her.

"I'm great. I need another cup of coffee," she laughs, gesturing at me to stand on the scale.

"I need my first cup."

She snickers and then we fall into an awkward silence as she takes my height and blood pressure and asks me a zillion questions that I've already answered. They should be in the computer system.

"The doctor will be right in," she informs, leaving me alone in the patient room.

I lean back on the table, giving me time to think about other aspects of my life. I don't know what it is about a doctor's office that gives me an 'impending doom' feeling but I'm reevaluating my life choices. I don't regret anything, but I should have moved my sister out here with me.

I didn't even ask her. I'll need to change that. I didn't leave her behind the first time, so I don't know why I did the second.

The hinges to the door creak. A doctor with long light brown hair walks in. She's staring down at my chart, her lips moving silently as she reads.

"Hello. Hello. How are we doing, Fitsgerald?"

"Just Fitz." I correct her. "Please," I add, not wanting to sound like an asshole.

She lifts her eyes from the chart, the dark greens lacking spark. She seems exhausted.

"No problem, Fitz. I read in your chart that you have a mark you need looked at, is that right?"

A light sheen of sweat breaks over my body at the thought of showing my dick to her. Not just because she's a woman but there is a voice in the back of my head that is screaming to ask for a male doctor.

"I don't mean to sound offensive, Doctor. Is there a male physician around?"

"Oh, don't worry about that. I've seen everything and anything. Truly, you are safe here with me, Fitz. If that is what you're worried about? I am the only doctor here for another few hours."

It isn't her ability to do her job that I'm worried about. There is a stabbing, clawing pain in my stomach that I'd be cheating on my mate.

The fake made-up monster I've conjured in my head. Now I think I'm cheating on someone who doesn't even exist.

I could tell the doctor right now that I need my head examined. I won't because I want more time with my fake mate.

This is fucking wild.

I feel protective over my monster. No other woman deserves to see me naked. If it's a doctor, surely it's okay, right?

"Okay. I'm sorry. I'm just nervous. It has nothing to do with you not being able to do your job. I don't think that—" I hurry to explain. "I think you're a great doctor from what I've seen. Just really great. I'm lucky. I'm so lucky to have you as my doctor, but this mark is in a vulnerable spot, and I'd hate for you to have the image of my dick in your head all day. Not that you would have it in your head all day—" I bury my face in my hands. "This isn't coming out right at all."

"Fitz." She pats my knee. "It's okay to be nervous. I promise you, I've seen hundreds of dicks, not in a sexual way, and have happily helped these men with their issues. I truly don't care about what your dick looks like. I want to make sure— like you do—that everything is okay. Okay?"

I feel like a teenage boy. This isn't like me.

"Now, take a breath and tell me what happened."

"I woke up with a weird mark on my dick and it's freaking me out a little. I haven't had sex in years, Doc." My face flushes from the admission. "By choice." I roll my eyes, wishing I could keep my mouth shut.

I tug the front of my sweatpants down. "See? What is that? I don't know. I can't tell you. It wasn't there yesterday."

She leans in, pressing her gloved hands along the black lines. "It doesn't hurt?"

"No. No pain. I haven't gotten a tattoo. I don't know what this is."

"It doesn't look questionable to me." She rolls her chair

away, shucking off her gloves.

I pull up my pants and point to myself. "Not question-able? I have nothing but questions."

"Sometimes as we age, things change. I'm thinking it's a birthmark. We will keep an eye on it. I want some bloodwork to see if anything has changed but other than that, I think you're fine."

I blink at her in confusion. "There's nothing to be done?"

"No. I think it's an odd development but that's it."

That's it.

Why doesn't that make me feel any better than when I walked in?

"Thanks." I don't bother to hide my disappointment.

"If you need anything else, you know where to find me. You're free to go. I'll have the nurse out front give you the referral for bloodwork."

"I appreciate it. Thanks for your help." I scrub my face with my hands, suddenly exhausted from all the mental gymnastics I've done since I rolled out of bed this morning.

"I promise, Fitz. It isn't anything to concern yourself about. I feel good about that decision. If I feel good about it, let it bring you some peace."

I nod, inhaling and exhaling as deep as I can. "You're right. Thanks for your help. I'm sorry for all my rambling or if I sounded like an ass."

"I understand. Showing any part of yourself physically to someone is odd and unsettling. Your discomfort is natural. Also, the image of your genitals is not in my head and has already been forgotten." She closes her chart. "Once you've seen one, you've seen them all."

We both laugh, easing the tension that is one hundred

percent coming from me.

"Have a good day. I'll call you when I get your bloodwork results in. Okay?"

"Okay. Yeah, thanks." I hop off the table as soon as the doctor leaves the room.

A low growl sounds from the back corner. I spin around, staring from one end of the wall to the other.

I'm at a doctor's office. It's probably the sound of a machine. I walk out of the room, down the hall, and through the waiting room. I give a small wave to the guy managing the desk and he gives a very happy grin in return.

I stop in front of the doors, learning my lesson from the first time, and the doors open. At least I saved myself from another sore cheek.

When I step outside, I inhale the fresh air, letting it settle in my lungs, and release the pent-up breath.

I feel very different today than I did yesterday. I'm protective of the dream Holly I've imagined. Possessive, if I want to be honest. I could have told the doctor the whole truth but that would mean losing the girl of my dreams.

I'm not ready for that. I'm not sure if I'll ever be ready for it.

"What the fuck?" I glance around to see if anyone else is in the parking lot. It's empty.

In the condensation on my driver's window, two words are written:

Doe Eyes.

"Funny. Hilarious." I wipe the words away with my hand and open the door. I've always been told I had feminine eyes. I get compliments all the time about them but some days, like today, it's more like a curse than a blessing.

Usually, I'll bat the hell out of my lashes and ask for a fucking drink to play along with the joke.

Not today.

Too much has happened, and too many questions are left unanswered for me to have a happy bone in my body.

And that's just wild because I love being happy.

Today, happiness is taking a backseat. Something is going on with me, and I intend to find out.

CHAPTER SEVEN

HOLLY

My poor Fitz. He's so confused. So lost. He's trying so hard to look for answers to all of his questions. Because of his curiosity, he had to see a doctor about the beautiful mark spreading from his cock.

By the time I'm done marking him, he will have a gorgeous, one-of-a-kind claim that only he will have. No one else will have that branding. It will be unique to him alone.

But my silly, panicked, sweet mate ran to urgent care and his doctor was a woman.

Another woman has seen his cock.

I can't have that. From here on out, he is mine. I am the only one allowed to see him bare like that. She's probably thinking about him now, wishing he was hers. She's probably dreaming about him, thinking of all the ways she could fuck him.

I'm not going to be able to let that go.

It took every ounce of self-control I had not to reveal myself in the patient room. There was nothing I wanted more than to wrap my tail around her throat, squeeze until her face turned purple, crush her windpipe, and watch her die.

Then, I saw Fitz on the table looking so afraid. He wasn't in the position to see such violence. I don't think he would have been able to handle it. He was already so worried about the mark. I couldn't add to his stress.

He will always be first in my life. His feelings. His mental health. His physical health. Anything and everything in between are my first priority. I'd never subject him to witness death.

It's why I'll always kill behind his back. I'm thoughtful like that.

He'll never have to witness such horrors. I'll protect his peace while taking pieces of his soul as mine.

I'm in the backseat of the truck, leaning my chin on the right shoulder of his seat. I know he can feel me. He keeps looking in the rearview mirror, narrowing his eyes as if he sees something but isn't sure.

"I'm right here, Doe Eyes," I whisper into his ear.

The truck swerves off the road. His big brown eyes are round in shock as they meet mine in the mirror. He is looking at nothing but I'm staring into lovely honey pools.

"What the fuck? What the fuck is happening?" he yells, pulling off the highway.

The truck bounces as we hit a ditch. I giggle as I tumble out of my seat, nearly hitting my head on the ceiling. It's like a rollercoaster.

A rollercoaster. Have I been on one of those before? A faint memory tickles my mind, but I can't place it. The faces are blurred and so is the background. All I can hear are musical notes from a carousel.

Maybe one day Fitz can take me. We can make our own memories. Oh my gosh, what if we could hold hands through the park? We can get ice cream cones. Oh, oh, oh! We could share one and my tongue can just accidentally slip into his mouth.

Sigh.

What a dream.

"Is there someone in the car with me?" Fitz voice trembles as he stares out of the windshield.

I sink back into the seat, not wanting him to know I'm here. He isn't ready.

He flips his blinker on to get back on the highway when someone pulls in next to him with their window rolled down.

"You okay?" the man shouts from the other vehicle.

I sneer from the back window, wanting Fitz's attention on me again.

Fitz rolls down his window next. "I'm fine. Sorry about that. I thought I saw something dash in front of me. My eyes were playing tricks." My mate grins, flashing the charm that makes so many people like him instantly.

The kind stranger chuckles, his laugh grating on my nerves. My talons lengthen, wanting nothing more than to slice his throat so he will shut up.

"I get that. My eyes do the same. Alright then, have a good day."

"Hey, you too! Thanks for stopping man." Fitz hangs his arm out the window, slapping the driver's side door with his palm before pointing to the guy as he drives away.

When we are alone again, I lean forward, closing my eyes to inhale his scent. He smells so fucking good. A hint of sweat, a dash of oil that must just be embedded in his DNA from working as a mechanic, and then a whole lot of me.

He reeks of being claimed. I love it. All I want to do is grip him by his hair, yank his head back, and bite him all over his lean body until he is begging for my cunt.

"It's too early for all this wildness happening all at once." He rolls up the window, puts his blinker on, and eases into a lane.

I decide to keep my mouth shut. I'd hate to scare him and cause him to wreck. What if we wrecked and he died? I wouldn't be able to live. He is the reason I escaped Purgatory. He is the reason for my second chance at life.

I'm going to make sure he has the best existence possible. I only need a little bit longer before I reveal myself to him. Just a little more time to strengthen our bond so he won't be able to leave me when he finds out the truth.

I'm doing him a favor. I'm saving him from being alone in a world that doesn't deserve his kindness, his smile, or his genuine soul. I appreciate every single particle that makes him Fitz.

I came back to life for his love.

And I plan to live for all eternity making sure his heart is mine.

I don't think he knows he has someone in his life that would do anything for him. No barrier exists that could stop me when it comes to protecting him.

"Ah, fuck it. Could be worse," he talks to himself—which I notice he does more frequently than not.

It's cute. I like it.

I sit my elbow on the middle console, holding my chin in my hand as I watch him.

"I could be dead," he begins to list how it could be worse on his fingers. "I could have gotten into an accident." He lifts another finger. "I could have ruined someone's car somehow and then I would have had to pay for it. I could have an STD." He shivers from the thought.

I curl my lip at him, wanting him to watch his mouth before I fill it with my tentacles.

"And that couldn't have happened because I haven't had sex in years. Not that I'd ever tell anyone but my doctor that."

Oh, Doe Eyes. I fucked you so hard last night, you came twice.

I do love that he hasn't been with anyone else in a while. Although, I still need to snag that list from his nightstand, so no exes pop up in our future.

 I bet they will.

They always do.

"I could have fallen down the steps or burnt down my house," he continues. "I mean, a sudden new birthmark isn't bad. I'm alive. I'm well. I deserve ice cream after the morning I had, but I need coffee first. Coffee ice cream?" He ponders for a moment, wrinkling his nose when he decides against it. "Absolutely not. Coffee doesn't belong in ice cream."

I have to cover my mouth to stop myself from laughing at him.

"I'll just go to Demi's Diner. I'll walk down when I get to the shop." His phone rings, cutting off his conversation with himself. He presses a button on the steering wheel to answer, "Hey, Rhett. What's up?"

Rhett is his friend, if I remember correctly. He is also a monster. I'm curious how he is a monster in broad daylight, and no one says anything about him. Is the town okay with beasts like me? Am I hiding for no reason?

"How did your doctor's appointment go?" Rhett asks through the speaker.

I cover my ears to mute the sound of his voice.

I don't like it.

"Oh, fine. She thinks it's a birthmark that popped up or something. Nothing serious."

She doesn't know how serious I am. She will when I'm done with her.

"See? I told you everything was fine. What are you doing now?" Rhett asks.

"On my way to the garage. I have tires I have to change and usually those aren't urgent, but the wires are showing. I'm not sure how this person was able to drive to the shop. The tires had to be sparking against the road."

A heavy sigh sounds from his friend. "Well, it's a good thing you found that urgent. I would have said too bad so sad. Alright, well, I just wanted to check-in. I might swing by the garage too. Mickey is getting sick of me hovering. I think it's almost time. My beasts feel it."

Beasts.

He's more than one. How? How is that possible? I thought I was the only one like this.

"That's great, Rhett!" Fitz cheers, pumping his fist in the air. "I'm so excited for you. I can't wait to meet them. Do you or Mickey need anything? I can bring it. Any time of day or night."

"I appreciate it. Right now, we are good, but I'll let you know if that changes."

"Alright, sounds good. I'm pulling into town now. I'll see you later if you're coming to the shop."

"See you later." Rhett disconnects the call just as we come to a stop at the same red light where I met the man who died in that horrible car accident.

Tragic.

Eye roll. Another overly confident asshole has been wiped from the earth. I am confident he won't be missed.

I take the time to look around, noticing a boutique just to the right of us. The outside is painted teal, the trim painted white, and in the window, there is a gold dress with thin straps hanging on a mannequin.

I want it.

The light turns green and naturally Fitz presses on the gas to pull forward. I stare at the dress in the window, watching as it gets further and further away from my grasp.

"Aw, someone made crosses for Ms. Livingston and the man who was killed in the car accident. I'll have to bring them some flowers. What a terrible thing."

If he buys her flowers, I'll tear them to shreds.

Or I'll replace them with dead ones, take the live ones home, and smell the flowers he got me.

Yes, I'll do that instead.

The blinker clicks as he turns right into the parking lot of the garage. Fitz whistles a tune I don't know as he drives around back, parking the truck in his usual spot. There is a lot of land back here and half of it is filled with everything from cars in amazing condition to pieces of what used to be a vehicle lying on the ground.

I turn my attention to Fitz and he's looking out the window to the yard, his eyes suddenly losing the spark that lights up his face. Without saying a word, he sighs, climbing out of the truck.

The door stays open as he stretches and groans. I take the opportunity to crawl up front, slide into the driver's seat, then slip out of the door. I press myself against the truck, my skin and scales changing to match my surroundings.

He shakes his head, his brown shaggy hair swaying from the force. "Wild," he whispers as he looks up at the garage.

The gravel under his boots crunches as he strolls to the back door. He lifts his keys, plucking through all the silver until he finds the one he needs to unlock the deadbolt.

The door swings open and Fitz disappears inside.

In true fashion, I follow because I never want him out of my sight. Rain begins to fall, peppering my skin with slow cold drops, and it ruins my camouflage. Light purple flesh peeks through the rain on my arm. It's as if the universe is trying to ruin my plan.

I rush into Snapdragons Garage, rubbing my arms to brush off the droplets. I had no idea I couldn't use that ability in the rain. My skin glitches, switching from the color of the shadows and concrete floors to my natural purple coloring.

Fuck. I watch Fitz vanish behind another door. On the front, there is a sign that says 'Front Office' and I debate if I should take this chance to leave. If I do, something bad might happen to him.

I can't leave him. He needs protection. I hate the rain. I hate storms. He's the only person in this world and the next who gives me a sense of safety, comfort, and peace.

A knock on one of the metal garage bays echoes through the space.

"We're closed. Only emergencies. It will be like that for a while, sorry!" Fitz says over the intercom so they can hear him outside.

"You're going to want to see me, Son."

I snarl at the tone of voice this man uses on my mate. How dare he? Doesn't he know there isn't a better man in the world than Fitz? I creep behind one of the cars, hiding myself just in case my chameleon ability is tarnished for the time being.

I peek over the trunk of a small grey car when I hear my mate stomping across the concrete floor.

"You have got to be kidding me," Fitz's tone is harsh and lethal, sending goosebumps down my arms.

My tentacles slip free, wanting him to use that tone on me.

He stops at the closed locked door and stares out of the window. "What the fuck do you want?"

My brows raise. I've never heard him talk like that to somcone before. He's... Fitz. He is sweet like a puppy. All he does is want to laugh, play, and sleep. I love that Fitz. This one... this one makes me want to kill whoever is standing on the other side of that door.

"Is that any way to greet your father?"

Hmm, could I kill his father?

Yes. Fitz will get over it. He'll see I did it for him. It seems like he'd be better off anyway.

"Last I checked, I disowned you the moment I walked out the door when I was eighteen."

"Well, I want to retire, Fitsgerald. You need to come home. Enough of this nonsense. You need to take over the family business."

Fitz spreads his arms. "I have my own business already."

"Changing oil? Going home with grease all over your

body? Please, this isn't a job for a man with a family fortune. Enough of this. Come home."

"No. I meant it the day I left. You're dead to me. You know the way out."

"Don't make your sister pay for the mistake you're about to make, Fitz. Maybe I'll bring my grandson into it. He's old enough to learn all the tricks of the trade now. What is he? Twenty? By now?"

Eli is twenty-one years old now, why doesn't his father know that?

Fitz opens the garage door and grabs his father by the jacket, slamming him against the wall. My tentacles rub over my clit, giving me a constant buzz of pleasure while I watch my mate defend his family.

"Don't you dare bring Heather or Eli into this. You left her, remember? You disowned her when she was pregnant. Eli has no respect for you. You have no right to do that. Leave her and my nephew alone."

"I will if you come to work with me. That's my offer. Wallsworth Candy Canes will not die because my heir isn't thinking clearly. We have expanded, you know. We're Wallsworth Candy now. Doesn't that have a nice ring to it?"

Fitz tosses his dad to the right with more strength than I thought he possessed.

"Take your family history, your money, and that fucking candy out of my shop. I never want to see you again."

"We'll see about that, Fitz."

Mmm, we will see about that.

No one threatens my mate or his sister. Whoever he claims as family, is my family. The man who calls himself Fitz's father is about to get a rude awakening.

And he'll never be able to see anything ever again.

Fitz rips his hat from his head and tosses it against the wall as he watches his dad drive away.

"Fuck!" he yells at the top of his lungs. He digs into his pocket and calls someone. "Heather, you two need to come move in with me right now. Dad just came to see me, and he said if I don't take the job, you would be at risk. Pack up. You're living with me. No arguments. Pull Elijah out of college and get him transferred here. We aren't risking Dad getting his hands on either of you." He hangs up, leaving no room for her to argue or say a word. He laces his fingers behind his head, trying to calm himself.

It doesn't work.

He takes a deep breath, then chucks his phone against the wall. It shatters to pieces, clinking on the ground. Plastic slides across the shop floor and a chunk of glass from the screen hits my foot.

I'm going to crush his father's bones just like his father seems to have crushed my mate's soul.

So many people to kill. My list is getting longer.

CHAPTER EIGHT

FITZ

It takes a lot for me to get angry. I consider myself a pretty calm, collected, fun guy. I think I'm a happy person. Probably too happy. I've been told I have 'golden retriever' energy once or twice—whatever that means.

Nothing or no one ruins every ounce of good I have inside me like my parents—my father—specifically.

He makes me forget about being kind or understanding. A vile hatred always takes over my mind when he enters my life. It's been five years since I've heard from him and you would think after we both got a few punches in, he would have taken the hint to never see me again.

The man is relentless. He never gives up when it comes to what he wants. He has been hounding me to join the family business, and I don't want to. I never want to risk putting myself in that line of work. Not if it means there is a chance I turn into a soulless, mean, conceited, selfish, bad, and irritating person.

If I see him in another five years, it would be too soon.

This time felt different. He seemed desperate. I'm too out of the loop with the company to know what's going on and I'm going to stay that way. I don't know what else to do when it comes to my father. I could try to file a restraining order. Maybe then he will take me seriously about wanting nothing to do with him.

If he died, I wouldn't care.

That statement is so opposite of who I am, but my dad brings out the worst of me. He brings out that part inside me that is too much like him. It's part of the reason why I go the extra mile for people. I do not want anyone to think I'm anything like that lying, cheating, self-centered asshole.

And like always, I find myself in a pickle after seeing my dad. I have no phone because I broke it.

I squat down, picking up the frame of what used to be my way to connect to the world. "Son of a bitch, Fitz. Why do you let him get to you like that?" I hang my head in shame, tossing the broken piece onto the floor again. "You're better than this." I stand, my knees popping to remind me I'm not as young as I used to be.

"Rhett is never going to let me manage this shop by my-self if my days are going to be like today." I start walking to the office phone to call Rhett and I'm trying to think about what to say to him.

I'll need to close the shop for the rest of the day. I have to get my house ready for my sister and I need a new cell phone.

"A wild fucking day." I pick up my hat from the floor, dusting it off by slapping it on my thigh when a loud crash from the back of the shop has me spinning around.

I don't say anything. I freeze not wanting to make a

sound. It could be nothing but with how my luck is going today, I doubt it. I've been trying to shake the sense of someone watching or following me. Since my dad showed up out of nowhere, I'm thinking it's him and some of his little buddies spying on me.

I take one step, wrapping my fingers around a crowbar Rhett keeps leaning against one of the pillars that is between two hydraulic lifts.

Another jarring metal sound echoes, this time coming from the other corner. I lift the crowbar onto my shoulder. Sweat beads at my temples from the adrenaline pumping through my veins. My heart is thunderous, booming inside my chest like a thunderstorm.

"I have a weapon!" I announce, wanting to give this person a warning. "And you know what—" I scoff, the insanity of my day making me chuckle "—I have not had a good day. It's only eleven in the morning. Eleven! The day has hardly even started and I'm over it. I'm sick of it. I'm ready to go to bed, but no. No, I can't because I have shit going on I can't explain. So what I'm trying to say is, I'm not really in the mood, okay? I haven't even had my fucking cup of coffee." I slam the crowbar on the ground to scare whoever is in the shop with me. "And not that you need to know, but I need a cup of coffee for my day to go smoothly. I haven't been this grouchy in a very long time. I woke up with a weird mark on my cock, had amazing sexy dreams, and I swear I'm hearing voices. I don't feel like myself. Please, do me a favor and just go. I don't have the energy to fight someone right now."

I stop talking, realizing I'm blabbering too much of my personal life away. I sound like a maniac. Look at me. I'm alone, holding a crowbar in the middle of the garage, and no one is replying to me.

Holding the crowbar out in front of me, I inch behind a car and then slam the metal down on the ground when I turn right. I close my eyes and keep swinging as I take small steps forward.

Peeking one eye open, my shoulders sag in relief when there's no one there. The only thing I've managed to do is put dents on the floor. My cheeks puff before I blow out a breath. I've never felt more ridiculous than I do at this moment.

I peek around the second car and that's when I notice oil droplets on the ground. I follow the trail around the third car, then the fourth, and it leads to the line of oil on the shelves.

There are small droplets. Nothing too hard to clean up, but it stops at the shelves. One bottle is turned on its side, dripping onto the ledge, then leaks over onto the floor. Picking it up, I tighten the lid and stand it up, then proceed to check all of the tops of the oil containers.

Maybe this mess is from yesterday. I did do a few oil changes. I could have sworn I cleaned up.

I laugh at myself and then wipe my forehead on my sleeve. "Fucking Hell, Fitz. Get your shit together." Seeing my dad has me on edge. I need to figure out what to do because my dad will go out of his way to make sure I have nothing.

He will make my life miserable. He will use all of his money and influence to take everything away from me, leaving me with nothing, so I have no choice but to crawl back to him.

I'd rather die than work for him or have my nephew work for him. He has made it his life's mission to make my life and Heather's life a living Hell. He wasn't a good dad when we were teens, and he has only gotten worse since we are adults now.

Leaning the crowbar against the wall, I grab a few cotton cloths, paper towels, a degreaser, and baking soda. After soaking up the excess oil with the paper towels, I pour degreaser over the stains, then add the baking soda. It creates a paste after I mix it all together. It helps lift the stains off the floor.

I shouldn't care about oil stains given the fact it's a damn car shop, but this business is new. I want to show Rhett he can count on me to keep the shop in working order and after how this morning has gone, I'm wondering if I'm capable at all.

When the spot is cleaned up, I place the materials I used on the shelf, then rush to the front office to use the phone.

I only know two phone numbers off the top of my head. My sister's and Rhett's. I place the phone against my ear and sigh in exasperation while staring up at the ceiling. It rings and rings, leaving me more anxious with every unanswered second that passes.

The door to one of the bays opens, allowing the light in. It's Rhett and Creed.

"Oh, fucking great." I'm not in the mood for Creed. He is an acquired taste that I do not think I will ever acquire.

I hang up the phone, noticing the handle has oil-stained fingerprints on it. I add a pep to my step as I hurry out of the office to greet them.

"What is that smell?" Rhett rears back as if he has been slapped. His face pinches together and he waves his hand in front of his face.

"It fucking reeks," Creed snarls, yet continues to sniff the air. He follows the scent until he is standing in front of me. "It's you. You reek."

I lift my arm and take a sniff. "I smell like fucking pine needles and sandalwood. What are you talking about? I do not stink."

Creed takes that as an invitation to step closer, completely invading my space. He sniffs again then gags. He has the fucking audacity to audibly gag.

"Yes, you do. I don't know what the hell you rolled in, but you need to shower."

I'm flabbergasted. "Rhett, will you please get your feral fucking cat away from me before I decide to do something about it?"

"What could you do to me?" His eyes glow with fury. Smoke drifts from his nostrils, showing that I have awakened the dragon—literally. "Before you could try, I would rip your skin from your fucking bones."

"Enough!" Rhett shouts, rubbing his temples. "I can't work in here. It does smell, Fitz. I'm sorry. It is causing my head to throb. It's overwhelming my senses." He stumbles backward, grabbing his chest. "My beasts are thrashing inside me. They hate it in here."

"Mine don't like it either but it could be you, Fitz." Creed curls his lip as he looks me up and down. "You say the word Rhett, I'll roast him. It won't take but a second since my fire is so hot."

I'm very close to snapping. I won't have a chance at all against Creed, but I'll die trying to get one punch in at this point.

"Will you please stop? Everyone lower your voice and

open the windows. Air this place out," Rhett orders with a loud, deep, monstrous boom.

Creed and I exchange judgmental looks, our shoulders bumping against each other as we walk to the doors that are closed. He gets to the one on the far right and I'm far left. I unlocked the bolt and lift the metal door. Creed does the same.

"I have no idea what you two are smelling but I don't smell it. I'm sorry. Maybe something died?"

"Did it die inside you? Because you are what stinks, Fitz," Creed once again adds his opinion when I didn't fucking ask for it.

"Creed." Rhett snarls at the delusional beast.

I cross my arms, a smug grin tugging my lips.

"Smell him, Rhett." Creed fists the front of my shirt, tugging me forward so hard, I slam against Rhett's chest.

The breath is knocked from my lungs. Rhett grips my shoulders, blinking at me in horror, his mouth curling into a frown that suggests he smells something bad.

And it's me.

He sniffs me again. He buries his nose in my chest, and he can only get away with that because he is my best friend. He pulls away, covering his mouth with his hand.

"Oh, come on!" I shout, plucking the front of my shirt to my nose. I inhale, smelling nothing but laundry detergent. "I have no clue what you two are smelling. Okay. You know what?" I take a deep breath, holding up my hands for us to calm down. "I can't deal with this right now. I was about to call you, Rhett. I have to close the shop for the day. I broke my phone."

"Again? Fitz—"

"—My dad came to see me." I cut him off before he can give me a lecture.

His eyes turn from reptilian to crimson, his fangs lengthening with only one purpose.

Rhett wants to drain my father's blood. I can't say I blame him. Rhett has always hated my parents due to how they treated me and Heather.

"What the fuck was he doing here?"

"He did what he always does. He is giving me an ultimatum. Either I work for him or Elijah does. My sister is at risk because if Elijah says no, my dad will go after her in every way. He will strip them of everything, so they have no other choice but to fall into his hands. I called her to tell her they need to move here. I need to go get my house ready. I can't have her so far away with him on the prowl again, Rhett. You know Heather and my nephew are my only family."

He steps forward, holding his breath as he grabs my shoulder. "You aren't alone. Whatever you two need but I'll need you to go home and shower. Creed and I can finish up here. Okay?"

"Okay. Thank you." I rub my neck, needing to ease some of the tension.

I want to tell Rhett one more thing. I want to say I think someone is following me but then, I don't want to be disrespectful. I know Rhett and Creed didn't necessarily go through the regular dating channels with their mates.

I don't want to offend them because that could mean my death.

Keeping my mouth shut is my best option.

"He isn't welcome here," Rhett growls. "We will get security installed in your house when I bring the rest of your belongings over later. You, your sister, and your nephew will be okay."

"If it means I can kill someone, I'm in," Creed says.

I snort, not surprised in the least. "Thanks, Creed."

He grunts in response. "I'm going to change these tires since you have been doing nothing all day."

I bite my tongue to stop myself from lashing out.

"Don't ever be afraid to talk to me, Fitz. We're brothers. I've got your back even if you do smell bad. Go home. Call me later."

I dig my keys from my pocket, nodding in defeat. "Yeah, thanks, Rhett. I'll talk to you later." I drag my feet toward the back door.

"I'm serious, Fitz. Everything will be okay."

I want to believe Rhett, I do, but I don't. Nothing ever is when it comes to my dad. Pushing the door open with my shoulder, the fresh air hits my face.

"You won't need security. You have me. No one will touch you, Doe Eyes. I'll make sure of it."

I'm not going to fight the voice in my head. Whatever I've made up in my head, the voice is there for a reason. I like the extra layer of protection. Maybe it's my subconscious gearing up for war. I'm not sure.

I no longer care.

I'll fight the enemy even if it kills me.

CHAPTER NINE

HOLLY

The way Rhett and Creed acted when they smelled Fitz made me happy. They are going to go insane when they come to work every day and smell me everywhere.

Not only does Fitz smell like me, but so does their entire shop. My sweet mate thought he made a mess from the oil droplets but those weren't from oil. The mess was made by me. Watching Fitz get angry at his dad had my tentacles dripping. It didn't take long for my ink to pour from me, so I made use of it.

I added it to every single oil container they had, every grease jar, and anything else dark I could find. Then, in every corner, in every room while Fitz, Rhett, and Creed were arguing, I swiped my ink on spots in the room they will never be able to see.

Fitz is fucking mine. That means wherever he is, he has to be protected. Where he works has to be marked so others know not to mess with him. I'm sure he would have been fine considering Rhett is his friend and has probably marked this place too with his own scent.

I growl internally. That means Rhett will probably want to remove my scent and will mark his shop again. That's what I would do, and it seems he is more like me than I initially thought.

I don't get in the truck with Fitz when he leaves. Instead, I launch myself in the air to fly home. My wings need to stretch. I soar high above Fitz until his truck is nothing but a speck in my line of sight.

Seeing him so disgruntled about his dad worries me. I don't like seeing Fitz unhappy. He doesn't deserve to frown when his energy makes people smile.

I'll fix this. Any problems he has, I'm the solution. He will never have to lift a finger again.

In a world full of chaos, I will be his sword that spills the blood that causes dismay to him.

In his kingdom of light, I will be his queen of darkness.

Our love will be considered royalty. I don't care who I need to kill to make sure our crowns are lifted in the air as high as possible. I will stack the dead bodies of his enemies beneath us so we can stand on their backs. Our reign will be loved and feared.

Through the ones that dare to try to overtake us, I will fly them high over our land and drop them from miles up in the sky. So they can see that their only hope of survival is me.

And I will not give them any hope.

Fitz stopping at a red light yanks me from my dream. He is only a half a mile from home. I'm going to continue without him so I'm there first. I'll grab some clothes and then pretend to do something outside to grab his attention.

The cool wind ruffles my feathers as I flap my wings. I spin and flip, loving that I'm getting this flying thing under control. It's fun. I don't think there is anything in the world that could give me more freedom than this.

The world from up here is so hypocritical. I can see how big and vast the planet is. The sky spans across a never-ending threshold while the town I call home is nothing but a fly on the wall when I look down. The dichotomy is beautiful.

Even though the distance between the red light and home isn't far, clouds not too far from here are churning from a fluffy white to an ominous graphite. Thunderclaps from miles away are felt in my bones, the vibrations reverberating off my ribcage.

Panic swells in my chest at the thought of being caught in a storm. An onslaught of memories assaults me. I was strapped down and forced to do unimaginable things. I was pumped full of DNA that changed me forever. The pain. The torture. My screams echo in my mind.

I lose complete vision of Fitz. A gust of wind takes me by surprise, side-swiping me from the left. I tumble through the air, my wings trying to extend to find their rhythm again.

I'm right above the highway and I'm falling directly into it. I can't have that happen. Too many questions will want to be answered. If people see me, I'll be a freak. I'll be taken and tested on. I can't live through that again. Anxiety spills through my nerve endings. My blood is replaced by the fuel of fear.

I won't go back. I refuse to go back.

A soul-draining scream shreds my throat when I use all my strength to move my wings against the heavy gust of wind. Feathers are ripped from my harpy wings, floating all around me.

Rain begins to pour. I fight the pull of my trauma try-ing to suck me down. Those memories of being in a sunless room, hearing nothing but the harsh beat of rain, the wicked howls of wind, the rolls of thunder, and loud cracks of light-ning nearly make me immobile.

I'm too unstable to fly. I can't get my wings to work. Not in this rain. My eyes burn from tears. The storm is about to rage, and it nearly has me in its claws. With an unstable for-mation, I'm able to tumble into my backyard. I'm not sure if I was seen and there is a part of me that doesn't care.

I roll through the wet grass and mud, skidding to a stop just before my back door.

"Gross." I pluck a few blades of grass from between my fangs.

I don't bother waiting around for lightning to strike me. I get to my feet, open the back door, and run inside before the storm can get me.

Slamming the door, I lock it for good measure. Gulping, I watch how the light fades from the sky, darkening with the bad intentions of the storm. Rain begins to pour so hard, that I can hear it beating against the roof. The wind smacks the rain against the side of the house, and I jump, staring at the wall where the pummeling noise is coming from.

Water slings from the ends of my hair as I spin around. Between all the noises, I can't seem to breathe. I cup my ears and fall to my knees, squeezing my eyes shut until it's over. I'll sit in this empty living room that has no furniture for the rest of the night if I have to.

I don't even have a bed. I only use the bedroom to watch Fitz out the window when he is in his kitchen.

The doorbell ringing surprises me, startling me so much, I fall on my ass. My tail wraps around my leg, my wings wrap around my body, and all I want to do is sink into the floor.

A loud pounding on the door happens next. It sounds too similar to the thunder outside. It all reminds me of being on that table, the pounding of a hammer to break my bones just so the scientist could see how long I took to heal.

A sob catches in my throat. I lift my knees to my chest, burying my face between my legs, and try to take a deep breath.

"Holly? Are you okay? I heard you scream," Fitz shouts from behind the door.

I lift my head from my hiding spot, staring at the door for a moment to see if I'm imagining things.

"I just want to make sure you're alright," he says again, his tone soft with a hint of worry. "Holly?"

I've waited too long to answer. I hurry to stand, realizing I'm soaking wet and muddy. I toss my damp tangled hair over my shoulder, slip and slide to the door since my feet are wet, then cloak myself in my human disguise.

I wonder if they ever found the camper's body.

Another worry for another day.

"I'll be right there!" I shout, dashing to the bathroom for a towel. I dry myself off, needing my chameleon ability to work.

I dry off the best I can, practically rubbing my skin raw. "Shit!" The towel gets caught on my fins near my ankles.

The cotton tugs and pulls on the sharp ends of the fins. That's when I notice how dry my scales are. A piece of a fin just broke onto the floor.

I haven't been soaking myself in the lake as much as I

should, even though it's in my own backyard.

"Okay, let's see if it worked," I whisper to my reflection in the mirror.

Focusing on my human disguise, I'm relieved when the camper comes into view and all of my monstrous features disappear.

Sprinting out of the bathroom door, I rush to pull on clothes and then I run down the hall. I take the corner too quickly, and I stumble, smashing my shoulder against the wall.

"Ow," I growl, snapping my teeth at the corner as if it bit me.

"You okay?" His tone is more curious than earnestly worried now.

I yank the door open to see a soaking-wet Fitz standing under the awning. His shirt clings to his body, the damp material leaving nothing to my imagination. Every abdominal muscle is outlined. His pecs are firm and defined with a slight curve to prove his manual labor.

There is nothing like the body of a man who does physical work. His hat is on backward, the wet ends of his hair curling. His freckles are most pronounced right now for some reason. I'm lost in the perfection of my mate.

"Hi," I croak out. "I'm fine. I dislike storms. That's all. They aren't attached to good memories." I wrap my arms around myself, forgetting about the murderous rage. It's still there but there's nothing I can do about it right now. "You risked your life to come check on me?" That's so sweet. He could have drowned in this rain waiting for me to answer the door.

He rubs the water off his face. "I wouldn't say I risked

my life. It's only water, but if you want to ride out the storm together? We can. My day got derailed and I could use a friendly face right now."

I know all about the horrible day he is having. "Oh? What happened? Are you alright?"

He adjusts his stance, his boots splashing the water pooling beneath him. "Want to talk about it over hot chocolate or wine? I can make us dinner or dessert. Maybe we can put on a movie."

I fight a smile, twirling my hair around my finger like a lovesick girl.

I suppose I am.

I am so lovesick, the only cure for it would be for me to stop existing. I don't mean death because I'd haunt him, or I'd try to come back to life like I did this time. No, I'd need to die in purgatory for my obsession with Fitz to cease to exist.

"Is this a date?"

A crooked grin takes over his face. His lashes are small spikes from being wet from the rain and they fan over his cheeks as he glances down, blushing.

"Well, I guess it is. No pressure though. You don't like storms, and I need a friend. You were who I thought to come to first. I'd like to get to know you better."

I'm not sure if I'll be able to control my disguise for that long but I'll try. I refuse to miss time with Fitz.

"I'd love to. I need an umbrella. Do you have one?" I can't get wet or he will see who I really am.

"I do. Let me run and grab it from the truck."

"I know, it's silly. I'm not afraid of getting wet. The storm, the rain, it all just—"

He steps closer, pinching my chin with his thumb and

index finger. I hold my breath, wondering if he is really this close to me, touching me, staring directly into my eyes.

"It isn't silly if it makes you feel safe." His thumb rubs over my chin, the rough skin of the callouses leaving a slight scrape behind with every sweep the pad of his finger gives. "Would me getting the umbrella make you feel safe?"

I swallow, realizing I'm nervous. My entire body feels flustered and hot. I'm not sure if I can continue to look him in the eyes. I might combust. Those long lashes blink just before his eyes hood, a sultry heat blowing the pupils.

He looks from my eyes to my lips back to my eyes only to drop to my mouth again. The tip of Fitz's tongue licks his bottom lip before he inhales a deep breath and takes a step back to put space between us.

"Give me a minute. I'll be right back with the umbrella." He never takes his gaze off of me as he slowly walks backward.

My mate chooses to step out in the rain rather than remain dry under the awning. Rain pours, soaking him in seconds.

"Don't move," he warns, taking another step.

I wrap my arms tighter around myself and smile. "I'm not going anywhere."

"Good. I'd hate to have to track you down when this is the best part of my day," he says, giving me that crooked shy grin I'm obsessed with.

He turns his hat around, the rain dripping from the bill. Tucking his head, he runs next door to his house, jumping over the step leading to his front door. I can't see him anymore which leaves me alone outside in the storm.

I jump when thunder shakes the ground. My heart

forgets the calm and chooses to beat at a pace only caused by anxiety. I lean against my door, close my eyes, and hold a hand to my chest.

The wind howls like a wild lone wolf in a snow-covered field. Regardless of how good the gusts feel against the heat of my skin, it doesn't tame the fear controlling my body. I'm frozen in place. This is unlike me. I have no reason to fear storms anymore now that I'm free.

The doctors can't hurt me anymore. I'm stronger than they could have ever been. I'm stronger than most of society.

Is this my punishment for my lack of humanity when it comes to claiming Fitz? Maybe.

I'll happily take this punishment. Fitz is more import-ant than my fear. I'll battle anxiety every day and deal with storms if it means I get to have him. There isn't anything I wouldn't do to make him mine even if it means living in his subconscious for the rest of my life.

I don't hear the heavy splash of boots because of my own blood rushing through my head. The whoosh of the umbrella opening has me opening my eyes to see Fitz standing direct-ly in front of me, drenched.

He turns his hat backward, lifting the umbrella only over my head. "It's okay." Fitz cups my face. "There's always calm after a storm. It will pass. Come on, Wildflower. Let's get you inside."

"Wildflower?" I ask him, stepping under the umbrella he kindly provided.

"Yeah. You remind me of my favorite flower, which we have already discussed, but also, something tells me you have a wild side."

The memory of me fucking him while I invade his

dreams tickles my mind. "You have no idea," I almost growl.

He steps into the rain again, holding the umbrella direct- ly over me so I don't get wet.

"I'd love to have even the slightest idea," he says.

"I'm not sure if you could handle my wild, Fitz."

We both turn to look at one another while walking through the storm to get to his house.

"I think you'll be surprised when you learn I can handle more than you could ever imagine, Wildflower."

My breath catches with hope. That dangerous fucking human emotion that has no business in my new form, but damn it, Fitz makes me hope.

I trip on the edge of his driveway. I barely have time to think to brace myself for impact. I won't have time to get away from Fitz before my monstrous form takes over in the rain.

I'm planning the worst scenario in my head as the driveway becomes closer to my face when Fitz's arm wraps around my waist. He catches me, forcing me to be inches away from his face.

His eyes do the dance again, dropping from my eyes to my lips. "Are you okay?" he rasps, the rain beating against the top of the umbrella to remind us we aren't alone.

I can't seem to find my voice which never happens. I'm part siren. I always have a voice.

Not now. Not when I'm so close to Fitz, his eyes roam all over my face as if he is memorizing it for himself.

"Wildflower?" he calls me in his gentle, deep, yet soft voice.

I could fall asleep listening to him, lulling me to sleep. Maybe one night, a very long time from now when he knows the truth about what I am. If he is able to love me for what I am.

"I'm okay." I glance up, noticing I'm still mostly dry while Fitz is choosing to be soaking wet. "You're soaked. Let's get inside."

"I'm just showing you rain doesn't hurt, but I'd love to know why you think it does. When you are ready to tell me, of course." He straightens us, leaving my heart trembling for him. "Come on, let's get you inside."

We step onto his porch and that's where I notice the empty plant pots lining either side under the awning. I'm shivering from the cold and I'm worried that any second, my human disguise will fade.

Fitz opens the door for me, and I remember when I broke into his house last night. He forgot to lock the back door. Granted, I doubt he expects anyone to hop the fence to break into his house.

But a girl wants what she wants.

I step inside, the warmth wrapping around me like I wish Fitz would. That's fine. I can wrap myself around him later. Why wait for him when I know I'll be getting my fill of him tonight?

Doe Eyes shakes the water from the umbrella, setting it right inside the door on a rubber mat. Getting to watch him in his home gives me reassurance that I'm not an intruder. I like seeing him in his element.

"Your home is beautiful," I say, breaking the silence between us. "I love the beams." I point to the ceiling, loving the color of the metal. "I wish my house looked this good. It's still empty."

"Empty?" Fitz takes off his hat, giving the cap a good

shake before hanging it on a hook over the coffee table.

He's an organized guy. His keys are in the bowl on top of the coffee table. His hat is strategically placed right above the keys. His coat is on a hanger next to the door. Everything is ready for him to walk out if he needs to.

I lift a shoulder, shrugging. "Yeah, it's no big deal. I'm still shopping for furniture. I am picky with what I like." Because everything I like is in this house and eventually, this house will be my home. Why would I spend the money I stole on useless furniture when I could spend it on Fitz?

"If you ever need any help, I'm pretty handy. I can help you repair or fix anything. If you need a truck for furniture shopping, I don't mind at all. I bet it would be fun to go together."

"You'd go shopping?" I question in disbelief, strolling into his living room to plop on his couch. "I thought men didn't like shopping?"

He unlaces his boots and then kicks them off. Each one thuds against the wall before falling to the floor. "I'll be right back. Hold onto that thought. I need to get out of these wet clothes. Actually, do you want some dry clothes too?"

I gasp, jumping off the couch. A huge wet spot is on the cushion. "I'm so sorry, Fitz. I wasn't even thinking. I ruined your couch." What was I thinking? I know better than to plop on someone's sofa soaking wet.

It's been too long since I've been around people. I've forgotten how to act. Even now, I feel odd pretending I give a fuck about the couch. I'll destroy this couch. It means nothing to me but it might mean something to Fitz. If it's important to him, then it is to me.

That's how I'll be living my life or everyone and everything will be at my mercy.

"I don't care about the couch, Wildflower."

The unexpected closeness of his voice has me gasping and spinning around. He's so close, that I smack against his chest.

"Sorry," I chirp, cursing myself internally for how I'm behaving. How am I becoming such a mess around him? I'm the one always in control.

The connection between us is different. Our bond, our claim grows stronger the more time we spend together, and I didn't expect for us to spend any time together while he was conscious. A man like Fitz could only ever love a woman like me in his dreams.

I'm not the kind of woman for him to bring home to his mother. Although, lucky me, he doesn't seem to have a good relationship with her.

"What's wrong, Holly?" He puts distance between us by taking a step back. "I didn't mean to make you nervous. I won't hurt you."

"No, I don't think you would. You...you do make me nervous but not in a bad way, Fitz."

He holds out his hand with that charming smile. "Come on. I'll give you some clothes and I'll pour us a glass of wine."

I need to run out of this house and away from him. Being around him is too difficult to keep my human cloak. Any moment, my hair could turn blue, my scales or fins could show, or my tail could decide to have a mind of its own.

And yet, I slip my palm across his because I'm not strong enough to run away from my mate. "That sounds perfect."

"Follow me." He tugs me behind him, following him up the staircase next to the front door.

I stare at a few pictures lining the wall. "These pictures are great. Who is this?" I point to him and a woman. His arm is around her.

I'm going to kill her.

"That's my sister."

Damn it. I can't kill her.

"You two look happy."

When he gets to the top of the stairs, he leans against the wall and crosses his arms. "We were. Things were simpler then."

I don't like the tone of his voice. It's resigned as if things aren't as simple now. "What changed? Has something happened?"

"That story requires wine and dry clothes." The sadness from his face is gone. He cocks his head in the direction we need to go. "Come on. I'm freezing in these clothes."

"How many bedrooms is your house?"

He swings open his bedroom door, flipping on the light. I want to brag about how I've been in this room and on his bed.

"Five. I know it's just me, but I always wanted a big family. I figured I might as well get a house that, hopefully, can hold that dream. Heck, two rooms are about to be taken."

The drawer to his dresser grinds as Fitz opens it. He plucks a black shirt from the top. "I hope you don't mind an old garage shirt."

"Are you kidding? You'll be lucky to even get it back." I snatch it from him before he can take it back. I bring the shirt to my nose and inhale. "Smells like you."

He grabs a shirt too, pushing the drawer shut while laughing. "Well, according to my friends, that's a bad thing.

They said, and I quote, "I reek today.'"

I step into his space, pressing my nose into the middle of his chest. Lifting my eyes to his, I can't help the possessive growl that rolls in my chest for him. My beasts are all too happy to be this close.

His Adam's apple bobs and I hear the slight change of his heart rate increase.

"They are wrong. You smell delicious to me." I need to be careful. If I lose control, it could mean the end of my entire plan to have Fitz fall in love with me.

I won't stop until he does.

CHAPTER TEN

FITZ

I'm a bad man.

I've always considered myself a decent, kind, and thoughtful person. I always put everyone else above me. Their happiness, their health, even their anger. I chose to pick up and head out of town with my sister when she was sixteen and pregnant because of how our dad treated her.

I'm curious what would have happened to me if she didn't get pregnant. We probably would have stayed there with our parents. I can't go down that road. I would hate the man I would have become working with my dad.

I've never considered myself a selfish man.

Until I knocked on Holly's door.

Now, this woman is standing in front of me. Her eyes are shining like beacons, shooting me with light that could reach the fucking stars. I know she is interested in me.

I'm interested in her too but that's only because when I look at her, all I see is the monster from my dreams. There's something wrong with me. This monster is sheer, kind of transparent like a shadow but I'm able to see everything. Before, I would see horns and then I wouldn't.

Now though, not only do I see horns, I see wings, a tail, fangs, and even fins at the bottom of her ankles. My mind has created the perfect monster. The one I crave. The one I want in my bed, in my arms, in my home, filling all the empty rooms with children.

Dreams aren't enough and now I'm hallucinating my dream woman with a human woman I have no interest in.

This is where I'm selfish. Why? Because I'm not going to stop spending time with Holly if it means I get to see my monster. Human Holly is very pretty, and any man would be lucky to have her.

I want what seems to be her unlikely shadow. I'm not ready to give that up. So when or if Holly decides to move away, I'll be done. I'll never see my monster again.

For now, especially after today, I want to live in my delusions.

"Um." Heat creeps up my neck and spreads across my cheeks. I step away, wanting to put space between us. This monster that I can see, I only see with her, and the closer the monster is to me, the more I want to take this connection a step further.

And no matter what, I can't do that to human Holly. That would make me a sick, fucked up man. I have to be better than that.

I hand her a pair of black sweatpants, then point to the door behind her. "That leads to the bathroom. You can change there. I'll change out here."

Her blue eyes can't hide the bright burning coals of my monster.

"Thank you, Fitz. I appreciate this," she says with a smile.

"I don't mind at all." I point my chin in the direction of the bathroom. "Go on. I promise I won't peek."

"Too bad." She strolls away from me, turning her head to her shoulder before opening the bathroom door. "I can't promise I won't." Holly steps into the bathroom and shuts the door, but she doesn't realize that she has to hear it click or it will crack open.

And that is exactly what it does.

I grab the back of my damp shirt, tug it over my head, then toss it into the laundry hamper.

Be good. Be good. Be good.

Knowing I could see her body is too much on my pathetic self-control that I don't seem to have when I'm around her. I unzip my wet jeans and then bend down to tug the bottoms from my feet, when the sleek curve of her back peeking through the cracked door captures my attention.

I fall onto the bed with a grunt, smacking my leg on the bedpost. Burying my face in the sheets, I scream, "Mother fucker!" while holding onto my shin.

"You okay?" she calls from the bathroom.

"Fine. I'm fine. Just hit my leg. I'm fine." I lean forward, peeking through the crack just in time to see her slide my sweatpants on.

Fuck.

Her ass is round and plump. Tiny lace black panties hug her cheeks. I'm overwhelmed with jealousy of that skimpy material having that much contact.

Her tail wraps around her leg so it doesn't get in the way. Well, I suppose I'm making the monster do that since she is a figment of my imagination. I continue to lean over the edge of the bed to see more, watching as she slips my shirt on over her light purple skin.

I mean, her human skin? Fuck, I don't know.

I need to get her out of my house. This isn't okay. I'm sick in the head using her like this. This sweet, innocent girl is being held hostage because I want to see my dreams come to life.

That isn't fair.

I managed to lean too far over the edge of the bed from my wandering eyes and face plant right onto the floor.

"Oh my God, Fitz. Are you okay?"

I groan, opening my eyes to see Holly hovering over me with a concerned expression.

"I'm fine. I just–"

"–Fell trying to catch a peek? Doe Eyes, if you want a peek, all you need to do is ask."

The nickname flutters through my mind, ruffling a memory. "Doe Eyes?" I repeat, trying to think of when I heard it. "Who told you to call me that?"

She turns her head to the side, giving me the perfect view of her horns. They are more like a mirage. If I reach for them, I know my hands would go right through them. They aren't real. No matter how much I want them to be.

"No one. I was looking into your eyes, and they remind me of a doe, that's all. They are big, brown, and full of innocence."

I get to my feet, shaking the static from my head. Holly's gaze roams down my body.

That's when I remember I'm only in my briefs.

"Ah, shit." I pluck the clean shirt off the bed, covering my torso with it. My cheeks become brighter. The fever of embarrassment has me sweating. "I–uh–you–I'm–" I can't figure out what I want to say. I'm nervous. My cock is half hard, my lust is in a frenzy with being so close to Holly while the more time I spend with her, the more confused I become.

"Do you need me to turn around?" She eyes me again, biting her lip, sending me very strong signals. "That's adorable. You have nothing to be shy about, Fitz. You are a very good-looking man." She turns around, giving me a little privacy.

I'm conflicted. I'm not usually bashful but I feel like I'm cheating on my monster–who isn't even real–and I can't enjoy a nice night with a new friend because of it.

I slip on my grey sweatpants, then tug my black Snapdragons Garage shirt over my head. "That was wild. Completely, wild." My words are muffled under the material of the shirt before I pull it down my torso. "I'm good. You can turn around. You didn't have to, by the way. The nickname really threw me for a loop. I thought I had heard it before. Sorry, it's been a really weird day."

"We can talk about it over that glass of wine," she says. "I've had those days too. I'm sorry, Fitz." The amber eyes my mind has conjured swirl behind her blues. "I'll be good. I promise. You can tell me about your day."

My cheeks expand with the massive breath I release. "I'd like that, Holly. Thank you."

"I'll always have your best interests at heart, Fitz. I hope you know that." She looks around the room, pointing to the broken bulb. "What happened?"

I love the change of subject. I'm relieved. "I don't know. I think I might have broken it. It's been a wild few days, if I'm being honest. I think I'm just tired. Come on, let's go downstairs so I don't make a bigger fool out of myself." I give her my back, walking out of the bedroom.

"I don't know. The night is young," she teases.

Smirking, I turn to reply when I see her at my nightstand. I open my mouth to say something, but her tail swishes from the sweatpants. It flicks, stretching out to me as if it wants me.

I rub my eyes with the palms of my hand so hard, I begin to see spots. When I look at Holly again, the tail is gone but I can see everything else still. My imagination won't quit.

"What are you doing?" I hate how the question sounds so accusatory. "I'm sorry for the tone. I shouldn't have snapped like that."

She spins, her blonde hair spraying over her shoulders. Teal paints a few strands, they fade in and out as if trying to mesh with Holly's human features. To me, the human skin almost appears to be armor as if it's trying to cover or hide something. That something—the monster my mind has created.

I'm not sure why my brain picked Holly, but this is as close to the real thing as I'll ever get. I'm not sure if I can let her go. I like being around her too much.

"It's okay. I shouldn't have snooped. I saw the pen and paper on your nightstand. I was writing my number down for you. You know, just in case you need some friendly neighborhood sugar." Holly strolls up to me, a piece of paper in hand, and slips it in my pocket.

I gasp when her finger skims the tip of my cock.

"Let's go see about that wine."

I'm dumbfounded and hard as fucking stone when she walks away. I need a second to calm down. Seeing the monster in my clothes has me ready to strip Holly bare. I wonder if I imagined it hard enough if she'd look like the creature I desire as I fucked her.

"No, fuck. Come on, Fitz. That's too wild of a thought. Even for you. What the fuck, man?" I hiss to myself, gripping the edge of the dresser.

I hang my head, taking a slow deep breath. My arousal fades enough but I'm one fucking lash flutter away from coming in my damn sweatpants.

"You got this. You're completely fine. You're fine." I leave the bedroom when something floats in the air out of my peripheral. Holding out my hand, a small fluffy white feather lands in my palm.

Her wings.

"You have got to be kidding me. I'm imagining feathers shedding now? I need to sleep for a week. This is getting out of hand." I drop the dream feather onto the dresser and head downstairs to see Holly sitting on the couch.

She has one of my favorite blankets tossed over her and a glass of red wine is in her hand. My glass is on the coffee table waiting for me.

"Sorry about that. I needed a minute."

She takes a sip from her glass. "We all need a minute every now and then, don't we?"

Holly looks too damn good on my couch. She's made herself at home. Something about this picture feels so fucking good, so right. Seeing her gaze upon me as if I've plucked the moon from the sky to slide it upon her left ring finger is a gaze I'm suddenly in love with.

I'm so confused about that. One moment I'm all about Holly, the next, I want to only be her friend.

Then, an epiphany hits me.

When my mind isn't playing tricks on me visualizing her as a monster—I only want to be her friend. Yet, when I see the creature of my dreams? I want to marry her at this very moment.

I'm one wild twister. Goddamn.

"Hey, you okay?" Holly crawls over to be closer to me, then wraps her arm around my leg. "Talk to me."

I don't even know where to begin. I'll go with what does make sense. "My sister is on her way here because of my father. She and my nephew, actually. I'm probably not in a great situation for a relationship." I take a big swig of the red wine she poured for me, the liquid smooth with a hint of sweetness to coat my throat.

How did she know where my wine glasses were?

"If it makes you feel any better, I can't remember any-thing except for the last few days. Well, okay, that's not true. I can remember little things, but they are blurry, and muscle memory is there."

I sit up, blinking at her in shock. "Okay, you win. What the fuck? What do you mean you don't remember anything?"

Her posture changes to a slouch. Holly's confidence vanishes in the defeat of her own nightmares. Her eyes gloss over, a sadness overwhelming them. Lightning cracks out-side. The crash is loud, proving how close it is. Holly closes her eyes, wincing with every bolt the storm brings.

Fucking Caden.

I take her hand in mine, loving how soft her skin is. I've never felt like this in my entire life. The purple flesh I love so much peeks through and a fin on the back of her wrist to her elbow captures my attention.

I wonder what creatures my mind is creating for this monster?

"It's okay. This storm won't hurt you," I reassure her, giving her hand a tight squeeze. "You're safe here."

Holly turns her head away, wiping a tear off her cheek. I slip a finger across her jaw, forcing her to turn her head.

"Come here." I reposition myself, making a spot for her next to me.

She eyes the empty space for a minute, unsure if she wants to be so close. Thunder vibrates the ground and the light above us shakes, the glass clinking together. Holly scurries to my side. I wrap my arm around her shoulders, pulling her close to my side.

"You're alright, Wildflower. I'm not going to let anything happen to you. You're safe here. Whenever you're ready to talk about it, I'll listen."

She places her head on my chest, reaching for the coffee table to set down her empty wine glass. "Thank you, Fitz. I appreciate that. I'm not ready to talk about it. I can't go down that dark road right now."

Whatever happened, it must be bad. The thought of anyone hurting her makes me want to go on a rampage. I feel very protective over her in ways I can't explain because I hardly understand these emotions. Do I like her? Or do I like what my mind is creating around her?

Regardless, anything horrible that happened to her has a weight of anger bearing down on my chest.

She lifts up onto one arm, staring down at me with a glint in her eyes I can't place. "If you really knew me, you'd run away from me as fast as you could."

I sit up, taking one last sip of wine before setting my

glass next to hers. I drift my hand up her arm, right be-side the fin. I wish it were real. I'd want to know if they are sensitive. Could I lick, kiss, and rub them? Could I make her orgasm?

Drifting my fingers up, nerves flutter in my stomach like dragonflies flapping their wings nonstop.

"I'm bad for you, Fitz. I'm warning you now. I'm bad for you."

I cup her face, tilting my head to lean in for a kiss. "Prove it," I dare her, my gaze dropping to her lips. A boiling heat invades my body, the kind that has me wanting to bend her over this couch and show her who she belongs to.

I fucking want that.

"If anything, I'm the one who is bad for you," I admit, the all too familiar guilt eating away at me.

She's the closest thing I'll ever have to what I want. I don't want to let this go.

"I've experienced things that are horrendous, even tor-turous, but you, Fitz, are anything but bad."

I lean in closer, our noses grazing one another. "You'd be surprised. The worst of the worst lives inside everybody. Hiding the villain to prove how good you are is an art form most have mastered." I rub my thumb across her cheek, the slight scratch of the calloused pad over smooth skin is whis-pering to me how different she and I are.

I don't care.

Just as our lips touch, my new cellphone blares from the counter. The ringtone belongs to my sister.

I move my mouth to the side, kissing the corner of her mouth where it creases. "I need to answer that. It's my sis-ter."

"I understand. I can go–"

"–No, stay here. I don't want you alone in your house during a storm." I stand, adjusting my cock as I turn so Holly doesn't see how much I want her. I'm ready to burn this house to the ground and fuck her in the warmth of the ashes if it means I get to feel her cunt spasm around me.

Holly wraps the blankets around her shoulders. "Thank you."

I unplug my replacement phone from the charger, swipe the screen, and answer, "Hey, Heather. Are you almost here?" I check the time glowing on the microwave. "You shouldn't be too far out."

"I can't get there for another few days, Fitz."

My heart drops to the fucking floor when I hear those words. I give my back to Holly and try to keep my voice quiet. "What do you mean you won't be here for a few days? You and Eli need to get here now. Dad isn't fucking around, Heather."

"You don't think I know that? Elijah is sick with a fever, Fitz. He can barely walk. He had to come home from class at SCU. He is vomiting. He can't keep anything down. I'm worried about him."

Elijah lives at home with his mom while going to school. He didn't want to leave her alone. He has grown into a good man. He works part-time while going to school and dealing with his duties of being captain of the SCU's swim team. He contributes to the household. I remember him telling me, "I won't ever feel comfortable leaving mom alone. She protected me. It's my turn to protect her."

I'm so fucking proud of him.

"What do you mean he is sick? I would rather him travel

sick than have his piece of shit grandfather kick your door down."

"His fever is one hundred and two. The doctors told me if it got any higher, I'd have to take him to the hospital. I can't risk traveling with him. He is in a fog right now. He needs help just to go to the bathroom. I have to wait, Fitz. I won't apologize for keeping his best interest—"

"—His best interest is getting out of that house!" I roar, yelling at my sister for the first time in her life.

I pull the phone away from my ear when I hear her take a sharp breath. "Fitz," her whispered voice wobbles.

Arms wrap around my waist. Holly hugs me from behind and the simple gesture has me relaxing. I place my hand on top of hers to calm myself down. Holly is magic.

"I'm sorry, Heather. I'm so sorry," I say with profound regret. "I'm worried. I'm scared. I can't let anything happen to either of you. You're all I have. Is Eli okay? Can I help him in any way? I love him, Heather. You know that and you know how Dad is. I just want you both protected. I shouldn't have moved away and left you two there. I should have brought you with me. That was selfish of me." Tears burn my eyes as regret slithers its way inside me, replacing my blood with terror.

"You did the right thing, Fitz. Rhett was kidnapped and he needed you when you found him. Dad doesn't know where we are, remember? If he is trying to find me, he will have a hard time. We will get to you, but Elijah's health comes first. I have packed our bags. They are in the car. I'll keep you updated, okay? I promise."

"Every few hours, Heather. Please."

"I can't check in when I'm sleeping," my sister teases,

trying to lighten the mood.

I roll my eyes, wishing she could see me. "You know what I mean."

"I'll call you in the morning. The security system is on. Gary is on standby."

"I know you did not just say your damn chihuahua is on guard watch. What is he going to do, Heather? Bite their ankles?"

"Have you had your ankle bitten? It hurts, you know."

"You should have gotten a bigger dog."

"Nothing is bigger than Gary's spirit. You should know that, Fitz."

Holly snickers behind me. I peek over to try to look at her, but she buries her face in my back. By the sound of it, she's inhaling. Is she smelling me?

"Who is that? Do you have a girl over there?"

Oh. No.

"Where did you meet? What's her name? What does she do? Do you like her? What's she look like? How long have you been seeing each other? I can't believe you didn't tell me—"

"—Okay. Love you, byeeeee," I singsong, hanging up the phone before she can say another word.

This time, I'm careful when I set my phone down, so I don't break it.

"Sorry about that," I mutter, twisting around in her arms.

I place my hands on her hips. My thoughts are running a million miles an hour. Could we make this work? Could I? Could I love her even though she is human? Is it fair to her if I try?

"You love your sister and your nephew very much. It's

okay. I understand. I know what it is like to care for someone so much that you would kill to protect them."

"Do you?" I slip my hand to her neck, wrapping my fingers around her slim throat with delicate ease. I'm careful. I don't want to hurt her. I crowd her against the counter, caging her with my weight so she can't get free. "I know I don't seem like the killing type, but I would. I love fiercely, Wildflower. I'm picky with who I give my heart to. I don't let just anyone in."

"I think you're wrong. I think you let everyone in, but you pick and choose between who to love and who to be kind to. There is a difference. Not everyone is deserving of your love. Not everyone is deserving of your kindness and yet, you give your kindness away to everyone."

"I don't like that you know me so well and we barely know each other."

"I know you better than you think, Fitz." Her gaze switches from me to the clock. "It's getting late. Want to put on a movie until we fall asleep?"

I yawn just as she says that. "I'm not sure if I'll make it through the entire movie. I'm beat. It's been a wild day."

"Let's tame it then." She tugs me to the couch from the kitchen, the corner of the counter grazing my hip.

I swallow the bite of pain as it scratches me.

"Lead the way, Wildflower."

When she turns to me, her human face is gone, and all I see is what I've been dreaming about.

A gorgeous beautiful monster with glowing orange eyes, horns, lavender skin, and fangs.

I'm completely in love with my delusions. All I want to do is dream so I can experience her again.

I'll fall asleep which will cause Holly to leave, and I'll be left alone to be in love with a woman who only exists in my mind.

Finally.

CHAPTER ELEVEN

HOLLY

Controlling this human facade drains my energy around Fitz. Sometimes, I'll catch him staring at me in ways that have me wondering if he can truly see me. That can't happen.

I'm running out of energy to maintain this form. It's why I need Fitz to go ahead and fall asleep. This is the longest I've tried to hold the disguise, and the attempt is draining me.

It's been about an hour since we sat down on the couch. Fitz is fighting to stay awake. His head keeps bobbing. The jerking of his head always wakes him up. It's absolutely adorable.

"Do you need anything?" he asks in a sleep-drenched tone.

Just you.

"No. I'm—" Thunder rolls above us. I yank the blanket to my chin, forgetting I'm a mixture of lethal creatures, and hide myself away from the storm. "—I'm fine."

"I won't let anything happen to you, Holly. If lightning

strikes, I'll stand in its way so it can't touch you." He brushes his fingers through my hair, tucking it behind my ears. Fitz yawns, scratching his chest. Those doe eyes I love so much become heavy. "I won't let anything happen to you," he says on the brink of sleep. The words are slow and barely a whisper. "I'll protect you."

"But who will protect you?" I ask in return, memorizing the sharp edges of his face.

He doesn't answer me. Sleep's power finally drags him to the darkness. His chest rises and falls in slow even rhythms. I poke him in the middle of his chest to see if he will wake up and he doesn't. His head remains tilted back with his arms crossed over his chest.

"Finally." I stand, watching as my arms fade from human to my natural state. I roll my head over my shoulders, groaning as a few joints pop into place.

A strong itch has me bending down to scratch the scales on my legs. The more I scratch, the worse the itch becomes. Extending my talons, I apply more pressure, dig deeper, and groan when I finally get relief.

But when I look down, dried scales dust the floor where I stand. I know it means I need to be in water more, but how often? There's too much to keep up with when it comes to these creatures who make my identity now.

I stare down at Fitz and the desire I've been swallowing all day burns my body from the inside out. Placing one knee to his left and the other to his right, I straddle him.

I love how fucking good he feels under me. Gently, I rock myself over his thick cock.

Fitz grumbles in his slumber. I know he feels me, and I know he wants me. I can sense it in our bond even though

he is fighting it. Why is he not giving in to me? I don't understand. I have a prime human form I take due to the woman I
killed. She is pretty. I know I could put her skin on, walk into
a bar, and have my pick of any man.

I don't want any man. I want Fitz. So why won't he give
himself to me when he is awake?

"We're going to have to change that, Doe Eyes. I can't
keep the human form that long anymore. It drains me of all
my energy." I scratch my legs again, wondering if being in a
form that isn't mine is what is drying out my scales so fast.

"I want you so much." I run my fingers through his hair,
the need to mate with him becoming stronger. I bend down,
licking his bottom lip before dragging my tongue to his ear.

He tastes like rain.

"I want to know everything about you," I tell him, kissing
the delicate skin just below his jaw. "Let me in, Fitz." I slip my
hand under his shirt, sliding my palm across his abs. "Let me
give you the sweetest dreams."

I sit up, watching his eyes open to take on a glowing
purple hue. A sly smirk tugs the corners of my mouth.

He's mine now.

"Such a good boy." I lift his shirt up, tug one arm
through, then the other, and toss it to the side for me to take
home later.

He's never getting his clothes back.

His body is on display and my fangs lengthen, wanting to
mark him on his neck. I want his blood. My mouth waters for
it and I don't understand why. I don't need blood to survive.
The scientists would have told me that much as they collected their data.

My nails scrape up his torso. His skin pebbles from my

touch and his cock hardens to full mast under me. I cage his head in with my arms, staring into his handsome face, and immerse myself in his dreams.

I want to see what he sees. I want to feel what he feels. I want his experiences to be mine.

What I see brings tears to my eyes. "Oh, Fitz." I graze my knuckles across his cheek, hating to know that even in his sleep, he doesn't even feel peace.

He can fool everyone else with his kindness, but it's only armor to cover up how broken he is on the inside.

"You've burdened yourself for so long. It's okay. Let me have your burdens. I'll carry them from now on." I lean forward, pressing my lips against his. I close my eyes, relishing in the soft give, the sweet taste of wine still lingering on his breath, and his stubble scratches my chin.

I press my forehead against his, holding my breath when I sink deeper into his dream.

I'm inside a mansion. It's one of those houses that swallows you whole with how big it is. The ceilings are high. Floor-to-ceiling windows line the wall to give a gorgeous view of the gardens.

It's pouring rain. No lightning. No thunder. Just rain beating against the windows.

The same man who came to visit him at the shop is yelling at Fitz and if I could kill him right now, I would.

People in dreams can't be killed. In real life? His father is on my list along with the list of women who dared to touch Fitz.

"You're nothing to me. Do you hear me?" his father yells at him, towering over him in height since Fitz wasn't done growing. His dad's hair is slicked back with streaks of black and silver. His eyes are a cold dead blue, nothing but bad intentions fill them. "You've never had what it takes to be a Wallsworth. You're weak." He shoves Fitz in the chest before rearing his fist back and punching his own son in the face.

I growl so loud that if Fitz wasn't locked in my succubus trance, he'd wake up.

Fitz takes the hit and barely moves. He stands strong like a statue. He wipes the blood from his bottom lip and scoffs, throwing his own punch so fast, that his dad couldn't prepare himself.

He hits his old man so hard, he stumbles, trips over a very modern coffee table, and lands on the couch.

"Fitsgerald!" his mother scolds, holding her husband as if he is a baby. "What has gotten into you? How dare you hit your father."

"How dare I hit him?" A manic laugh leaves young Fitz. "You are just as bad as he is. You can't even see how terrible of a man he is. He has his venom injected so deep inside of you, that you can't see him for what he really is. He shoved and punched me. Over wanting to protect Heather, you know, your daughter!" He points to a girl behind him who is sitting on a recliner.

She's sobbing quietly. Her cheeks are wet with tears. Her brown eyes match Fitz's with the same dashing of freckles across her nose. This must be Heather. The two took after their mom because they look nothing like their father.

Small favors I suppose.

"She is no daughter of mine," his mother hisses. "She's nothing but a wild whore. She knew better than to get pregnant. We taught her better than that. We have rules. We have a reputation to uphold. Do you know what it would look like for us to go into society with a pregnant sixteen-year-old daughter?"

"Because then you'd see how much you failed at parenting," Fitz shouts. "How dare you—"

Heather sniffles, grabbing his hand. "It's okay, Fitz."

"It isn't okay. It isn't okay," he repeats, taking her hand in his. "Accidents happen. I don't care what these uppity fucks say, you aren't a failure. You aren't a problem. You're my sister. I'll take care of you."

"Take care of her? How the hell are you going to take care of her and a baby at your age? Do you know what people will think?" His dad blubbers, wincing when his wife places a handkerchief against his lip to stop the bleeding.

"That's the difference between me and you. I'm willing to be what you two aren't. Good. And I don't care what I have to do to make sure Heather is okay, but I'll do it."

"You won't make it a week without us."

"Go pack your bags, Heather." Fitz helps Heather to her feet.

"Fitz, I'm scared," she says, sounding so much younger than sixteen.

He wipes the tears from her cheeks, giving her that familiar charming smile I love. His dimples show, making him appear so much younger than eighteen. His hair is shorter than it is now. His face has a youthful plumpness to it that doesn't stay as humans age.

"I know. Everything will be okay. I'll make sure of it. Go pack your bags. We are leaving as soon as possible."

"She isn't going anywhere. She is a minor. You can't take her, or I will report you for kidnapping," his sorry excuse for a father sneers. He laughs from the couch, pushing himself up to stand. "You have no power here. You have always been weak. You've always been a doormat. You'll be nothing without me. People will walk all over you until you are pressed into the fucking dirt. Your kindness will get you nowhere in life. Kindness doesn't make money."

Fitz steps into his father's space, narrowing his eyes at the older man. "Kindness builds community, loyalty, and love. Everything good comes from that. You can keep your wealth when it is attached to such evil and stupidity. Go ahead and call the cops. I'll tell them everything illegal you have ever done. I'll take you to court for custody."

"You couldn't afford it."

"You'd be surprised at what I can afford. Fucking test me and see. Stay the fuck away from me, from Heather, and from her child. You are pathetic. You'll never get to know your grandchild." Fitz shakes his head with sadness and disappointment in a slow gesture as he steps away from the man he called his dad. "I know you don't care and that's fine. Maybe that's why I care so much because I grew up in a home where nothing—not even your own children—were cared for. Have a good fucking life you sorry piece of shit, human being."

I'm lost in the hatred burning in his eyes.

"Get the fuck out of my house," his father seethes. "And take my whore of a daughter with you."

"Gladly. I'll give her the life you never could. I'll give her a life full of everything you emotionally are unable to give."

"Wait. Wait! No, let's...let's talk about this. There must be an agreement we can all come to." His mother wipes her palms on her white skirt as she stands. She walks around the coffee table, placing herself between Fitz and his father.

He looks just like her. The same color hair, eyes, and freckles. It's obvious they are mother and son.

"We can... we can get Heather's issue taken care of. Then, we can be a family again."

From the shadows, I watch Fitz's face turn from hatred to disgust. He steps away.

"Fitsgerald, please–" his mother tries to reach for him, but he shrugs off her attempt.

"You two are monsters. How dare you talk about that without Heather in the room? That isn't your decision to make."

"The hell it isn't my decision," his father bellows, tucking his hands in his pockets. He turns around, strolling the bar at the other end of the room. The walking dead man pours himself two fingers of scotch, downing it in one swallow before pouring another glass. "She's a minor. I'll find a doctor to do it. Everyone can be bought for the right price."

"I'm not doing that. I'm not getting rid of my baby."

Fitz rushes to Heather's side, taking her bags. "No, they aren't. If that's not what you want, that's fine, Heather. That's okay. You aren't alone. You have me."

"I want my baby, Fitz." Heather's bottom lip trembles as she tries to hold in her emotions. "I know–" she swallows "–I know I messed up. I know I got pregnant too young. I know that. I–"

"–Who is the father? Certainly not that boy who helps his father with the garden," Their mother asks with a laugh.

Heather doesn't look away ashamed. She stands tall and proud.

Good for her.

"So what if he is? He is nice. He loves me," she says.

"What the fuck do you know about love?" his father roars, stomping his way across the living room to confront her. "He got what he wanted stupid girl. He wanted an easy piece of ass, and he got it. Why do you think he hasn't been around?" He raises his hand to slap her when Fitz steps in front of her, taking the hit.

A tear rolls down my cheek, debating if I should continue to invade such a private dream. I can't seem to stop when it comes to my mate. I want to know everything. He didn't deserve any of this and neither did Heather.

There's a malicious glint in his eye as he takes a swig of scotch.

"What did you do, Dad?" Heather questions in a horrified whisper. "What did you do to him!" She screams, trying to push Fitz out of the way.

"He'll never be a problem again. You'll get an abortion. You and your brother will stay here. We will be a family. Fitz you'll be the heir to the company. That's the plan."

"Fuck you and your plan." Fitz becomes nose-to-nose with his dad. "We're leaving. You have no heirs. Not any-more."

His Dad punches Fitz again, the skin-to-skin contact has me gasp when a burst of blood flies from my mate's mouth through the air. Fitz laughs, spitting blood on the ground.

"Is that all you've got? I've taken better hits from my girlfriends."

I growl, not liking that mention. Now isn't the time or place for jealousy.

His father hits him again.

And again.

"Stop it! Stop, you're going to kill him!" Heather sobs.

Fitz takes hit after hit until he can no longer stand, falling to his knees only to receive a hard kick in the gut.

"Fitz!" Heather screams at the top of her lungs.

His dad grips him by the root of his hair and my own hand slips across his head, rubbing the same area his father controlled him by.

"How do the hits feel now?" He shoves Fitz down to the floor, rearing his leg back.

Fitz begins to jerk underneath me. With every kick he takes, his body tenses and spasms.

"Hey, hey, you're okay," I whisper into his dream. "You aren't there, Doe Eyes. You're safe. You got your sister out. You did it. Follow my voice, Fitz. Come to me. Let me take care of you."

The nightmare fades from his father, morphing into a beautiful sunset.

I'm able to breathe again. He's safe.

"Oh, Doe Eyes. I can't see that again. You scared me. I'm so sorry that happened to you. I promise to make them pay for what they did. No one touches you like that. No one will ever put another hand on you. Only I'm allowed to touch you." I drag my finger across his jaw. "And I promise to never harm you with my hands. My only want in this life is to make you happy, to give you everything you could ever want."

I seep into his new dream, wanting to prove to him just how good my hands can make him feel. "I'll work my entire life to erase the hate he gave you with my love." I drag my hand down his chest then back up, my body aching for more of his body.

Now isn't the time but I have no choice. I need his come to survive. It's my succubus nature. Especially, now. I have my mate, and that knowledge only makes me hungrier for him.

In the dream, he is sitting on the tailgate of his truck, watching the sunset. The sky is painted in reds, yellows, oranges, pinks, and purples. The sun is a glowing circle lowering itself behind the mountains.

I sit on the tailgate next to him and he turns his head to me, his hair curling just above his brows.

"You're back. Did you miss me?" He wraps his arm around my waist, tugging me to his side. He buries his nose in my hair and inhales. "I've missed you."

"I've missed you too. Is this your favorite spot?" I ask, placing my hand on his thigh. "It's beautiful."

"Yeah. I come here when I need peace. I love all the colors in the sky. The sunset reminds me that the day is nearly over, and tomorrow is a fresh start. This day will be considered the past as soon as the sun rises again. I get to be a better person than I was yesterday. I sit here and numb my mind. I try to think about all the ways I can be better instead of all the ways I have failed."

"You haven't failed, Fitz." I prompt him to look at me, smiling at him with all the love I have in my heart for my Doe Eyes.

He sees me for me. My fangs. My horns. My body. My tail. Nothing is hidden and I've never been looked at the way Fitz looks at me. His gaze, his attention, it's as if I'm the only person in the world that matters to him in this very second. I'm addicted.

"You're the most extraordinary man I've ever met. You're so kind and considerate. You have nothing but good inside you. You're so much better than me. If you knew..."

He cuts my sentence off by kissing me. Fitz cups the back of my head, his tongue gliding across mine.

In real-time, he is kissing me as if he isn't dreaming. What does surprise me is the movement of his arms. His hands are mimicking the way he is kissing me in the dream. His cock is hard, and the impressive girth has me gasping as I rock back and forth.

Falling into his mind again, I press him down in the bed of the truck. I imagine a blanket under us, and it appears along with a few pillows. He rests his head, slipping his hand to the back of my neck, controlling how deep our kiss is. He moans and I swallow his sounds, feeding every creature who lives inside me now.

A vision slams into my mind, forcing me to break the kiss. It's Fitz, surrounded by four men at the garage after it's been closed.

All men have weapons. They attack Fitz at the same time, launching themselves at him. He swings and fights, but his father pulls out a gun.

The loud crack of a bullet has me gasping, opening my eyes to stare down at Fitz. I check him all over for wounds, my eyes blurring with tears.

Did I just witness my mate die?

"No. I refuse. I won't lose you to him. I'll be there. I'll protect you." I taste the salt from my tears as I kiss his swollen pink lips. Needing him more than ever now. Being this close isn't enough. Being inside his head isn't enough. Having him inside me isn't enough.

I need more.

"I won't lose you to him," I say against his lips. "He almost took you once." I slip my hand down his cheek. "This time,

I'll be the one to take him to the depths of hell for you. I'll do anything for you, Fitz."

Closing my eyes, I fully give myself over to the dream.

We kiss until we can't breathe. We're groaning and gasping. I rock against his cock, my tentacles wanting to be freed from the sweatpants. His hands roam up my shirt, fingering the chains attached to my nipple rings. He tugs them, once, twice, and I moan, arching my back.

"Fitz," I mewl his name. "Do you want me?"

"So fucking bad, Wildflower. Give me what I need. I'll do anything."

"Anything? Only good boys say things like that." I kiss down his chest, sucking one of his nipples into my mouth. "Are you my good boy, Fitz?"

He tugs down his pants, his fat cock slapping against his stomach. "I'm so good. What do I need to do to prove it to you?"

"Undress me."

He rips the shirt from my body, then pulls my pants down, and off. His sweatpants are wrapped around his ankles.

In reality too.

I gently lie Fitz down on the couch, smirking when I straddle his face.

"Be a good boy and lick every tentacle. I want to feel your tongue inside me before I ride your cock. I'm so hungry for your come, Doe Eyes. Will you give it to me?"

"Fuck yes, I'll give you whatever you want, Wildflower. I'll fucking paint you with my come and lick it off if that's what you want."

I gasp, playfully covering my mouth with my hand. "Why

would I have you lick it clean?" A tentacle wraps around his throat, tightening until his face turns red. "When you can just spit into my mouth so I can be full of you in more ways than one." His eyes roll to the back of his head, my tentacles unraveling from his throat.

He gasps, licking his plump lips. His eyes water from being choked and a tear slowly drips from his lower lash line. A tentacle swipes it away from his cheek and I'm able to taste the warmth along with the salt.

Delicious.

My tentacles reach for him, forcing his mouth open. One wraps around his tongue, two others spread his mouth wide, sliding in to feel how wet and warm he is. Those doe eyes roll back again as my suckers massage his tongue.

"Suck," I order. "Be my good boy and make me come down that throat."

He palms my ass, using the flesh as leverage to yank me down onto his face.

"I don't want to smother you," I groan when he sucks the tip of my tentacle, lavishing it in his spit. He hums, sucking me like I would his cock. "Oh, Fitz. That feels so good. You're a filthy boy, aren't you? You love having a monster fuck you."

He slowly nods, slurping a tentacle down his throat as if I'm a meal he can't wait to eat.

Back in reality, he is doing the same thing. His hands remain on my ass, gripping me so hard, I'd think he might be awake. The purple shine from his eyes says differently. He licks and sucks like he is conscious too. Now, I'm wondering if my invasion in his mind is working.

It has to be. If he saw me, he'd push me off him so fast.

"Sit down, Wildflower. Smother me with that pretty

cunt. I want to feel those suckers on my tongue." He gives my ass a smack and my tail slithers up his legs.

He spreads his thighs, but I continue up his body, allowing it to push between my pussy and his mouth.

"Watch me, Doe Eyes. I'm going to ruin you for anyone else. Do you understand me?" Curling my tail inward, it glides through my lips becoming soaked in my arousal.

I moan when I press it inside myself. I slap his chest, digging my claws into his pecs. To my surprise, Fitz sucks a tentacle into his mouth again. His fingers find my clit, giving it hard and slow circles.

"Fitz." I increase the speed of my tail fucking me.

"You're so fucking beautiful, Wildflower. Are you going to come for me?"

"No."

He spanks me again, growling with my tentacle between his lips. The vibrations travel through the suckers, zinging the nerves of my clit.

"Why not?" He releases a tentacle with a soft pop before paying attention to another.

I yank his head back by his hair. "Because I want your tongue deep inside me when I do. I'm going to stain it with my come so every time you speak, everyone will know you're claimed. That you're mine. That you belong to me." My tail slips from my cunt, drenched in my ink, and it glides down Fitz's cock.

He is so fucking thick. I love that it isn't long and huge. It's perfect. He's perfect. He fits me just right, stretches me wide until he takes my breath, and makes me come harder than any other man ever could.

Without warning, without ease or consideration, I push

my tail between his legs, shoving my tail into his tight hole.

"That I own you. Me. No one else."

"Fuck, oh fuck, Holly. Oh my God," he cries out, clenching around me.

The voltage of lightning outside shines light through the windows, illuminating Fitz's body. It shines from the light sheen of sweat. His hands roam my body, tugging on the chains attached to my nipple piercings.

Oh, he loves this.

"You feel so real," he moans, bringing me back into his mind.

I plunge my tail in and out, loving the pinch of pleasure in his face. The space between his brows crinkles. His eyes become so expressive. They round in shock before rolling back again. He bites his bottom lip, groaning every time I brush his prostate.

"I'm as real as you want me to be, Doe Eyes." I settle over his face, lowering myself to his mouth. "Make me come. You aren't allowed to until I say. If you do, I won't show up to your dreams for a week."

"Holly," he practically whines. "I'm already on edge. I don't know if I can hold it back."

"You better if you ever want to see me again," I state with a hard bite. "You're talking too much." I shove my tentacles in his mouth, filling it to the point that his lips are as wide as possible. "Your will is mine. So if I say wait to come, you fucking wait, Fitz." I yank my tentacles free, spit dripping from every sucker.

His lips are swollen and wet. "Whatever you want, Wildflower."

"Good boy. Now, take a deep breath. I'm going to suffocate you."

His eyes become glassy as his face turns hungry. His hands are locked onto my ass, gripping them so hard, he will leave bruises behind. I'll have his mark on me, and I can't wait. My mate doesn't wait for me to sit. He urges me forward, shoving me onto his face.

"Fitz!" I cry out as his tongue plunges deep inside me.

He moans when my tail hits his prostate which has me tossing my head back, shouting to the gorgeous sunset sky. My tentacles suction cup to his cheek and neck, helping bring him closer. His nose brushes against my clit, and the teasing pressure has my wings expanding.

His eyes widen and his desire for me becomes stronger. I smell it.

"You like my wings, Doe Eyes?" My question is breathless and needy.

I stroke my feathers, plucking one from the root. I drag it over his chest. "Do you think I could make you come just by doing this?" I stretch my arm back, tickling the tip of his cock before dragging it down the gorgeous plump shaft.

He whimpers into my cunt; his tongue freezes deep inside me when I caress his cock with the feather.

"Mmm. Fuck. Don't stop." His words are muffled by my pussy.

I continue all my assaults. Fucking him with my tail, teasing his cock, and his pleas for more has the warning signs of my orgasm becoming bigger.

Rocking my hips against his mouth, my suckers stick and massage his tongue.

"You're so good with your mouth, Doe Eyes. You're such a good fucking boy." I toss my head back, my body tensing, my suckers secreting my ink when my orgasm slams against me.

I drop the feather from my grasp. "Fitz. Oh, fuck, Fitz. I'm coming. You're such a good boy making me come. You feel so good. Drink me. Drink me down. Fuck. Oh, God." I roll my hips wanting to extend my pleasure.

Glancing down, black iridescent ink drips from the corner of his mouth, down his chin, and he gulps me down as if it's the best drink he has ever had.

"Good boy," I praise him, stroking his chest with my talons.

His big brown eyes light up with joy, giving my ass one final squeeze. I slide from his mouth, his lips, tongue, and teeth black from my ink. I bend down, licking his lips clean.

"Do you like how I taste?" I kiss his succulent lips, nipping the flesh with my fangs.

"I want more. You're my favorite flavor, Wildflower." He squeezes his eyes shut, breathing in and out through his nose. His bicep is flexed.

Curious, I look back to see him gripping his cock so hard that the tip is a deep shade of red.

I can confirm he's squeezing his cock outside of the dream as well.

"What do you think you're doing, Doe Eyes? Don't strangle that pretty cock. That's for me to do."

"I'm too close. I'm going to come. The taste of you was too much."

"What kind of mate would I be if I didn't give my good boy relief?" I purr, kissing down his chest.

"Please," he begs through broken breaths. "Please, Wildflower. Please," he continues to ramble and plead. "I'll do anything. What do you want? I'll do it. I'll do anything for you. Please, make me come. Please," he practically sobs, fisting the blanket under him.

I kiss down his chest, shifting my tongue into a tentacle, leaving small suction marks all over his torso.

"You look so pretty decorated by me," I croon, licking the valleys of his abs.

His fingers brush through my hair, holding it away from my face. "And you look so gorgeous against me. I'll wear your marks proudly, Wildflower. Leave scars for all I care," he says.

"Mmmm." I circle his navel. "Don't go giving me ideas." I circle my tongue around his cock, gripping it with the suckers.

"Fuck," he groans, his back arching off the bed of the truck. "Those goddamn suckers are going to be the death of me."

I swirl and suck him deep until he hits the back of my throat. My tongue splits in two, wrapping around the thick stalk. The suction cups move, wave, and massage. My mate trembles beneath me. His heart rate skips a beat and that tells me he is close.

"Holly. Holly. Holly," he shouts my name, and it echoes into the space of the mountain.

He fills my mouth with come. I drink it down, needy and thirsty for him.

"Fuck. There's no mouth that exists like yours."

I lift off him, come dripping from my tongue, and I let it coat his cock. "You're out of your mind if you think we're done. I'm still hungry, Doe Eyes."

"I wouldn't be a good man if I didn't feed you." He picks me up by my hips, my tentacles already stretching to reach his cock.

We watch as they swirl around him. He sucks his top lip before lifting his eyes to meet mine. We lock gazes and I ease down on him, inviting him into me.

Those big brown eyes roll back again. "I can't wait for these suckers, Holly. I'm already on the edge again just by sliding inside you. I won't last. I won't." He struggles to breathe, slapping a hand down on my ass. "Fuck!" He pours into me, shocking me with his second orgasm.

The tentacles and suckers pull his come to my womb, needing him to breed me.

"The more the better. Give me more, Fitz." I begin to ride him, his come leaking out of me to create filthy wet sounds.

In reality, the couch is ruined by my ink. His body is stained from it. His come drips from his cock, down his sack, and onto the couch. We're making a mess. The grip of his fingers sinks into my hips, holding me tight to rock me back and forth faster.

And faster.

And faster.

My orgasm is close again. Fitz tweaks my nipples, tugging on the chains. With a growl, he sits up and sucks my left nipple into his mouth. He tugs the right chain. Then the left. He kisses across my chest to give attention to the other, continuing to drive me crazy as he pulls on the chains.

"You're so tight, Wildflower. No one has fucked me like you have. No one has felt as good as you do."

"And no one will ever fuck you again, do you hear me? You're mine, Fitz. Mine. No one will ever feel this thick cock stretch them. It's mine. Tell me."

"It's yours."

I rock my hips. "Again."

"My cock is yours."

I fuck him faster. "Again!" I scream, my orgasm barreling closer to destroy me.

"My cock is yours. I'm yours. Yours and yours alone."

My tentacles, my suckers, my muscles clamp around him. My ink squirts all over his skin, adding to his permanent mark.

"Fitz!" I cry so loud that I pull myself from the dream. "Are you going to come? You better breed me, Doe Eyes. I need you to."

"You want to be pregnant with my child, Holly? Is that what you want?"

"Yes. God, yes." I become louder with my cries of pleasure.

"I'll give you all the kids you want. Imagining you pregnant..." he growls, thrusting his hips to meet my pace.

I stare down at Fitz. Sweat drips from his temples. His hair is a mess. His tongue is stained. My claws made red lines down his chest. Circular marks are all over his defined torso.

The black tattoo on his skin from my ink grows, veining up to the bottom of his pec while another part wraps around his back.

He groans, the warmth of his come painting my depths.

"Yes," I moan, drinking him down. "Good boy, Fitz. Good boy filling me." I bend down to give him a kiss and fall into his dream again.

He wraps his arms around me, covers us with a blanket, and we watch the sunset.

"I think I love you, Wildflower. I'll be happy if I only ever see you in my dreams."

"I love you too, Fitz. Your dreams are home."

My plan has worked, but now what do I do?

I'm not ready to tell him the truth. Maybe staying in his dreams is what is best.

CHAPTER TWELVE

FITZ

"Ow." I rub the back of my neck, a pinched nerve causing me pain.

I lift my head, continuing to massage the aching muscles. "That explains it," I grumble with a yawn, stretching my arms to work out the kinks of sleeping on the sofa.

I don't typically sleep in the living room but last night with Holly, I felt so relaxed and tired. I have never felt that way before. Even though I have so much to worry about, she still made me feel at peace.

"Holly," I whisper when it hits me that I did not fall asleep alone. "Holly?" I raise my voice, looking around the room for any sign of her. "Holly!" I yell, standing to my feet.

I check the kitchen, the bedrooms, and the bathrooms downstairs. Running, I take two steps at a time hoping she is in my bedroom. Maybe the couch was uncomfortable for her.

"Holly? Are you okay?" Opening the bedroom door, I'm prepared to slide in next to her. I want to wrap my arms around her and pull her close.

Or maybe she can be the big spoon. I love being held. I can't remember the last time where I was the one being cuddled.

But the room is empty.

She isn't in the bathroom. The door is open, and the light is off. The house is quiet.

Holly isn't here.

There's a sting of disappointment knowing she left without saying goodbye. I plop down on the side of the bed, trying to recall the moment she left. My head is numb. I can't remember anything. I must have slept like I was dead.

I lie down and stare at the ceiling fan.

Yikes. I need to clean the blades.

Blowing out a breath after a second of gathering my thoughts, I sit up, scratching my bare shoulder.

I freeze.

The morning fog in my mind lifts just enough for me to remember I slept with a shirt on.

"I swear I did," I grumble, rubbing a hand down my face in exhaustion and slight confusion. "I remember getting dressed, giving Holly clothes, we went downstairs, talked, and..."

Everything after that is blank.

I scrub my eyes and yawn again. I need to get up, get ready, and call Heather. I'll knock on Holly's door later. I hope I didn't do anything wrong last night for her to get up and leave. I wanted her to stay. I didn't want her to spend the night during a storm alone.

Which reminds me, I need to talk to Caden. He needs to calm down with all these damn storms. Caden is a storm kitsune. He creates storms which gives him energy, but it rains almost every day now. I miss the sun on my skin.

The smell of my automatic coffee pot brewing motivates me to get up from my big comfortable bed.

"Ugh, this sucks. Mornings are not for me," I groan, hanging my head as I drag my feet to the bathroom.

Flipping on the light, I wince, closing my eyes to slits to protect them from the harsh brightness. I grip the vanity, taking a deep breath to prepare myself for the day.

Looking at my reflection, I reach for my toothbrush when I notice my torso.

My toothbrush falls from my grip. I can't remember to breathe.

"What in the ever-loving fucking wild is this?" I screech, jumping backward and grabbing at my skin.

I twist and turn, seeing where all the hickey-like spots end and begin. "I'm losing my fucking mind. I'm losing it. Holy fuck, I have a disease. This has to be contagious." I stare at myself in the mirror in pure panic, noticing perfect red dots all over my body. They kind of look like hickies. How that would be possible, I have no idea.

The black mark is what grabs my attention the most.

It's spread.

"Holy wild. Holy wild, Holy wild," I chant in absolute dismay, fumbling with the strings at my sweatpants before tugging them down to my knees.

"Ah!" I'm not proud of the high-note scream, but others would too if they saw what I'm seeing on my cock.

I grab myself, twisting and turning, completely forgetting it's attached to my body until I tug too hard and grunt.

"Shit, sorry," I groan in pain, apologizing to my fucking

self.

The black mark looks like splattered ink. The largest darkest spot is my cock. More than half is onyx with a few spots that vein out like lightning. It's those veins that travel up my body and now they have grown, stopping right under pec.

I grip the counter when the room starts to spin. Spots fill my vision as worst-case scenarios run through my mind.

Is this the plague? It can't be the plague, right? A skin disorder maybe? Cancer?

I slap my forehead when that thought crosses my mind. "Of course it isn't cancer, you fucking idiot." I catch my reflection in the mirror, watching my chest rise and fall as I take deep calming breaths.

This is wild. How does this happen?

"Take a shower, relax, and go to the doctor. Everything will be fine," I say to myself, picking up my toothbrush again. "Just fine. You're fine, Fitz." A manic cackle escapes me as I load my toothbrush with too much toothpaste.

Right as I open my mouth to begin brushing, a dark color captures my attention. "What the fuck?" I stick out my tongue, eyes widening when I see it's black. "What the fuck?" I scream through a mumble. I touch it and then rub it with my fingers. It won't come off.

"Oh my God. What the fuck is going on? What is this? Am I dying? I have to be dying."

I scrub my tongue with my toothbrush and the frothy white paste begins to turn grey. There's nothing I can do about it. I don't think I'm dying. I guess if I keel over later that will answer all of my questions.

I'm going to drive myself insane with this. All I can do is

move forward and keep my mouth shut so I don't get asked too many questions.

I brush my teeth in a daze, same with the shower, and not even the fun bubbles with iridescent colors bring me out of my trance.

With the same energy, I get dressed.

"Dressed and Stressed should be your motto, Fitz." Buttoning my jeans, I continue my morning routine on autopilot.

The feather on the nightstand captures my attention. I pick it up, analyzing it to decide where it could have come from. I remember thinking it was her wings, and I've never felt so fucking stupid in my entire life.

The feather is probably from my pillow. It's the only reasonable solution.

"Because monsters aren't real, Fitz. At least, not for you." I slam the light off with my fist, rage burning away the morning fog I typically feel this early.

I don't usually pity myself but I'm so tired of being let down. There is always fucking something that sets me back. I grew up with awful abusive parents. I took a beating from my father the same night I took my pregnant sister away from that house. I was only eighteen years old working two jobs and getting five hours of sleep between each shift. I helped raise my nephew Elijah and being so young, that wasn't easy for me or Heather. Then, my best friend went missing and was turned into a monster.

I got him back and I couldn't be happier, but now with all these unknown things happening to me, I'm not sure how to stay positive. I'm tired of always having to keep my head up, of always pushing through and forward. I'm so sick of waiting to get out on the other side. I'm done fooling myself that this 'other side' I have made up in my head is better than the side I have been on my entire life.

One step forward, one hundred steps back it seems. I'm tired. To my bones. To my soul. I need a reset. I'm not sure how much longer I can continue to live like this. This fixation I have on wanting a monster mate is out of control. It's unhealthy. The hope for her is what will ultimately kill me because I know monsters exist. I see Rhett and Creed nearly every day.

Knowing they exist only reaffirms my dream.

I'm starting to think it is too unrealistic to have what Demi and Mickey have.

"It's time for the real world, Fitz."

Going downstairs, I don't even bother with my coffee. I'm too resigned. I think I'll go to Demi's Diner instead. Maybe being around others will lighten my mood after I go to the doctor.

Snagging my hat, I plop it on my head as I snag my keys. It's cool out so I put on my jacket too, tucking my wallet inside the pocket. When I open the door, the cold air hits me, taking away my breath for a second.

The harshness from the blast of bitter cold pulls me from my stupor a little. For some reason, all I can think about is planting a variety of different colored hollyhocks in front of my porch. If I plant them now, maybe by summer they could bloom. Seeing them would bring me so much happiness, reminding me of a time when life was hard yet so good.

When it was just my sister and I living in a one-bedroom apartment and barely making rent, our neighbor would bring us freshly picked hollyhocks from her garden every single week.

They were the only pop of color in our bland apartment. We couldn't afford anything else. The walls were blank. We couldn't afford to put photos up anywhere because we couldn't afford to print them. I gave my sister the closet and I lived out of a suitcase.

I remember asking her why she kept bringing these flowers to us and I'll never forget what she said.

"Hollyhocks symbolize fortune and eternal life, but not only that, they bring love and healing. I notice you need them all. These flowers will give you what you need in your soul. Think of them like armor, protecting you when you have no idea you need protection. Just wait and see."

So many years later, I can't help but wonder if her wild theory was right, and I'm starting to think I need to take a page from her book.

Every week when she came over was my favorite time. I was always curious about what color combinations she would come up with. I became fascinated. All from a simple flower. Do I think those flowers got me to where I am?

No, they are only flowers. And yet, they made me believe in myself and that's all I needed. Without that neighbor bringing those gifts to us every week, I'm not sure where my sister and I would be. That simple act of kindness lifted us from the mud we found ourselves in.

Thinking of hollyhocks reminds me of my new neighbor. My attention swivels from the empty lawn to Holly's house.

I'm curious what she is up to. Why would she leave without saying goodbye?

I need to leave her alone. This isn't fair to her. The monster I see reminds me so much of the symbolization of the hollyhock flower. Resigning myself to a normal life, I swing the key ring around my finger while I head to my truck.

It's time to put her out of sight and out of mind. That's easier said than done. I'm addicted to the vision my mind creates when she is around. I want more. I want to stare at her all day, bathe myself in hopes that she is real, and dream of her time and time again.

I'd be so lost in the dreams of her, I'd never want to wake up.

Too bad that isn't a choice.

Climbing into my truck, I take one last look at her house, drive away, and put her in my rearview.

***

I press the Bluetooth button on the steering wheel. "Call Heather," I say with clear and concise dictation so the damn computer can understand me.

"Calling Heather," the truck's 'voice' replies.

It rings three times before her voice comes across the speaker. "Hey, Fitz."

"You sound tired. Is Eli doing okay?"

"No... We're... I won't be there today, Fitz. We can't be."

I rub my chin with one hand, keeping the other on the wheel. "I'm worried, Heather. I need you to be on the lookout, okay? Arm yourself."

"Why is this different than all the other times he has found you, Fitz?"

"Because out of all those times, he has never threatened to come for you. This time he did. That's how I know he is serious. The moment Eli is better, you come to me. I have the space. I never should have left–”

“–Stop. You sacrificed so much for me and Eli. You deserved to go do something for yourself.”

“I’ll come to you now. I’ll help you guys get here. Do you need money?”

“No, you send plenty every week even though I tell you not to,” she scolds. “We’re okay. I promise I’ll update you. I need to go. The nurse is calling for us to go into the room.”

“Okay. Promise me you’ll be extra careful?”

“Fiz, I promise. I swear to you. I love you, okay? We will be there as soon as we can.”

I ball my fist as tight as I can, doing my best to remain calm. I’m very protective of my sister. She’s the only one I will change my morality for. I will kill to protect her and my nephew. I don’t care what that would mean for me as long as they are safe.

“I love you too. Let me know what the doctor says.”

“I will. Next time, I’ll have him call you when he is feeling better.”

I grin, excited to talk to him. “Perfect. I can’t wait. Give him a hug for me.”

“I always do. Talk to you later.”

The call ends just as I pull into the urgent care parking lot again. It’s empty because only I would come here this fucking early. Everyone is smart enough not to wake up at this ungodly hour.

I thud my forehead against the steering wheel. “These mornings are getting worse and worse. At this point, I might stay in bed.” I drag my ass out of the truck, pocketing my keys.

The skin on the back of my neck tingles. Every hair

stands up on its end and I freeze. I swear to all things wild; someone is breathing on the back of my neck. I lift my arms to show I'm not a threat. My mouth becomes dry. My heart pounds in my chest but to my surprise, it isn't because I'm afraid.

A small tremble irritates my body as that warm breath ghosts across my pulse on the side of my neck. I swear something slides down my back, bringing me nothing but comfort.

Closing my eyes, I allow the feeling to inject me. Peace eases the panic in the back of my mind. A soft pressure haunts my skin at the base of my throat. Inhaling a sharp breath, I open my eyes and spin around.

Nothing is there.

Only a nearly empty parking lot, the morning fog, and a few frogs croaking in the woods.

"What the fuck is going on?" I ask myself, absolutely dis-combobulated at how I have found myself in this situation.

I'm not going to be delusional to myself. I don't know what, but there's something happening to me. I felt it. I'm going to go with my instincts. Maybe I do have a monster.

I just haven't seen her yet.

"You don't need to be afraid," I announce to the empty parking lot.

If anyone were to see me right now, they would label me unstable.

"I know you're here." Someone is fucking here. "I won't care if you're a monster DNA experiment. I'm totally cool with it. I love it, actually." Oh, so fucking much. "I'm someone you can trust. I have friends like you." I stand in the middle of the parking lot under a dimly lit streetlight calling out to my little monster. Excitement burns me from within. "I'm wondering if maybe you're my mate? Maybe you don't know what that means. My friends didn't until they were taught by other paranormals but if I am your fated mate, it means I'm destined to be yours. I want that, you know. I want to be destined to you."

Everything that has happened makes so much sense if a monster is involved. It checks all of my boxes.

The question is will my monster come out and play? All I need to do is gain her trust. I'm pushing her, maybe. I need to respect her space.

Except I don't want to respect her space at all.

"I'll be looking for you," I say before stepping through the sliding glass doors of urgent care.

"Oh, you're back," the kind nurse I saw yesterday chirps with a big smile. "Same thing?"

My face burns bright red. "Yes."

"The doctor will be right with you."

"Thank you." I turn to sit in one of the chairs, wanting nothing more than to plot how to trap her.

"You'll be seeing a new doctor today, though. I hope that is alright," the nurse casually announces.

Quirking my brow, I turn to him. "Why? I'd rather see the last doctor if you don't mind. She is familiar with...my issue." I tread carefully, not wanting everyone to know about my medical concerns.

"She didn't come in. It's weird. She hasn't texted. It isn't like her. The on-call doctor is here."

"Oh, wow. I hope she's okay. I'm so sorry to hear that."

"Me too. She was sweet. She made coming to work easy, you know?"

I nod, understanding exactly what he means.

"I'd rather see the other doctor. I'll come back later." If I'm right about my monster, then my marks have to be from her. It's the only thing that makes sense.

"I understand," he says, bending down to place his elbows on the counter. "I know this is out of left field, but would you want to go out sometime? You're cute. You have innocent eyes I want to corrupt." His eyes roam up and down me.

"Uh, I'm flattered but I'm taken. I hope you have a good day."

He pouts. "All the cute ones always are." The chair he is in rolls directly in front of a computer. "Have a great day."

I give him a wave, having to stop myself from skipping out of there. Granted, I've never skipped, but I do run into the fucking 'automatic' doors again.

"Mother fucker." I rub my nose.

A small giggle sounds behind me and the flush from my cheeks spreads to the tip of my ears. When the doors open, I dash through them. My boots scuff against the pavement, the fog a giant phantom snake slithering throughout the parking lot.

There it is again. That feeling of being watched. A big smile spreads across my face, but I don't think she wants to be close to me right now. I'll keep my distance.

For now.

I climb into the driver's seat and then hang out the door, studying the parking lot one last time. "I hope I see you soon. I look forward to it," I announce, the words echoing between the trees.

Slamming the door, my cock plumps at the thought of

her. Her skin is my favorite color, and her wings look so soft. I want to hold onto them while I fuck her from the back. Unless she doesn't look that way at all.

I could be wrong and if I am, I'll go get help to see why I want this so much that I'm imagining it.

The headlights pour through the dense fog as I drive to the main road. I'm no longer in auto-pilot. This revelation has zapped me with a bolt of energy. Did lightning strike me? Are all these marks because of a storm?

That would make sense too but it's not nearly as fun.

This is so fucking wild.

I stop before taking a left onto the main road, noticing two figures in the depths of the fog. Rolling down my window, I shout to the hitchhikers, "Hey. Do you need a ride or anything?"

They stay hidden, keeping their faces turned away from me. "No, we are fine. Just taking a walk."

An eerie energy has me on high alert.

I pat the side of the truck with my fingers. "Alright, then. Be safe." I roll up my window. I'm not sure what is up with them, but they aren't from around here.

Doesn't mean they are bad people but there is a heaviness in the air surrounding me about them. I can't stop glancing in the rearview. The two men are standing in the middle of the road, watching me until I can no longer see them.

They don't sit right with me, and I can't put my finger on why.

Pulling into Demi's Diner for a to-go coffee, I keep the two newcomers in mind. If I come across Jake, maybe I'll let him know.

Heading into Demi's, the first person I see is Creed. He is sitting in the same booth he always sits at. Caden is coming out of the kitchen with a tray filled with plates of breakfast. Mickey isn't here because she is very pregnant, but her brother Milo is and he is the one that greets me.

"Hey, man. Long time no see," a bright smile stretches across his face.

"Hey," My gaze darts over his shoulder to peek at Creed. He's so fucking weird. In a good way.

And in a bad way, let's not fool ourselves.

Bringing my attention back to Milo, I yawn, covering my mouth with my hand. "I'm sorry. I haven't been sleeping well. Can I get a large coffee to go?" I ask him, peering over his shoulder to spy on Creed.

He isn't there.

"You still smell fucking terrible."

I jump, slapping a hand to my chest. "Jesus, Creed. You scared the fuck out of me. Don't you know not to sneak up on people?"

"Yes," he states. "But I don't care."

"Of course, you don't," I grumble. I'm so not in the mood for him. I lift my arm to take a sniff. "I smell fine. Fucking sandalwood, asshole."

"You do not smell like sandalwood." He sniffs me but this time he makes a show, getting everyone's attention.

With loud deep head turning inhales, Creed smells me from head to toe. A few people turn around in their booths, lifting their brows at us.

"Don't mind him. He is being treated for his issues. It just takes time." I give the patrons a quick smile and a wave, hoping it will get these spectators to look away.

"Don't listen to him," Creed growls, lifting his nose from my stomach to speak. "He reeks. I'm doing everyone a fucking favor."

I slap him on the back of the head. "I do not reek. You're being very rude and intrusive."

He bites me.

He fucking bites me!

"Mother fucker!" I shove him in the chest, staring at the teeth punctures in my jeans. "You bit me."

"You wouldn't stop insulting me. I'm doing you a favor." He lies down on the ground going as far as sniffing my damn shoes. "You stink. I don't know what you stepped in, but as Mickey and Demi would say to one another, "Girlfriend, I hate to tell you this, but you smell." He snaps his fingers, adding a bit of sass. "Or something like that."

I roll my lips together to keep from laughing. "You do know they aren't serious when they call each other that? It's a joke, Creed."

"Joke or not, the message works."

"Here is your coffee." The person who brings me my coffee isn't Milo. It's Caden.

Perfect.

"My God, Creed. Leave the man alone," Caden states. "Don't you have somewhere to be?"

"Yes. Right here. Wherever Demi is."

"You can leave her side. She won't blow up or anything."

Creed sneers, inching closer to Caden. "No, she fucking won't. Because I'm here." He points at me, narrowing his eyes. "I don't know if I like you. You do stink. Deal with it." Creed marches to his usual booth, snarling at a customer who is simply trying to eat their breakfast.

"He makes my head hurt," I grumble, only to see Creed flick me the middle finger while he drinks his own cup of coffee.

Damn, I forget he has advanced hearing.

"He makes all of our heads hurt. Don't worry. It isn't only you," Caden explains, not paying attention to Creed's murderous glare. "You okay? You seem...I don't know. Different. You usually come in happy and chipper. All life is good and shit. Today, you have a cloud hanging over your head."

"Maybe the cloud is from all the damn storms you keep here, Caden." I take a sip of my coffee, and I can feel my morning demon slipping back into his slumber.

That's better.

"Why don't you say it louder for the customers in the back?" he whispers through a fake smile and clenched teeth since the bell rings from the door opening behind. "Hi, thank you for coming to Demi's Diner. Please pick a seat and I'll be with you shortly."

The new customers take the booth in front of Creed and Caden points a finger at me. "Listen, Fitz," he hisses a-matter-of-factly. "I know you think us monsters are happy all the time and you think we have no worries—"

"—I don't—"

He lifts a finger to silence me. "—But we do. I'm a storm kitsune. I need the rain, the thunder, and lightning to power myself. Some days when it rains, it means I'm sad. I'm fucking sad, Fitz. I'm allowed to be sad. I can't always control the rain when I get in these moods. So why don't you stop thinking we are invincible and start seeing us as beings with actual feelings."

"I'm sorry, Caden. Mostly my points of reference are

Creed and Rhett. I do need to be more thoughtful. You're right." I take a longer swig of coffee so I can hide the embarrassment on my face. "Why are you sad? What's going on?"

He waves my concern away. "I'm fine and it's okay, Fitz. Rhett and Creed are your first experiences with the paranormal. I can understand why you think feelings work differently with us, especially with Creed."

"He can hear us, you know." I lower my voice in hopes Creed doesn't come over and snap my neck. I just know he has been waiting to kill me.

"I know. I don't care. I have this safety net called Demi, and you have a safety net called Rhett. It's all the other people who need to be concerned. Granted, Rhett has more humanity. I think it varies from monster to monster. Kind of like humans, you know? They are varied. Some feel more deeply than others and some only have the capacity to only love one person. Demi is Creed's one person. That's it. That is who he has space for in the new form he was given. We–" he gestures a finger from me to him. "–Have the ability to care for others. "

"I'm an asshole," I reply.

Shame is all I am drinking from this cup of coffee.

He shakes his head. "No, you aren't. Creed is a dick, but we love him anyway."

"You know I can hear you," Creed shouts from his booth.

"Yeah, yeah," Caden ignores him, leaning forward. "And he is right. You stink."

"I don't smell anything." Milo comes out of nowhere, sniffing my shoulder.

I'm so tired of being sniffed.

"You smell fine to me. Like sandalwood." Milo pats me on

the back, heading to the booth filled with new customers.

"Just a hint," Caden whispers. "The last time this happened was when Mickey got marked by Rhett. No one else could smell his scent but paranormals. If we are the only ones who can smell it, you have a paranormal in your life, my friend."

"I don't know who it is. Only Rhett, Creed, and you."

"It isn't us, obviously. Be on the lookout. You don't know their plans for you."

Oh, I have an idea what her plan is. The only thing I want is to be awake so I can enjoy all the fucking things she will do to me.

CHAPTER THIRTEEN

HOLLY

"Please," she begs with tears pouring down her face. "Please, take whatever you want. Don't hurt me."

I'm standing in front of Fitz's doctor. I might have found out where she lived because I smelled her scent all over my mate. All I had to do was follow her rancid trail through town to find out where she lived.

She's sitting on a dining chair, every inch of her shaking from fear as she stares at me. I'm in my natural form. There's no need to disguise myself when my plans for her only benefit me.

The doctor isn't tied to a chair. If she wanted, she could try to run away from me. She hasn't.

She knows she has no chance in this situation. I can outrun her. I'm stronger. I can fly. I can swim faster.

I. Am. More. Superior. Than. She. Could. Ever. Be.

There is nothing she can do to get away from me. That's just how I like my victims.

Stressed and subdued.

"I'll give you whatever you want," she sniffles. "I have money. You can have the money."

"I don't want your money." I slide my finger along the kitchen counter as I walk around the island to stand in front of her. I lean down, trapping her in her own chair by gripping the armrests. "There is nothing you could offer me."

She squeezes her eyes closed, a cloudy black line drifting down her cheek caused by mascara.

"I-I-I have never seen you before," she stammers. "I don't know what I did to you."

"You saw my mate naked. You touched his cock," I snarl, inching closer to her face. "I don't like other women touching what doesn't belong to them. Would you?"

"It-it-um-it wasn't like that. I didn't fantasize about him. It was medical only."

I tilt my head to the right, then the left, debating if I believe her.

I don't.

What I know about humans, considering I have been one before, is that they know how to lie to protect themselves.

"Would you bet your life?"

"Yes!" She scoots to the edge of her chair. "I will put my life on that statement. I did not view your husband—"

"—Mate." I correct her. "That's so much more meaningful than a husband." I'm not sure how I know that. My beasts are roaring in my mind how important Fitz is to me. He is more than what these humans call spouses.

"I didn't view your mate sexually. I was only making sure he was okay. That is my job as his doctor."

I stare into her eyes, wanting to know the truth. I'll happily let her live if she is honest. Encroaching her space, I maintain eye contact until her eyes glaze over. The scientists who experimented on me told me I could put people in a trance due to my harpy DNA and extract the truth.

This is the perfect time to try to see if that's true.

"Lift your right hand and press your index finger to your nose," I order in a calm tone.

She does exactly what I say.

Perfect.

"Did you touch my mate with more than medical intentions?"

"Yes," she answers in a monotone voice.

"What did you do?" I sneer, anger curling my fingers around the armrests until the wood of the chair cracks.

"I loved how thick he was. I held him in my hands longer than necessary. I loved the weight of it. I couldn't stop thinking about how big he would become. Fitz is handsome. If he wasn't my patient, I would have asked him out."

I pull away, breaking the connection, and terror rounds her eyes. They fill with tears, and she shakes her head so fast, dislodging those tears.

"I didn't mean that. That wasn't true. I didn't mean that. I didn't. Please—"

"—You meant it," I growl, flapping my wings to pull me into the air.

My feet lift from the ground and I'm able to snag her by the shirt with my talons. I drag her through her house to get to the back door. She screams at the top of her lungs, kicking her feet and grabbing my wrists to free her.

"Please. Please, I won't ever see him again. I won't talk to him again. Let me go," she cries.

I don't give a fuck about her tears. If I could, I'd drink the salty liquid to fuel the hate I have for her.

Shattering the glass to the back door, the whore of a doctor screams at the top of her lungs. I lift her into the air, higher and higher, getting her away from the other humans who can hear her screeches.

The sky is grey and cold, the wicked air becomes thinner the higher we climb. She struggles to breathe as I bathe her in the clouds. When I'm over her house, I lift her until we are nose to nose.

"You used your power to abuse a man I love. That's what you did, Doctor," I sneer in disgust. "The only woman who can use her power to abuse him is me."

Her eyes widen when she knows death is near. She punches me in the shoulder and with every hit, they become weaker.

"The difference is, I didn't take advantage of him as a trusted professional. I am his mate. I can do whatever I want to him, and he will love every minute of it." I lean forward, whispering in her ear, "As for his cock," I moan, licking her cheek. "It gets so thick." I keep her up with one hand while reaching between her legs with the other. "I bet you wish you could have seen it. It is impressive. He reaches spots inside me no man has ever been able to touch before. He fucks like he hates me though." I apply pressure to her clit with the palm of my hand over these flimsy scrubs she's wearing. "But guess what?"

Desire swirls in the air between us. Even on the brink of death, she wants my mate and that is why I cannot allow her to live.

I inhale her desire from her lips before giving her a long tongueless kiss. I break away, swallowing the spiteful arousal permeating from her.

"You'll never get to experience his stretch like I do."

And then I release her, happily watching her fall away from me. Her arms reach for me pathetically, horror painting her face.

I follow closely enough that if I got a little closer, she'd be able to reach for me and live. Before I get too low, I arch my wings, slowing my pace.

She gets further.

And further.

Her screams become an echo in the distance until finally coming to an end as her body smashes against her roof.

Even from here, I can scent her death.

Karma is bliss, but the aroma of her whore blood is better.

CHAPTER FOURTEEN

FITZ

I'm at Rhett's house, sitting on the bench near the lake as he swims in his crocodile form. I take a swig of beer, fighting the urge to fall asleep because I'm so exhausted.

Rhett is pulling Mickey through the water, his tail wrapped around her so she can get some relief. She still hasn't given birth. The poor woman is miserable. Rhett is dragging her around to give her body a rest. Her ankles are so swollen. Not that I would tell her that.

I care about my life, and I have no doubt Mickey would want to kill me but she wouldn't be able to, so Rhett would do it.

"You still smell bad." Creed takes the spot next to me, cracking open a beer. He has Storm, his feral fucking child, attached to a leash, letting him fly over the lake. The kid dives head-first into the water, zooms out, and throws fire-balls in the sky. "And why is your tongue black?"

Creed continues drinking his beer, all while his own har-ness strapped to his chest is being tugged on.

"And you're still a pain in my ass," I reply, gulping another mouthful of beer. I shouldn't be here. I have too much on my mind. "Why my tongue is black, is none of your business."

"It's what Demi told me earlier today. It's why I'm here, unfortunately. She deserves some peace since she is pregnant again. Storm can be a handful sometimes. And why isn't it my business? You're walking around with a black tongue."

"I don't know why it's black, okay? I woke up with it like this. There are many questionable changes happening to me, and I have no answers."

"That sucks. Maybe you're dying. Hey, if you are, I'll put you out of your misery quickly. I won't let you suffer. I'm nice like that."

I roll my eyes. "Wow, thanks for having my back. You're so thoughtful."

"I know. I wish others could see that. I am a thoughtful person."

Thoughtful as a fucking rock smashing a windshield.

I look out onto the lake and see Storm light a tree on fire.

Creed crushes his beer can, places it on the ground, and stands. His wings burst from his back, and he launches himself into the sky. "Don't you dare keep blowing that fire, young man! Do you know what you will do to this ecosystem if you burn it down?" he yells, sounding completely different than I expected him to.

I'm not sure what I thought he would do, but I didn't think he would actually sound like a parent. He's so... Creed.

Luckily, the tree Storm lit on fire was growing out of the water. Creed uses his wings to wave the water onto the burning branches.

"No fireballs. We talked about this," he warns. "And if I see another, I'm telling your mom to zip-tie your wings together so you can't fly."

Never in my wildest dreams did I think I would be here listening to conversations that should never exist.

Yet here I am.

I down the rest of my beer, plopping the can next to Creed's on the ground. I'll take them to the recycling bin when I head home. I bury my face in my hands, blowing out a stressful breath.

A loud growl has me tilting my head up to see Creed and Storm barreling toward the water like a cannonball. The splash is huge. Water sprays all over me, soaking my clothes, my hair, and my face.

And I can't help but laugh.

My phone rings, blaring my sister's ringtone from my pocket. I scramble to answer knowing this phone call is going to give me an update on Eli. Her name brightens the screen and with shaking fingers, I swipe to answer it.

"Will he be okay?" I ask without wasting any time.

Creed, Rhett, and Mickey are staring at me with concern. Storm is too little to understand so he continues being a menace to society.

"Sorry it took so long to call back. It's been chaos. Elijah just got out of surgery."

"Surgery?" I shout and stand at the same time. "What do you mean, surgery?"

"He's okay, Fitz. He needed his appendix removed. He is okay. He is alive. He is still asleep. If he is up for it, I'll have him call you later. We should be able to get there soon. He'll need to rest the moment he walks into your house though."

"Of course. I just want him safe and okay. He will heal? No complications during surgery?"

"No, no, nothing like that. Everything went as expected, Fitz."

I pinch my eyes together to try and stop the onslaught of emotions. I wouldn't know what to do with myself if Eli had died. There would be a part of me that would never be able to heal.

"That's a relief. I've been so fucking worried." I fall onto the bench, plopping down hard on the old wood. "That's good." Rhett shifts into his human form, wrapping his arms around Mickey. He lifts up a thumb to signal if everything is okay.

I return the thumbs up and a big grin washes over his face.

"No word from Dad yet?" It's the one issue that's been eating away at me. I know he is waiting for the perfect moment to strike.

"Nothing yet. Maybe he didn't mean the threat. He doesn't usually think this far ahead. He attacks before he thinks. You know that."

I shake my head in disagreement, staring out onto the lake where my friends are. "This was different. You're going to have to believe me."

"I'll always believe you," she yawns. "Sorry, I'm so exhausted."

"It's okay. You need to rest. Get some sleep while he is."

"I'm going to. I'm not going to leave his side though. This entire experience made me age twenty years. I swear, Fitz. I don't know if I've ever been so afraid as I was when they took him into surgery."

"I wish I could have been there. Get some rest, okay? I'll see you two soon."

"I love you."

"I love you too, Sis."

Ending the call, I lean back onto the bench and stare up at the sky, releasing a giant breath until there isn't any air left in my lungs.

"Everything okay?" Rhett calls out from the middle of the lake, rubbing Mickey's stomach.

Life is wild.

All the emotions and ups and downs this invisible force brings are exhausted. Some days, I'm not sure how to ride this rollercoaster anymore. Some days, surrender seems so much sweeter than dying to survive. However, if I kept that mindset, I'd miss out on the good parts of life.

Like watching Storm light Creed's face on fire. It doesn't hurt Creed but it sure does make me feel so much better.

"I'm going to go. Let me know if those babies make an appearance," I shout to Rhett.

Rhett kisses Mickey on the cheek, whispering something in her ear that makes her smile and nod.

What I'd give to have a love like that.

Mickey continues to float on her back while Rhett swims to shore to see me off. He's naked when he steps onto shore. I can't help it. I stare at his cock because it's a fucking jelly-fish and never in my entire life have I seen anything like that before.

He snaps his fingers. "My eyes are up here, Fitz."

"Yeah, but your jellyfish cock glows neon blue and it's down there." I point. "You expect me not to look? How can I not look? It's like telling somebody not to turn around when they see someone they don't like. It only makes me want to look more."

Rhett's laughter bellows, snagging a folded-up towel lying peacefully on the grass. "I guess that's understandable. Want to touch it?"

I rear back, wide-eyed, and excited but not sexually. Who else gets to touch a jellyfish peen? "For science?" I ask, maintaining the humor.

"Anything for Science."

He stares at me.

I stare at him.

A quick second of me thinking about if I want to touch it has my hand twitching. We both toss our heads back with laughter.

"I'm not touching that damn thing. You're out of your mind. Like I want to get shocked?"

"I'd kill you if you did!" Mickey shouts from the lake.

"Storm, don't make me muzzle you. No biting!" Creed continues to battle with his son.

Rhett wraps his towel around his waist, tucking the corner in so it doesn't fall off. "You need to tell me what else is going on with you, Fitz. I know when you're hiding something."

I rip off my baseball cap, thinking about what to say to him, and run my fingers through my hair, debating on the truth.

"Well, my nephew just got out of surgery—"

"—Not that." He lifts his hand to stop me from talking. "I heard that conversation between you two when I was in the lake. I'm glad he is okay, but there is something else you aren't being honest about. What is it?"

I sigh, raising my shirt to show him what I've been dealing with.

He's silenced.

I lower my shirt, clearing my throat. The silence expands until it becomes heavy and awkward.

"That's why you fucking stink," he says as it dawns on him. "You have a stalker."

I correct him. "No, no," I shake my finger. "I have a monster who is nervous to reveal herself. There's a difference."

"Is there?" He smirks. "Because I still stalk Mickey, and Creed stalks Demi every day. I'm surprised he is here now that I think about it." His brows pull together then turns his head to see Creed playing with Storm.

To me it looks more like fighting, but what do I know?

"Be careful, okay? We are dangerous, Fitz."

"You're no more dangerous than a regular human being, Rhett."

"That's not true and you know that. Don't fool yourself." He closes the distance between us with his giant crocodile feet. "If I wanted to, I could rip your head off from your body before you could speak your next word. I have nothing but primal urges and instincts. If anyone looks at Mickey, if a man's eyes linger too long, I have blood on my hands. I'm not like Creed. He doesn't care who he kills. I don't either but it doesn't mean I don't wish things were different. It doesn't mean I don't wish to feel more human. Granted, I feel more than Creed does, but you need to be careful. I hope whoever this monster is, they are your fated mate and they aren't here to hurt you, but it makes sense. The smell and the markings, they have claimed you. You don't know who it is?"

"No clue," I say. "And I don't know if there is a monster.

Maybe I'm losing my mind."

"You aren't. We are really great at evading if we don't want to get caught. It's only a matter of time. When is all this happening? Do you know?"

"I wake up like this," I answer, lifting my shirt again to show how far the black mark travels. "It's like lightning."

"It's probably happening while you sleep. I'm not sure what kind of a monster can do that. What are your dreams like?"

My cheeks redden immediately with embarrassment.

Rhett grins, flashing his fangs. "I see, well, that answers that. Try to find something in that dream that helps bring you back to reality. Wake up to see the truth, Fitz. You'll have your answers. If you find out that your mind is gone, that's okay, I love you enough to take care of you. You look exhausted so why don't you go get some sleep." He winks. "Keep me updated."

I salute him with a finger. "Will do."

"And stay away from the shop. I've closed it. You have other things to focus on. And to be honest, it's still airing out. I'm not sure what your monster did but it fucking reeks."

"Rhett! Come swim!" Mickey shouts.

I give Rhett a slap on the arm. "I'll see you later. Have a good time. I'm going to go home and crash. I can barely keep my eyes open." I sway on my feet, exhaustion hitting me like a brick wall. "I really need to go."

Rhett steps in front of me to stop me. "You look like you have worked three days straight. Why don't you take the spare room? I don't feel comfortable with you driving."

"I'm fine. It isn't a far drive. Remember, I'm only across the lake. I'll get the rest of my stuff later if you don't mind."

"We will leave it in your room for when you're ready. No rush. This will always be your home, Fitz."

I step in and give him a hug, slapping him on the back. "Thanks, man. I appreciate it."

He shoves me away, covering his mouth and nose.

"Oh, come on. It doesn't smell that bad. You're being dramatic." I begin to walk away, my vision blurring with the need to sleep.

"It is for us paranormals! Anyone else's scent is atrocious!" my best friend yells.

I happen to like that I smell like someone. I am obsessed with the fact that there is someone out there who wants me so badly that they mark me to warn everyone else away. I belong to someone.

I've never belonged to anyone. I've always been isolated and alone in a sense. I've always had to depend on myself. That's how I was raised. By watching what my parents said and how they acted, I learned the only person I could trust in the world was me. No one else was going to support me. No one else would save me. And no one else would love me.

What is it like being loved?

Not friend love or parental love, whatever that's like, but the all-consuming, rageful, will do anything for you, kind of love. The love that knows no bounds. The love that will kill everyone if it means my heart got to beat one more time. The type of love people heal from.

I want that.

I need to heal because I'm tired. I ache. I'm sore. My heart beats, sure, but my blood is tired of feeding a lonely soul. I'm battered. I'm damaged. All my pain is my own doing, I realize that. I've always been the life vest. This time it's me who is drowning.

It's me who needs to be saved.

By the time I'm climbing into the truck, I question how I got here for a second. I'm so tired. Maybe I should take the spare room in Rhett's house. Even as the thought crosses my mind, I press the button to start the engine. A pull is tugging me home. It's only a five-minute drive.

I can do it.

"Wake up. Fitz." I scrub my eyes, yawning as the energy continues to be drained from me. "What the fuck is going on?" I've never experienced this kind of lethargy.

Putting the truck in drive, I sit up close to the steering wheel to look out the windshield. I need to be able to see where I'm going. My vision blurs. My eyes droop. The truck swerves off the road.

I yank the steering wheel the other way. The tires burn against the pavement, skidding across the black road as I try to get control. Not even the adrenaline is enough to awaken me.

I miss a tree by an inch, the branches and leaves scrape against the passenger side of the truck. Intense scratching, like nails on a chalkboard, has my ears ringing. The road, the trees, the sky, everything begins to swirl together as the need to sleep inches closer to being victor.

"Stay the fuck awake." I slap myself in the face, the fresh sting on my cheek gives me a bolt of energy. Tingles spread down my neck, jumpstarting my body enough to get a clear head.

I can see the road.

And I am not fucking on it. I'm driving on the side of the road, kicking up grass and mud as my tires spin to gain traction.

I slap myself again. "Son of a bitch," I yell, hitting the same cheek I did before. The fatigue is a villain trying to drag me down, but the pain is what is keeping me awake.

Getting enough clarity, I jerk the wheel to the left, the large truck bouncing from the uneven ground to get onto the road.

"Stay awake. Stay awake," I chant, pinching the under-skin of my arm. "Fuck, that hurt. I swear, if I see my mate, I'm going to spank her for doing this to me."

The real question is, do I have a mate? Wouldn't she be watching me right now? Following me? Looking in the rear-view mirror, there isn't another car behind me or in front of me.

I'm alone.

Where is she?

I'm worried that I've made all this up. What if I was the one who did this to my body? I need to set up a camera in my bedroom, then I'll have all the proof I need for my theory.

Turning right onto the road that leads to my house, I stare at the sign that wasn't there before.

Hollyhocks Rd.

Only one person could have done that.

Holly.

"Holy shit, you fucking idiot," I whisper in realization.

It's Holly. The monster I've been seeing when she is around is her. It has to be.

"This is fucking wild." I practically bounce in my seat to get home while still fighting how tired I am.

It's as if gravity is pushing me down to the ground and I'm fighting every fucking second of this force.

My house and Holly's come to view. Her old yellow Volkswagen van sits in her driveway, proving she is home. Maybe she isn't if she has wings... I still have a feather on my nightstand.

It isn't from my pillow. It's from her.

I've never been more sure about anything.

Pulling into my driveway, I'm not sure if I turn off the truck or not when I open the door. I don't know if I shut the door either. I'm too tired. I'm swaying back and forth, stumbling towards my front door.

Losing my footing, I trip over myself, slamming my back against the faded red brick wall next to the door.

Deep breaths in and out.

I'm so tired. I scramble for my house key. The metal clinks together, the loud clinking has me covering my ears and the keys fall to the ground. Even the scratch against the concrete walkway against my keychain has me wanting to faint.

I can barely stand.

Sliding down the wall, the material of my Snapdragons Garage shirt tugs on the brick, no doubt ruining it.

I'm too tired to care. I'll take a quick nap on my porch. Right here. Just a few minutes.

That's...all...I'll...need.

***

I'm standing in the middle of an empty store. There are mirrors all along the walls and the floors are slick polished concrete. There are long silver poles evenly spaced between one another. Surrounding the poles are thick mats. The lighting is dim and sultry. Circular red couches strategically surround every pole.

A soft slow beat begins to thump the speakers anchored to the wall.

"Sit down, Doe Eyes. Let me put on a show for you." Holly's voice cuts through the music, forcing me to move my legs.

I do as I'm told because I want to be her good boy.

The floor is cold against the pads of my feet as I walk over to the couch, plopping down on the red velvet cushions. The material is soft and warm against the palm of my hand.

A finger under my chin forces my head up. I'm staring into glowing amber irises while falling in love with her horns. Holly's blue hair cascades down her shoulders, the left side of her head is freshly shaved and I fucking love it. I bite my lower lip, leaning forward to rob her of a kiss.

Her tail slithers over her shoulder and it shoves into my chest to push me back.

"Behave, Doe Eyes."

The tail wraps around my throat, giving me a slight squeeze.

"Sit down. Keep your hands to yourself. And watch the show I put on for you. Can you do that for me?" she asks, taking a step onto the mat platform.

I nod in a daze.

She grins. "That's my good boy."

She's wearing a sheer black top with emerald gems decorating the middle to cover her nipples. Her cleavage is pushed up, the dim lights shining on the tops of the swells. My mouth fucking waters. I want more.

The panties match, the emeralds glittering with wealth, and hiding the tight pussy I want to sink into it.

I rub a hand over my mouth while taking a deep breath to maintain control. I have to be good, or she won't give me what I want. I'm her good boy and I have to behave as such.

"If I'm going to dance, I need something pretty to look at." Holly snaps her fingers and my clothes disappear.

I'm sitting naked on the couch now. My reflection in the mirrors shows the state I'm in. My legs are slightly spread, giving me a view of my erect cock standing straight. I reach for my shaft for a quick touch when her wings stretch out in front of her and pin my arms on the couch.

"Don't you dare touch yourself," she growls. "I'll touch you when I'm ready. I'll make you come when I fucking want you to come." Her shifted tentacled tongue swipes across my cheek, and I moan, wishing she would suck my cock. "And when I do, you'll pump me full of every drop. Won't you?" she croons, kissing the shell of my ear. "Are you going to breed me, Doe Eyes?" She hums, straddling my lap, and my cock jerks with a bead of precome dripping off the tip. "I need you to. I want you bound to me in every single way."

I'm gasping for breath, my chest rising and falling in anticipated beats. "I want nothing more. Fuck me, Wildflower." I reach for her thighs to pull her down on me when her wings slam me down.

She's put me in my place.

And I fucking love it.

"I can't breed that pretty little cunt if you won't let me."

A villainous laughter ignites her. "You're so cute if you think you have any say in what I want to do and take from you." Her lips find mine and they form together. The softness of her lips against mine feels like home.

I never want to be anywhere except with Holly, our bodies touching, and our lips connected. I push against her wings to be freed. My arms twitch to wrap around her and pull her close. She doubles down, pressing me harder onto the couch.

"Behave," she warns in a flirtatious quip.

She's a vision, and I can't focus on anything other than her body so close to mine. "You make it so difficult to be good." I inhale a deep breath, leaning forward for another kiss.

Right when our lips brush together, she presses her hand against my chest and shoves me back.

"Being good is supposed to be difficult, Doe Eyes." She stands, wrapping her hand around the silver pole.

Her gaze lands on my straining cock. Precome drips freely at this point, creating a slick spot against my stomach. Holly's nostrils flare, her tongue flicking out as if she wants to suck my cock. The suckers seem alive with how they move.

My fingers dig into the couch to find some damn self-control. A quake shivers my body as I watch her wrap her leg around the pole.

I like this dream.

I like this dream a lot.

"Fuck," I curse in a harsh gasp when she flips upside down, spinning slow and steady to the beat of the music.

She hangs upside down, her ankles crossed over one another, and her tail disappears behind her back. The straps of her bra become loose, and with a sly grin, she flips again, her legs squeezing the pole how I wish she'd squeeze my face with her thighs while I plunge my tongue into her cunt.

Her tail wraps around the pole, her ankles still crossed, but we are face to face now. She slips the loose straps down her arms, dangling the bra in my face before tossing it into my face.

I pick it up, press it against my nose, and inhale her sweet scent. A spurt of come jets from my cock. I try to breathe through it and control the rest of my orgasm. "I want to be good. I want to be, Wildflower, but you've got me on edge. You smell so fucking good." I moan, burying my nose into her bra again.

"So stop smelling me so you can be a good boy again because right now, I'm not convinced."

I toss the bra over my head to show her how compliant I am. The music picks up pace and she begins to move, her hands roaming up her body. She cups her breasts, playing with the rods piercing her nipples. The chains that are usually attached to them aren't there, and I miss them. I love tugging on them to watch her mouth part in pleasure.

I'm obsessed with this monster. I never want to wake up.

"Wake up, Fitz. It's just a dream," I hear Rhett's voice whispering in the far distance of my mind.

I ignore it. There's no way in hell I'm letting Rhett ruin Holly pole dancing for me.

"Fuck, Wildflower. You look good up there. I want to kiss every inch of your skin and make you come on my tongue."

She flicks her tongue out, splitting it into multiple tentacles. They stretch from her mouth, the tips tickling my shins. Holly drops to her knees on the mat, her tits bouncing from the motion. Her dark purple nipples have me forgetting I'm not allowed to touch myself. I reach for my cock for a quick stroke but Holly is there, her wings pinning me to the couch once more.

"I said not to touch yourself."

"I can't help it," I groan. "You make me ache, Wildflower. Please," I beg, her tongue tentacles swimming up my thigh.

She licks a rope of come from my thigh. Her eyes roll to the back of her head and come drips from the suckers as she rolls my seed over her taste buds.

"I love how you taste," she says, scooping a lone drop from my inner thigh into her mouth.

"What do—" I swallow, fighting for my fucking life to continue to be a good boy. "—What do I taste like?"

Each tentacle shifts as her tongue wraps around my cock one by one. The suction cup of the suckers has me arching my back. I slap my hand onto the couch and shout, "Fuck, Holly! Fuck!" I almost sob from the extreme grip her tongue alone gives. "Ah, God. Fuck. Holly." I try to push away from her because it's too much.

My attempt doesn't work.

When I try to pull away, her tentacles stay in place. My cock tugs and the tight hold she has on me causes my orgasm to tense my cock.

"You have to stop. You have to—I'm too—I'm too close—"

"Wake up, Fitz." Rhett's voice is back, ruining my damn life.

I ignore him again.

She chokes me down the back of her throat, her tentacles still wrapped tight around me. When she sucks me into her mouth, her tentacles stroke at the same time. I'm seeing stars. I'm not sure how much longer I can hold on.

Holly hums around me, the vibrations making me cry out

again. "Holly!" My hands grip her by the back of her head, grasping the roots of her hair.

No one has ever looked so good on their knees.

"Is my thick cock too much for you? Look how wide your lips are spread. I love knowing how close I am to splitting you open." The intense suction has left circular marks behind that are similar to the ones on my torso.

"Wake up, Fitz. You need to wake up. Remember the conversation with Rhett." The voice is my own this time and it causes my surroundings to sway.

Holly unwraps her tongue from my cock. "Focus on me, Doe Eyes." She crawls into my lap and the silk touch of her body against mine solidifies how she is meant for me. "You need me."

"I always need you, Wildflower. Every day that passes when I don't get to dream of you, the more tired I become. Can't I just stay here forever?"

She cups my face with her hands as she hovers above my cock. Reaching between us, I fist my cock, aiming it at her entrance as she lowers herself down on me.

"Wake. Up!" The plea is louder, creeping closer to my consciousness.

We both gasp when her warm wet channel grips me as tight as her tongue did. Those damn tentacles stroke from the inside, the suckers giving me light kisses while she begins to rock back and forth.

I don't stand a chance.

"Wake up. It's a dream. She's in your bed right now. Wake the fuck up, you idiot!" I yell at myself.

That sounds familiar. I wanted to know who was doing this to me. Is she the reason I'm marked?

There's only one way to find out.

I force myself to wake up.

CHAPTER FIFTEEN

HOLLY

Out of nowhere, the dream is pulled away from me, and my horns are gripped to keep me still.

I forget how to breathe when I stare into Fitz's angry brown eyes. He's so full of rage that the gold flecks in his eyes shimmer.

"Fitz," I begin to explain, somehow, someway, but the betrayal shining in his eyes silences me.

All while I'm stretched to the brink from his cock while I sit on his lap. He yanks me down by my horns until his breath heats my lips.

Without saying a word, he flips me over by controlling me with my horns. He shoves me face-first into the bed, his cock still buried to the hilt. His touch on my horns makes me whimper. He feels so good.

"Did you really think you could fuck me in my dreams and I'd never wake up?" He slams into me, using the horns as leverage.

I shout into the mattress as he hammers into me,

stretching me wide just like that doctor wished she could have felt.

He still controls me with my horns, yanking me by them to pull me to his chest. "You thought wrong, Wildflower." He pushes me onto the bed again, shoving my face into the pillow to drive into me. "How dare you tell me to be a good boy when you are such a bad fucking girl."

Our skin slaps together with every thrust.

"You wouldn't have had to sneak into my dreams if you knew just how much I wanted a mate of my own. All this time, you could have knocked on—" he fucks into me harder, trying to get as deep as possible. "—My. Fucking. Door." He punctuates each word with his cock barreling into my womb. "And I would have opened my arms for you." He releases my horns and a slight ache throbs along my skull from his rough manhandling.

His touch sends a kaleidoscope of colors shooting across my eyes as he drags his calloused fingers down my wings.

"You're so beautiful," he says with awe, stroking the feathers in tandem with his thrusts. "You could easily destroy me." He grips the base of the wings that protrude from my back, rolling his hips to a slow sensual pace. "What's fucked up is that I'd let you." Fitz kisses my right shoulder, then my left before dragging his tongue to my throat.

He sucks the skin hard, pulling it into his mouth to make his own mark.

My pussy ripples with lust. He grunts as the suckers massage his cock.

He lets the skin go with a soft pop, kissing the heated spot he left, he whispers into my ear, "I'll take this over dreams any day, Wildflower." He flattens his chest against my back, his wide warm body swallowing mine in a cocoon.

His hands caress my arms until his fingers lace with mine.

"I've wished for you for far too long to be hidden in your fears. There's no need to be afraid of not having my love when you have had it since before you saw me for the first time." He pulls out of me, leaving me empty and throbbing for his girth.

I whimper from the loneliness, wanting him to slide inside me, to give me that stretch that I crave so much.

I squeeze my eyes closed, fighting the pleasure, fighting the emotion welling in my eyes from his words.

Gripping me by my horns, he manhandles me onto my back, forces my knees apart, and grabs his cock. Fitz teases and taunts me with his dick by gliding it between my soaked lips. The flared crown rubs over my clit, a groan scorching my throat from the teasing.

"You want my cock? How about it's your turn to be good? Do you know how to be a good girl for me?"

"I can be as good as my nature allows me to be," I reply in stammering breaths.

He curls over me, wraps his hand around my throat, and licks from the base of my horn to the tip.

I shiver.

"You're going to have to fight your nature, then. Because only a good girl will get my cock. Will you be good?"

Licking my lips, I give a slow nod even if every beast is clawing at my chest to take control of this situation. Fitz deserves my submission. He deserves more than me, but I'm too selfish to ever let that happen.

"Good," he croons, gripping my chin. "Wrap those tentacles around my cock just how I like. You're going to be bred and filled by the end of the day. If you're not, we're going to stay secluded in this bedroom until you are." He drags a finger down my chest, and stomach, then slips two fingers inside me.

My mouth parts from the intrusion. The pleasure doesn't distract me from what he ordered me to do. My tentacles stretch and wrap around his cock. He shivers. Those broad shoulders hunch when he looks between us to see how we are connected.

The tentacles have a mind of their own. They move on their own accord, squeezing and stroking him. The suckers leave marks behind, the soft skin of his cock claimed in another way.

"You've left all these marks on me. Are you worried people won't think I'm taken, Wildflower?"

"It's not you I'm worried about. It's everyone else. I'm not done claiming you either. Your mark can't be seen yet," I say with a bitter hiss.

He sits up, tracing the black outline that starts at his cock then up his left hip, over his ribcage, and then it stops below his pec. "This?" he questions, acting clueless. "I don't know what you mean. I got this tattoo ages ago." That damn smirk shows his dimples, and I fall more in love.

I growl, pouncing on him like a wild animal. His fingers slip out of me but my tentacles keep a tight grip on his shaft. "It is not a tattoo. It is my claim. This mark proves you're mine. I own this body."

He grins again, a mischievous glint in his eyes.

"And in order for the mark to be complete, it needs to be visible." I dig my sharp talons into his shoulder, the tips breaking the skin. A small bead of blood forms, and I moan in ecstasy at the scent.

My mate doesn't even flinch.

I bend down, lapping the blood up with my tongue. The iron bursts over my taste blood, seeping into every single one as his DNA melds with mine. It's as if he is inside me, stroking every pleasure spot beneath my skin. My orgasm comes out of nowhere.

"Fitz," I cry, heat bursting across my cheeks when my ink squirts all over his cock and lap.

I've made a mess.

This man takes his hands and rubs my ink all over his skin as if it's lotion. "You came just from the taste of me?"

I sway on his lap from the buzz of my orgasm and barely manage to nod.

"That's so fucking sexy–" he growls, throwing me onto my back, and thrusting inside me.

We gasp in unison.

My tentacles stay wrapped around him with every drive of his hips. He grips my horns at the base, using them to drive forward harder with every thrust. He twists one nipple between his fingers, tugging on the piercing.

"I miss the chains, Wildflower. Where did they go?"

"Took them off," I barely manage to say. The words are hoarse.

"Next time–" He tweaks the other nipple, tugging it so hard a slight tremor of pain has me whining. "–Don't"

"Whatever you want, Mate."

"Good Girl," he praises, taking my lips into a passionate messy kiss.

Our bodies slide together, sleek with sweat and ink. I

sink my teeth into his bottom lip, snarling down his throat. He wraps both hands around my neck, squeezing carefully, and controls the kiss. Our tongues collide and the tentacles wrap around the pretty black appendage.

The sounds he makes have me dripping with arousal, ruining his sheets forever.

"Fuck, I love everything you can do," he groans through tight teeth before plunging his tongue into my mouth and licking my fangs. He breaks the kiss, lifting one leg to his shoulder which drives him in an extra inch. "I can't wait until I'm fucking you in the sky. I want you everywhere, on every surface, in every air space, in every body of fucking water, I'm going to fuck you."

"I need your come, Doe Eyes. Give it to me."

"Not yet," he sneers, flipping me onto my hands and knees. "I'm nowhere near finished with you."

He must love my horns because he grabs them again, ramming into me with every bit of strength he has. His desire is thick in the air, and I inhale it as if it were smoke from a cigarette. The succubus inside me feeds on the delicious lust swirling around me.

Humans love the smell of homemade bread. His scent is like that to me. I can't inhale it enough and when I don't smell the aroma, I miss it. He's warm and comforting which increases my need for him.

My tail slips and slides against his stomach that's wet with my ink. Fitz notices what I'm doing and snags the tail in his grip.

"What do you think you're doing with this, Wildflower?"

"I'm going to fuck your ass with it, Doe Eyes. The last time I did it, you loved it. You wanted more. Begged for more."

He quirks a brow. "Is that so?" Fitz spits on the very tip, using his hand to spread it. "Prove it."

Fitz guides my tail behind him before letting me go, allowing me to take control of what happens next. To his surprise, I overpower him to switch positions. He's on his knees, and I wrap my legs around his hips. My tail caresses the bottom of his cock, his heavy orbs, pushing across the sensitive crease before circling his tight hole.

Sinking back onto his cock, all of our sounds pour down each other's throats. Our arms wrap around each other, pulling one another closer until it is physically impossible to get any closer.

My tail circles his rim, and I hear a sharp inhale of breath before he buries his face into my neck. Hot puffs of warm air flutter along my collarbone. His blunt nails dig into my shoulders just above where my wings and back connect.

"Look at me, Good Boy. I want to see your face when I fill you."

Fitz raises his head, his eyes glazed over, and his cheeks are hot and red. Sweat beads across his forehead.

His face has a look of surrender on it. My mate loves to submit, I think. He's taken care of everyone his entire life and now it's my turn to take care of him.

I push the tip of my tail inside him, and he tenses, clenching down naturally.

"Oh, Holly. I don't know if I can," he struggles to say.

I rock against him, his very hard cock seeming to like what I'm doing very much.

"You can and you will. You're going to love it. Be a good boy and relax for me."

He does just as I say, and I slip in deeper, the triangular end of my tail pressing against his prostate.

"Holly! Fuck. Oh, fuck," he whines as if he can't take all the pleasure he is receiving. "I can't hold on much longer. I can't."

I spread my wings and engulf us in their canopy. We are in our own world, alone, just us breathing in each other's breaths.

I've never felt more at home.

His forehead rolls against mine before he pulls away from me. His eyes drop to my mouth and his thumb drags across my bottom lip. He dives in, kissing me in a way that erases every kiss I've gotten before him.

He possesses all my pain and his love overwhelms any fear.

My suckers massage his cock every time he drives in and out. I claim every upward and downward stroke, wanting to milk him of every damn drop.

"I have my own monster," he mumbles against my shoulder before kissing my collarbone. "You don't know how long I've wanted you. You're everything."

He holds me tighter, his cries becoming louder when my tail moves faster.

"Holly. Holly." He shakes his head. "Oh, that's it. Fuck, oh, God, you feel so good. Give it to me, Wildflower. Make me come. Let me fill you up. I want nothing more than to get you pregnant." His hand cups my stomach. "I want to see you round with my child. I have a feeling I'm not going to be able to get enough of you knowing you'll be carrying my son or daughter."

I roll my hips against him harder. His face pinches as he

holds his orgasm back and his fingers dig into my hips, helping me move faster. I use my wings to gain speed. A strong breeze is created, making a mess of the blankets. Everything on his dresser falls to the floor. The lamp on his nightstand crashes to the ground too, the bulb shattering. The blankets twirl into a tangled mess, but it doesn't stop us from devouring one another.

I hit his prostate one more time and he tosses his head back, his cock thickening with his orgasm as he pours himself into me. With a growl, he picks me up and slams me on the bed, lifting my leg onto his shoulder to drive his come into me.

The suckers lining my channel taste his salty-sweet release. My tentacles wrap around his base, creating a thick knot, and when he thrusts into me as hard as he can, the makeshift knot connects us.

My orgasm bursts inside me next. "Fitz! Oh, more. More. More. Your cock feels so good. Oh, God," A loud cry sounds from me.

I arch my back as wave after wave of pleasure electrifies my body. I ink, squirting all over his cock again.

"Fuck!" he shouts, driving him and the knot inside me as he comes again. "Those suckers are a weapon, Wildflower. You could make me come with those alone."

"I'll have to try that another day." I suck his bottom lip into my mouth before it turns into a slow, lazy, heated kiss.

He rocks slowly, pushing his seed further inside me. Our tongues twist together. He licks and teases me before giving me his lips again.

"I love you wild," he murmurs against my lips. "As in, it can never be contained."

I drag my knuckles down his cheek. "I love you too, Doe Eyes. I've loved you since the moment I scented you."

He smiles, showing those damn dimples that make me weak in my knees. His fingers roam through my hair, petting me gently. His eyes dart from my horns, face, and wings, then back to my eyes.

"How long will we be locked together like this?"

My tongue flicks out to lick the sweat from his neck, but I want more. The appendage shifts, splitting into multiple tentacles again, and they wrap around his neck.

I can taste his lust through his sweat. It's warm like cinnamon. His pulse thumps in chaos, but not in panic or fear.

Desire.

And with direct contact, the scent infiltrates my taste buds, sating the craving that's always gnawing at my stomach for him.

"Holly," he groans, flexing his cock inside me one more time.

My mouth waters when his orgasm can be tasted from two of my holes. Spit drips from my bottom lip. I unwrap the tentacles from his neck and shift them into my regular tongue.

"I couldn't help myself." I wipe the corner of my mouth. "I love how your skin tastes. How you taste."

"You can taste me anytime, Holly." He cages my head in with his arms. "Do I have those hickeys all over my neck?" He touches his pulse where I sucked the hardest.

"Yes," I purr in delight. "You look pretty with my necklace around your throat."

He blushes, biting his bottom lip. His shaggy hair falls in his face, and I brush it out of the way so I can see his eyes.

"Did you know you have four hundred and eleven freckles on your face?" I twirl a finger in one strand, loving that the beautiful brown locks are slightly damp from how hard we fucked.

He tilts his head, chuckling, running his finger across my jaw. "And how do you know that?"

"I counted them while you were sleeping," I say obviously.

I mean, how else?

"I should be concerned about that but I oddly find it comforting."

"Good because you have almost a thousand across your shoulders. I lost count because you turned over." I roll my eyes, huffing.

"Aw, I'm sorry, Wildflower. One day, I'll let you count every freckle on my body if you want."

I grin so wide, that I know I'm showing all my teeth, including my fangs. "I can't wait. When? Now?"

"Another day, I have too many questions, Holly. You need to answer them."

"What do you want to know?" I question, doing my best to be serious but his chest is so defined and so wide, that I can't help but rub my hands all over him.

He lifts my chin, forcing me to look at him. "Focus, beautiful."

"It's hard to focus when I have you on top of me and inside me, handsome."

He growls. "You don't play fair."

"I never have, but what is it that you'd like to know?"

"What creatures are you and what abilities do you have? I know you can do something with dreams." He kisses my forehead.

I nod. "I'm part succubus. I can feed off desire and manipulate dreams. Then, I'm harpy which is the reason why I can fly. I also can see the future sometimes. Not all the time. It happens randomly. I'm part chameleon. My skin can adapt to the colors of my environment which is why you wouldn't see me when I've been standing by the wall every single night. Then, there's the siren DNA. I don't use that too much unless I want to use the siren's voice. Lastly, I'm part squid. I'm sure you can fill in the blanks with what I can do." I tighten the tentacles around him.

"You're part siren?" he asks in worry, lifting up one of my arms to see one of my fins. "You need water, Holly. When was the last time you went swimming in the lake?"

I shrug a shoulder. "Never. I've been too busy kill—I've been too busy," I correct myself, hoping he doesn't notice.

He lifts up, quirking a brow at me. "No, go ahead. Finish your sentence. Who have you killed?" Fitz's eyes widen when he realizes. "You caused the accident of that man and the girl who walked into traffic, didn't you?"

"I didn't like how she had her hands all over you. She deserved it." I lean onto my elbows and kiss his chin. "I'd do it again too. Just like I killed that doctor."

"You killed my doctor?" He doesn't sound scared.

Oh, no. My mate is turned on. His desire swarms between us, and I inhale it as if I haven't been feeding from him for hours.

"Do you like that? Do you like that I killed for you? Oh, sweet mate, I have so many others to kill for you too. Anyone who has ever caused you pain will greet death. Do you want to know what I did?"

His cock tenses inside me and is followed by a groan. That delicious flavor of his come tingles my mouth since I can taste him between my legs. "What?" he rasps.

"I flew her high in the sky, used my siren voice on her to see if she violated you, and she did. She said she loved how thick you were and was curious about how big you'd get. I couldn't allow her to live another day knowing she had touched you. So I dropped her. I listened to her scream until her blood could be smelled beyond the clouds."

"Fuck, I shouldn't find that so fucking attractive, but I do. I really do. I must be one sick fuck to come from your admission."

I lick his lips. "That's okay. I love it when you're disturbed. It makes my existence so much better." I nibble his lips with my fangs.

"Wait, who else do you need to kill?"

"Your father. He is number one on my list. Then, your exes who teased you about your cock. Off the top of my head, four more people."

"You made me write their names down. I didn't understand why I did that. You can't kill them, Holly. They are all grown with husbands and children of their own."

"So?"

He chuckles, grabs my chin, and kisses me again.

I love his kisses. I'll never reject them.

"So, I haven't thought about them in ages, but you can't do that to those families."

I snarl in disagreement.

"They don't need to die when they haven't bothered me in fifteen years. Don't kill them. Okay? Promise me."

I grumble, toying with my hair.

"Holly," he singsongs playfully. "Promise me."

I blow out an annoyed breath. "Fine. I promise I won't kill them. Your dad is still on my hitlist though."

"You can do whatever you want to him. I don't care."

"Really? You mean it?" I grip the back of his head and kiss him senselessly. "Thanks, Doe Eyes."

"Anything to sate you." He deepens the kiss, slow and easy as if we have all day to lie in bed. His tongue flicks out, teasing mine.

When he breaks the kiss, I'm breathless, and the suckers inside me flutter against his cock.

"Your existence has brought me happiness," he whispers against my lips.

We hold onto one another for a while until the tentacled knot locking us together begins to unravel. Fitz is thoughtful as he pulls out of me, taking his time to ease out. He looks down, watching as the black ink veins up his body, wrap around his shoulder, and then swirl down his left arm.

It finally stops at his ring finger.

"Wild," he says, turning his arm over to see that the black ink has used his veins as their map.

"You're all mine now."

"Wildflower, I've been yours. You just had to trust me enough to show you."

I tug his arm, lying him down next to me, and I can't look at him. I'm ashamed. I draw small circles on his chest with my finger. "I didn't know how to reveal myself to you when I barely knew how to look at myself. I was turned into this. I was human once too, you know. I have so many urges, mostly violent, but with you, the violence fades. How could I show you what I looked like? I'm not normal."

"That's what I love, Holly." He scoots closer, pushing my hair behind my ear. "When I found out DNA experiments existed—"

"Your friends?" I cut him off. "Creed and Rhett?"

He smirks, bopping my nose with his finger. "How long have you been stalking me?"

"All day every day," I admit. "I didn't want to leave you without protection, especially when your dad came back."

His happiness fades and the rare bitter scent of his rage returns.

I don't like it.

I want his happiness back.

"Yeah, you saw that? That makes sense. I knew I felt someone around."

"I'm always around, Fitz. You'll never be alone again." I place my hand over his and I'm not sure what caused it but he breaks.

A soft sob breaks free from him, and he sits up, turning away from me. Not wanting him to hide from me, I follow him, folding my wings out in front of him. I spin him around by his shoulders, hating to see the tears fighting not to fall from his lash line.

My sensitive, Doe Eyes.

The gold in his eyes seems to glow, somehow brighter than ever before.

"What is it, Fitz? You can talk to me."

"You said I won't ever have to be alone again," he answers, looking away from me. "I've always been alone."

Hate is a mistress fueling my need to kill anyone who has ever made my Fitz feel like this.

"You promise?" he asks, scooting closer. "You promise that I'm your mate? You can't leave me? You'll love me, always. No matter what. Because I have never been in love with anyone before, and I'm in love with you. I survived once with everything ripped away from me but if you leave...I wouldn't want to survive in this world again."

I hiss at the thought of us ever being a part. "Not even death could keep me away. I've crossed Purgatory for you once and I will always do it again if it means I get to be by your side. I am yours until the universe ends. My phantom will be your shadow for all eternity. You'll never be alone again. In life or death. My bones ache to be in your gravity because you are the only thing that can keep me grounded."

"I've never had that before."

"I know." I press my forehead against his. "But you are the roots in my heart. You are the part of me that is human. You are my sixth DNA."

He comes in slow, testing to see if I want a kiss.

There will never be a time when I don't.

CHAPTER SIXTEEN

FITZ

I'm wildly in love with a monster DNA experiment and she's better than any dream.

I'm in the kitchen, dancing on my feet to no music. I've never felt lighter or happier in my entire life. I knew dreams existed, I did, but they don't for me. I had made peace with that.

Then, Holly happened.

I finally have my dream.

I plop the pan on the stove, pour a dash of olive oil in there, and turn the knob to get the metal hot. The coffee beeps signaling that it is done.

"Perfect. Perfect," I say to myself when I flip the bacon.

"You are far from a morning person. I should know. I've watched you wake up in the grouchiest of moods."

I crack an egg on the side of the pan and give her a wink before the egg begins to sizzle. "I think all I needed was a reason to start getting up in the mornings, Wildflower." I put the lid on the pan to cover the egg, so it cooks perfectly.

She's standing on the side of the island, arms crossed as if she's cold. I groan when I see her in my shirt. All of that silky lavender skin is bright against the stark black of the Snapdragons Garage shirt she has on. It falls to her knees and the sleeves fall off her shoulders.

"Goddamn. I've never seen that shirt look so fucking good before."

She blushes, her cheeks turning a darker shade of purple. "I love your shirts. They are so cozy, and they smell like you. I can't help myself."

She tugs the collar to her nose and inhales. "Home."

I tug her to me and cup her delicate face in my hands, knowing she's far from fragile. "Home, Wildflower. We're finally home." I kiss her deeply, my hands roaming down her wings. She's cut holes for them in this shirt.

That's fine. I'll buy her all the Snapdragons Garage shirts we have if she wants.

I can't help myself, I get a handful of her ass and squeeze. Memories from last night flood my mind, and I remember grabbing her ass as I slid in to the hilt.

"Fuck, you look so fucking good." I cup the back of her head and pull her into a kiss.

Picking her up, I sit her on the counter. We knock over a few bowls, but I don't care. Our mouths move together as I lift the shirt to her hips.

"No underwear. You filthy fucking girl," I growl, spreading her legs apart so I can see her gorgeous cunt.

She's wet.

I scoot her to the edge of the counter and drop to my knees. Her legs wrap around my neck, and I waste no time diving in. I suck her clit into my mouth, commanding a loud roar from my mate as she tosses her head back. Her fingers roam through my hair, gripping at the roots when I insert two fingers into her dripping wet cunt.

It's the first time I can feel the suckers with my hands. Her tentacles reach out for me, wrapping around my neck like they did yesterday. They tighten around my throat, cutting off my ability to breathe ever so slightly.

I reach down with my free hand and grab my cock, stroking myself while I finger fuck her. The suckers are soft, warm, and wet. Sizes vary between them too; every round edge feels different than the other. It's as if my tongue is getting massaged.

Her cries have me tugging on my cock faster, wanting to join her in bliss when she rips my head back by the roots of my hair.

"Don't you dare come if you want to be a good boy. I don't want you to waste a drop. You need to be inside me when you do."

I groan into her cunt, releasing my grip on my aching cock. Spreading her legs, I finger fuck her faster while sucking on her clit harder.

"Fitz. Oh, fuck. Oh, God. You're—I'm—" she cries out into the kitchen and the first squirt of her ink spills into my mouth.

She's sweet like blackberries. God, I could spend hours on my knees for her and never get tired of drinking her down.

I rip my mouth away as she continues to pulse, spilling ink everywhere. Gripping my cock, I line myself up and drive inside her as she orgasms. The ink claim on my arm begins to move too, slithering and waving like a snake. All the way down to my cock, the mark moves faster while her orgasm continues.

Wrapping my arms around her, I bring us to the floor and place her on her back.

"Oh, God, Fitz. I can't stop. Oh, I can't stop." She cups her tits roughly, kneading them with more pressure than usual. She plucks her nipples through her shirt, her voice becoming horse with how loud she is screaming.

Ink leaks all around my cock and onto the floor. Her tentacles wrap around my base again, forcing me to ram inside her. Her cries become even louder somehow, another strong intense wave of pleasure draping over her.

"Fuck, Holly. You feel so good. You're clamping around me—" I gasp with how good she feels as she comes. "What's happening? Why do I feel like I can't get deep enough?" I pump into her so hard and fast; she slides along the floor.

I wrap a hand around her shoulder to keep her in place. Her tentacles pull me in with every stroke I give. The sensations are all too much. I curl over her, capturing her lips to swallow her cries.

Another knot is formed at the base of my cock. The next strokes become more difficult. Using all the force I have, I ram into her, locking us together.

I bend down, burying my face in her neck, "Holly. Ah—damn it—" I groan into her ear as I come. "You feel so fucking good. You're doing such a good job taking me right now. You're being such a good girl." I moan as another orgasm is pulled from my body. "You're taking every fucking drop, Wildflower. I wish you could see how beautiful you look right now. You're spread so wide. You barely take my thick cock."

She whimpers, rolling her hips up and down. I can see

the edges of the tentacles. They are tight around my cock, and they will not allow me to leave her body. Not that I want to. My favorite place is being inside her.

Her orgasms become slower and further in between as she continues to make me come ever so often. I'm not sure how long we lay there locked together, having back-to-back orgasms.

All I know is the eggs are burnt and there's smoke filling the house, but I don't fucking care.

I collapse when the tentacles finally let me go. "I don't know what came over me seeing you in my shirt but holy fuck, I can't wait to do that again."

She snickers, then yawns. "I'm exhausted. I think...I think that might have been me needing your–"

"–Come?" I puff out my chest, a little too proud at that moment.

"Yes. Would you be mad if I went back to bed?" She almost seems drugged. She's slurring her words and unable to keep her eyes open.

She can't wait for me to answer. Holly falls asleep on the kitchen floor. This hasn't happened before, but I'm going to go out on a limb here and think that maybe this is part of the pregnancy process for her?

I stand and reach for the burner to turn it off so the pan doesn't catch fire. Bending down, I pick her up in my arms, walking through the ink all over the floor. I don't care. I hope it sinks into the wood and stains.

Climbing the stairs, I hold her head to my chest and place her on the bed.

"Whatever is happening to you, just know I'm here, okay?" I fluff the pillow behind her and kiss her cheek.

I head to the bathroom, snag a cloth, and wet it with warm water. Squeezing the excess out, I hurry back to take care of Holly. I'm not going to let her sleep with ink running down her thighs.

Parting her legs, I clean the marks from her inner thighs. I love how soft and supple the skin is here. It's flawless and a tad shade lighter than the rest of her body.

I reach between her legs and clean her there too. She gasps and one of her tentacles sneaks out, slapping me on the arm.

"Okay, sorry. Didn't mean to overstep." I think the tentacles might have a mind of their own.

Covering her with the blanket, I kiss her forehead. I never want to leave this moment. This place. By her side. I know a lot of people would be mad about what she has done. For most, they would need time to wrap their heads around the situation, but not me.

Why would I be mad when this is exactly what I want? Sure, she fucked me in my sleep but I'll be honest, I can't wait for her to do it again. I look forward to it. Her abilities are so fucking attractive. I would lock myself in this house for her to have her way with me until she decided to allow me outside if that's what she wanted.

If she wants a good boy, I'll be the best fucking boy she has ever had.

She'll never have a reason to leave because I'm going to give her millions of reasons to stay.

My phone vibrates in my pocket. I stand, tiptoeing out of the bedroom, then close the door to not bother her.

Fishing my phone out of my pocket, Rhett's name flashes across the screen.

"Hey, man. Is it time?" I take the steps downstairs slowly so as to not make a lot of noise. "Is Mickey in labor?"

"No. These kids are stressing me out and they aren't even here yet. She's sleeping right now but I can't leave her side. I'm calling to ask for a favor."

"Anything." The scent of burnt eggs has me crinkling my nose and smoke hangs thick in the air. I need to crack a window.

Rhett is talking but I'm not listening because I walk into the kitchen and see the mess Holly and I made with ink smeared on the countertop. It drips onto the floor. The spot in front of the oven is where most of the mess is. I also need to get cleaned up since it's all over me but I'm not ready to rinse Holly's scent away just yet.

"Fitz, did you hear me?"

I snap out of my appreciative gaze. "What? No. Sorry, man. I got distracted." I crack the window above the sink to air out some of the smoke. I'm able to see Holly's house next door and see two figures walk around her car.

They remind me of the two men I came across on the road leaving urgent care. I keep an eye on them while listening to Rhett.

"Wait, do you have a mate?" he asks.

I grin. "I do. She's amazing. I'm not sure how I pulled myself out of the dream but I did. I have everything I've ever wanted."

"I can't wait to meet her, Fitz. No one else deserves love more than you. I'm happy for you. Tell me about her?"

"Thanks, man. I appreciate it. She reminds me of Creed and you. She's wild like Creed but has a clearer head and is able to think things through, like you. Holly is beautiful. She has lavender skin, horns, wings, a siren voice, and the ability to invade my dreams because she's part succubus. She's strong, Rhett, and protective. I love her. It's crazy but–"

"–It isn't crazy. That is how it is supposed to be with fated mates. Love is immediate. I really am happy for you, Fitz. You've taken care of everyone else for so long. I've always wanted this for you. For someone to take care of you."

I clear my throat, not wanting to get too emotional. "Thanks, Rhett. That means a lot. "Okay, what did you need me to do before you make me emotional?" I chuckle, wiping under my eye.

I can't help it. I wear my heart on my sleeves.

"I need you to go to the shop for me. Remember not to work. I really need you to bring me the order book. I have a few phone calls I need to make."

"I can do it, Rhett. Don't sweat it. I'll call them."

"No, please." He drops his voice to a whisper. "If I don't find something else to do besides hover over Mickey, she might kill me."

Laughter barks out of me as I pour coffee into a thermos, spilling a little on the counter.

Eh, I'm not worried about it. It can be added to the mess for all I care.

"No, problem. Give me around an hour?" Peeking out the window again, the two men are still in her driveway, talking to one another with animated hands.

They are arguing.

"That's fine. Thanks, man. I appreciate it."

"Sure," I check out of the conversation, watching these two people at Holly's house. I don't want to wake her but I'm worried. "I'll call you later." I hang up the phone, tossing it on the counter.

"People are wild. Fucking around on someone's property. You've got to be kidding me," I grumble under my breath.

My phone vibrates on the table, and it is Rhett calling me again, but I ignore it. I need to see what these two men are up to. When my phone stops ringing, it starts again, and this time it's my sister's name on the screen.

No way in hell am I ignoring that.

I answer it as I walk into the living room. "Hey, Sis. How is my nephew?"

"I'm fine, Uncle Fitz. Really." Elijah's deep voice takes me by surprise.

"Hey, Eli. It's good to hear your voice. Are you feeling okay?" I open the lid to the ottoman, snagging my gun, and tucking it in my waistband.

"I feel a lot better. Tired. Mom said we are coming to live with you because of Grandpa?"

"Yeah, you guys are coming to live with me. I know that messes up your classes, but we will figure it out."

"Actually, the rest of the year I'm doing classes online. The school has been really great about the surgery and they are working with me. I can't wait to come live with you."

I'm excited too. I've missed out on his life since moving away. I'm a little nervous to introduce him to my friends and Holly. Hopefully, it rains so that the spell Caden and his witch friend cast works on them.

What if they have mates too?

"I'm excited too, Eli. You're going to have to catch me up on your life when you get here. When will you two be on your way?" I march to the kitchen window again, peeking out to see them walking around her house now.

"A few days. They said it could take up to a week for me to be discharged. I spiked a fever last night, so they are keeping an eye on me."

"Do you still have a fever?" I'm worried. He has never been sick like this before.

"No. I'm fine. I got up and walked around. I feel fine, but they won't let me leave yet. I'm bored. I just want to come see you."

"Focus on getting better and you'll be here before you know it. Maybe I can get you a part-time job at the shop? I know it isn't much but—"

"—That would be awesome! I'd love to work with you, Uncle Fitz. I've missed you, you know. It isn't the same without you."

I smile, my heart twisting with how much I miss him. "I couldn't agree more. We're all better when we are together. Stronger too."

"Grandpa is serious this time?" His voice becomes hard with anger. "I won't let him touch Mom."

"I won't either. I won't let him get to you either."

"The doctor just walked in. I have to go. I'll call you later, okay? I love you."

I'm the luckiest fucking guy on this planet. Not many men his age are so in tune with their emotions. I always told him growing up that it's okay for men to show how they feel. It's healthier to express our feelings so we don't bottle them up and become bitter, angry, and resentful.

"I love you too, Kiddo. Text me what the doc says."

"Will do."

He hangs up the phone, and I blow out a stressful breath, tucking my phone into my pocket. I'm happy Heather and

Elijah aren't here right now. I don't want them to see what's going on or why I have a gun tucked in the back of my waistband.

Snagging my baseball cap from the hook, I put it on backward, unlock the door, and step outside.

It's a warmer day than usual. It's why Rhett, Mickey, and Creed were swimming yesterday. I think it's the last warm weather front we will have until the snow comes because the nights are turning frigid.

I step out from the porch, leaning against the beam and crossing my arms. The two men are pacing next to her car, talking to each other but I can't tell what they are saying.

Stepping onto my front lawn, I make myself known. "Hey, there. How are you doing?"

They turn to look at me and both have bright yellow eyes. Their cheeks have feathers, and they try to hide themselves by keeping their heads down.

I can see them.

"We need to know where the girl is who lives here."

I can't tell which one speaks but it doesn't matter. "I don't know. I haven't seen her."

"You haven't seen her? She lives next door," he sneers, taking a step forward.

His friend stops him from getting closer by grabbing his shoulder.

"Just because she is my neighbor doesn't mean anything. I'm barely home as it is. Maybe I can leave her a message for you."

"I think you're lying. You reek of the scent we found in the woods."

I have no idea what they are talking about, but I do feel

caught. I forgot about her scent. Of course they can smell her.

"That was our van. I want to know where the fuck the money is."

Holly hasn't told me the entire truth about how she got here. I don't know anything about the van or money.

"I'm sorry, fellas. I have no clue about the van or money. I'll let her know your concerns though."

"How about you stop the bullshit? Either you give her to us or I'm going to kill you and burn everything in this house and your house down." Smoke drifts from his nose, reminding me of Creed.

He's part dragon. I wonder if this guy is too.

"There's no need for the hostility guys. I'm only trying to help you."

In a blur, they are both standing in front of me.

Oh, shit.

They are part vampire like Creed and Rhett. If I'm not careful, I don't stand a fucking chance. I can't hide the slight fear stuttering in my heart. I'm fucking human. Anyone who says they wouldn't be scared in this situation is a fucking liar. Unless they have the ability to match these two standing in front of me.

"I smell her on you. Did she tell you what she did to our mate?"

My heart falls out of my chest when I hear those words. I continue to play stupid. "I don't know what you're talking about guys. I really don't. I don't know who you are looking for."

He pulls down his hood and snakes his hand out so fast, I don't have time to defend myself. His nails lengthen, the sharp points threatening to sink into my jugular. I'm afraid to swallow. His claws might rip my skin open with a simple movement.

"I smell her all over you. Not only do you know her, you're claimed. She's your mate."

"A mate for a mate, Rolo?" The other guy finally speaks up. "I think that's fair."

"You know what? I think you're right. And then, I'm going to take your mate," he snarls in my face. "After I've killed you. And I'm going to torture her for what she did."

My eyes narrow at him. "Good luck with that. She is going to chew you up and spit you out."

He growls, picks me up by my throat, and then throws me across my lawn. My back slams against the tree in my yard. Pain ripples down my spine and I grunt when I hit the ground.

The gun falls from my waistband and onto the grass behind me. I stay where I am so I can at least have access to a weapon. I'm not sure if bullets will kill them but I have to try to slow them down.

I pat the ground behind me, searching for the Glock. Every second feels like a century. They use their advanced speed and right as I wrap my fingers around the barrel, lift the gun, pull the hammer back, and aim, glass shatters from up above me.

Pieces fall onto my head, a larger shard skewing my forearm.

"Fuck!" I shout, having to drop my weapon.

Holly lands in front of me, wings spread like a guardian angel. Her wingspan is impressive. Fully stretched wide, they must be the largest wings I have ever seen. Her feathers shine in the rare light beaming from the sky.

"You made a mistake threatening my mate," Holly hisses.

"We will leave you alone if you give us the money you stole from us."

"You mean the money you stole first?" Holly asks, morphing into the human I met her as. "Does this help you have this conversation?"

I still see her beast just like I did before, only it's more like a shadow. I understand now. She was trying to disguise herself around me. I wasn't losing my mind. I was seeing her for her only I didn't know it at the time.

"I can take her form because I killed her. I will forever be able to take her form."

Both men are stunned, sadness hueing their violent eyes as they stare at her.

"She was kind," Holly says. "She was so sweet complimenting me, but I had just crawled out of a fucking grave and all I had was my mate's scent pulling me here. I had to get to him, and she got in my way. I killed her. I took your money. And I don't plan on giving it back. How did you find me, anyway?"

"GPS tracker on the van, you stupid bitch."

I clamp my teeth together when I yank the piece of glass out of my arm. Blood flows freely, dripping onto the grass. I have to support my wrist with my uninjured arm as I lift the gun, aiming it at one of the men.

I pull the trigger, a loud crack echoing for miles. Jake will be called soon. There's no mistaking what that was. The bullet slams into his chest, right where his heart is, and while it doesn't kill him, it surprises him.

"No one calls her a stupid bitch." I struggle to stand,

lifting the gun again.

Holly's voice changes, a soothing tone that must be her siren voice. It doesn't work on me but the two men relax, staring at her as if they are in a trance. She changes into her normal form, and I like it so much more than her disguise.

I knew there was something special about her when I met her.

"What are you doing?" I question with a bit of impatience. "Kill them."

"I need answers only they can give. I'm sorry for not telling you about this." Regret is etched into her face as her brows tense before she looks away from me to our company. "I notice you're DNA experiments. Where did you come from? I was sure I was the only one?"

"Another creature killed everyone and set the prisoners free."

"He's talking about Creed," I inform her. "That's what Creed did."

"So you didn't come from the facility I did? Did you travel to that campsite in the woods?"

The two new DNA experiments nod.

It dawns on me that there wasn't one testing facility but two.

"What did your scientists look like?"

"One had glasses, another had one eye, the other–"

Holly lifts her hand to silence them, and they listen.

"That's not possible. I had the same scientists. They couldn't have been in two places at once," she talks to herself more than she talks to me.

"Unless the scientists rotated, Wildflower. It's possible."

"I think I was the only one from where they kept me. I

never heard anyone else. What if I'm wrong and they are still trapped? What if there are more like me?"

"Then we will go check." I cover the wound on my arm with my hand to stop the bleeding. "But we need to deal with them." I point to the two men who are very subservient to her siren voice. "And your van. We need a new license plate. I didn't realize you were a criminal," I smirk. "Kind of hot."

She smirks at me before pulling her wings back until they are nearly flat, then flaps them to create wind. Holly aims her head down, horns straight, and she jets through the air, stabbing her horns through one threat. She flies higher, ripping the body from her horns and detaching his head from his body.

Blood rains from the sky before she drops the carcass and swoops down, snagging the other by her talons. He screams from her tight hold on his shoulders and as he is screaming, she twists his head off too. His cries for help become lifeless gurgles as she finally rips his head from his shoulders.

Holly lands, dropping the head next to his body, and wipes her hands on my shirt she's wearing. Her feathers are covered in blood.

"No one threatens my mate." She kicks their dead bodies and then walks towards me.

I should be terrified.

I'm not. I'm ready to fuck her on top of their bodies if she wants.

When she's close enough, I snag her by the back of the neck and haul her in for a kiss.

"Oh, you have got to be kidding me."

The unknown voice has us stopping mid-kiss. Holly spins

around to protect me and I look over the top of her head to see a skeleton figure standing next to the bodies.

"Lorcan?" Holly asks in surprise and disbelief.

Lorcan. I know that name. Rhett and Creed told me about him and The Four Horsemen. Lorcan is a Void, a reaper who works for Death.

"Girl, what the fuck is this? You escape and cause chaos? You've always kept me busy."

Holly squeals, running to give him a big hug, and I wish a bullet could kill him. I don't like him touching what's mine.

"You're leaving a mess just like Creed and Rhett. I'm here to take their souls but The Four Horsemen will come for answers. You know you just can't go around killing people." Lorcan places his hands on his hips. "I'm going to have to ask my boss for a raise. You monster DNA experiments keep me busy. Do you think it's easy to have this job? I like to relax too, you know. I've got to go. We will get together soon." He snaps his fingers, disappearing with the bodies, and leaving us alone.

A few seconds of silence ticks by to soak in what just happened.

I finally speak. "So you killed a woman, stole her van, and the money they robbed from a bank?"

"Yes."

"And you bought this house with that money?"

"Some of it. Nothing is in the house. It isn't even furnished. I only bought it to be close to you."

"God, you are fucking crazy, and I love it," I growl, pulling her into another kiss. "Before I was interrupted, I was on my way to the shop for Rhett. I'm going to take your van and make sure there's no mistake it's yours and not the woman you killed. I know you're tired. Why don't you stay and nap? I'll be back."

"I'll come with you. I don't feel okay leaving you alone. Keys are under the pot on the porch to the van."

"It's probably best if we shower first. We both have blood all over us."

Her eyes sparkle with mischief, and she launches herself in the air, slipping into the window she broke.

"Cheater!" I shout after her, running through the door and then up the steps.

I should be more bothered by what happened. I've learned one thing in all the time I've been on my own.

Evil deserves to die, and I refuse to shed one tear over their deaths.

CHAPTER SEVENTEEN

HOLLY

We stop in front of one of the silver garage doors. "What are we doing here again?" Fitz puts the Van in park and opens the driver's side door. I grab his arm, staring at him as if he is delusional for leaving my side. "Where are you going?'

"I have to open the garage door to get the van inside. I'll be right back." His hand roams across my cheek, then his fingers run through my hair. My eyes flutter closed from how good his touch feels. His lips meet mine in an unexpected kiss. When he dares to move away from me, he presses his orehead against mine. "Like I'd ever be able to stay away from you, Wildflower. I have to protect you, though. It's only a matter of time before the authorities find this van and connect you to a murder. And then add a robbery on top of that."

"I didn't rob the bank. I only stole the money they stole."

"Doesn't matter. You're the one they will pin the crime on."

"I'll kill the cops who try to arrest me then," I say with a 'duh' tone.

He laughs, leaning away from me to grab the handle of the door. "You can't kill everyone, Holly."

"Why not? I kill them if they threaten me or you. I would think that's fair."

"The way you think is very similar to Creed. I bet you and him will get along."

"Does he also kill?"

"More than you know," Fitz grumbles.

"Smart. Nothing can be pinned on me if everyone who comes after me is dead. It makes sense."

"I know it does." He pats my leg in defeat. "I'll bury all the bodies."

"You'd do that for me?" I light up like Christmas day.

"I'd do anything for you. Including scrubbing the VIN off the van and figuring out how to slap a new license plate on it. I'll need to do a few other things too. It could use a different paint job. That would throw them off the tracks."

"Aw, but I like the yellow."

"I know you do. It has to be done, though. Okay? Unless we just want to sell it for parts and keep it in the back here."

I gasp in horror. "It's a classic. You can't...you can't do that!" My hand is on my chest. My heart is racing. He can't be serious. "Please, don't do that. Change the color but can you keep some of the yellow? Somewhere?"

"I'll do anything for you if you don't know that by now."

My heart melts, wondering how the hell I got so lucky with such an open-minded mate. "Give me your injured arm, Doe Eyes."

"I'm fine."

"Don't make me make you. Be a good boy and give it to me."

His nostrils flare, lust swirling in his light brown eyes. He stretches out his injured arm that he refused to let me heal in the shower. I won't allow him to be scarred because of me.

I unwrap the blood-stained bandage, hating to see such a deep wound on my mate. Bringing his arm closer to my mouth, I lick the wound, tasting the metallic iron and the spices that make Fitz smell like Fitz.

My saliva heals the cut. The skin meshes together. All that's left is smooth, freckled skin.

I love those freckles.

He sticks his tongue out at me and a buzz of pleasure shoots down my spine when I see it's still black.

No other woman would be able to stake her claim like that.

"You look so proud of yourself." He winks at me, opening the door, and something about that wink with that baseball cap turned backward has me wanting more than a kiss.

"Oh, I am."

He holds the door, eyeing me up and down before groaning. "You can't keep doing this to me. And you're wearing my damn shirt. I'm a goner."

"I only want to wear your shirts. They smell like you."

"Then my shirts are all yours. Especially if you don't wear anything underneath."

"Why would I do that? I need to be able to fuck you anytime I want."

He slams the door, lacing his fingers behind his head, stressed. I grin, loving how much I drive him crazy.

Fitz's back muscles flex under his tight shirt as he lifts

the garage door. His biceps bulge, stretching the T-shirt's sleeves hugging his arms.

Fuck.

My mate is delicious.

Climbing into the car again, he eases the van inside. "Miss me?"

"Even when you're near me."

He takes my hand, brings it to his mouth, and kisses my knuckles. "Why don't you go lie down? I know you're tired. I can see it. Do you feel okay?"

"I'm exhausted. I don't know why."

"There's a bedroom in the back. I'll tuck you in and you can nap while I work on the van."

I yawn, realizing how exhausted I am. I only woke up from my slumber because I sensed Fitz was in trouble. I think it's a way my body completes the pregnancy. I'm not sure. I've never gone through this before.

"Yeah, I'll take you up on that. Unless you need my help?"

"No way would I ever let these beautiful purple hands get oil on them. That's my job, Wildflower. Don't get out of the van," he warns, stepping out only to walk around the front to open my door.

He stretches out his hand. "Come on. Let's get you to bed."

When I stand, I sway, another wave of pure exhaustion hitting me as if I'm drugged.

"Woah, I got you, okay?" He swings me into his arms, carrying me across the floor.

My head nestles on his chest, and I allow my eyes to close. His heartbeat is comforting. I want to live and die in these arms.

As he walks, I smile with confidence because there is still a hint of me marking my territory. I put my ink everywhere. In the oil and grease containers. I've swiped it on all the walls, under desks and chairs, the equipment, the bathrooms, and the fence lining their property.

His friends will smell me forever and something about that has me giddy.

The scent isn't as strong as I'd like it to be but that's okay. Fitz is mine. As long as he smells like me, it's fine. I'm happy.

He opens the office door, revealing a long stretch of hallway with bright lighting. There are a few pictures on the wall and I'm able to peek at them as we walk by. A human version of his friend Rhett is in one photo, and I have to say, being a monster suits him better. He has long blonde hair and a big award-winning smile while standing next to Fitz in front of another shop.

There's a story there that I want to know about.

When we get to the backroom, there's a couch lining the wall and a full-size bed on the other side. A few boxes are stacked to the side but other than that, it's clean. It doesn't smell like Fitz.

Luckily, I have his shirt on so I'll be able to fall asleep.

He yanks the covers back and lies me down, covering me up and tucking me in just like he said he would.

"Sleep well, Wildflower. I'll wake you when it's time to go, okay?" He continues to brush my hair with his fingers.

"Mmhmm," I hum, already falling asleep when my head hits the pillow.

I barely feel the phantom of his kiss or hear the hinges of the door squeak when Fitz leaves.

The vision I saw of four men confronting my mate

returns, leaving me restless and worried. Predictions don't always have to come to fruition. The future can change. One vision doesn't determine his death.

I turn to my side more anxious now.

He'll be okay. I'm here. As long as I'm here, he will be safe. I'm worrying for nothing.

I take a few deep breaths, relaxing in the darkness of the room. They must have blackout curtains in here because I can't see my fingers, and I'm wiggling them in front of my face.

My eyes finally close and exhaustion takes me under.

I don't know how long I'm asleep for but a loud gunshot yanks me from my sleep, stealing all the air from my lungs.

Blood is in the air.

And some of it belongs to Fitz.

CHAPTER EIGHTEEN

FITZ

(*While Holly is napping*)

Leaving her in the bedroom alone aches more than I thought it would. I want nothing more than to slide in next to her, wrap my arms around her, pull her close, and nestle my face in the silk of her wings.

I stop at the desk, staring at the mess Rhett left. Papers are scattered everywhere. I can't even see the keyboard to the computer.

"Wild, Rhett. You know better," I tsk, gathering the papers to look for the order book he needed. "I can't find shit in this mess. This is why I need to oversee the desk. How does he work like this?" I grumble, finally finding the book.

It's under a stack of papers under the damn keyboard. "How do you manage this, Rhett? No, we need to hire someone to manage the desk. This is not okay." He scratched 'order book' on the front of the cover with his talons.

A sticker would have worked. A marker.

But no, he had to use his talons.

I don't flip through the book or become nosey. I trust Rhett with what he has to do for the business. I toss the book in the driver's seat of the van and begin looking for all the places the VIN is. I'll need to do a VIN clone. I'll worry about the title and registration later.

Luckily, I know a guy, but I want to do as much as I can with everything I have here at the shop.

Obviously, the primary place for the VIN is the lower left corner of the windshield but there are a few other locations where it could be too. Engine bay, driver's door frame, trunk floor, and a few other places. It also depends on the make and model and since I don't know this year of Volkswagen van very well, I'm just going to look in every single nook and cranny.

I'm going to start with the easiest place. All I need to do is heat-up the VIN sticker and use the tip of a razor blade to peel it back.

"Where is that damn hair dryer?" I mumble to myself.

It's right in front of my face.

Like everything is when I'm fucking looking for it.

I get to work, heating the sticker while peeling it back with a razor blade. I'm not sure how long it takes. I'm not keeping track of time, but a shadow catches my attention out of my peripheral vision.

Turning off the loud hum of the dryer, I look up, rolling my damn eyes when I see no other than my mom and dad standing in the entryway of the garage door.

"You two are either the most persistent people or the stupidest. You know," I shake my finger at them, setting down the dryer. "I'm going to go with stupidest."

"Is that how you speak to your mother now?" She feigns being emotionally hurt.

"Please, Mom. You and I both know you aren't capable of actual feelings. No need to pretend."

"Don't speak to your mother that way," Dad harrumphs, reaching for the garage door to close it.

"You stopped being my parents the moment you beat me to near death. You stopped being my mom when you did nothing but allow Dad's abuse. You stopped being my parents when you threatened Heather at sixteen. You aren't my parents and even if I did have any love for you, I wouldn't respect you. Just like I don't respect you now. What the hell are you doing here? I don't think I could get any more clear about the business. I'm not fucking interested."

"Fitsgerald, is that a tattoo? How dare you ruin your body—"

"—We aren't talking about me. What do you want?"

"This is your last chance to come work for the company," my dad threatens. "We need you there. I know you have a trust fund. We need that money for the business."

"Not my problem you don't know how to manage your fortune. Your problem isn't my problem."

"Remember you have to, or I will go after your sister."

I toss my head back and laugh. "No, you won't. You don't know where she is. Do you really think I was stupid enough to leave her without knowing she would be safe from you? You underestimate me." I wipe my hands out of habit on a stained rag. "You always have, and I've always proved you wrong."

"Wallsworth Candy won't fail because of you."

"No, it failed because of you. You. Not me. I wasn't part

of this. You two—" I point at them, "are a disease. Do you hear me? You're a fucking waste of space. The more you stand in front of me, the more I hate you. You are so selfish. You are incapable of seeing the problem you caused and want to point fingers at everyone else. You are incapable of accepting your mistakes. You want others to fix them. You're willing to force me to do something I don't want to do. You went as far as pulling Heather and Elijah into this." I take a step back so I'm close to a few items that can be used as a weapon.

I don't have my gun on me. I left it at home.

I thought the threat of violence was over for the day after thing one and two circled like vultures around Holly's house.

"Get out before I call the cops."

"You won't be calling anyone anymore."

To my surprise, Dad pulls a gun on me, aiming it directly at my chest.

"Really? You're going to shoot me? How would you get the trust fund then, Dad? If I die, all my money goes to Heather and Elijah. That's how I have it set up."

"I'll kill them too."

"You're a monster," I sneer.

"No, they are monsters." He swings the gun from left to right.

Three other shadows flank me. I turn my head from one side to the other, confused about how my dad knows anything about monster DNA experiments.

All of them have the skin of a snake and reptilian eyes. They remind me of Rhett.

"What the fuck is going on?" I do my best to keep calm.

My heart is racing. The air is thick with the promise of war and looking at the five-to-one odds, I'm a goner.

My mom won't do anything to me. She is all bark and no bite, but my dad and his monster cronies? I'm done for. I can't fight for my life when the fight is already over before it even begins.

I can't let him know I know about the DNA experiments. He'd latch onto that bit of information and want to know who my friends are. I can't do that to Rhett or Creed. And I will die before I ever say Holly's name to this man.

My family's money issues start clicking in my head. All the details start forming a picture. All the puzzle pieces slide together with no issue. Wallsworth Candy is having money issues because they funded the monster DNA experiments.

It's my family that tortured the ones I love.

The information has my head spinning. Guilt is a burden weighing on my heart, twisting my stomach into knots.

Dad strolls up to me with confidence, his pristine suit unwrinkled. For a guy complaining about money, he doesn't seem to mind paying for brand-name clothes.

He stops in front of me, the barrel of the gun touching the middle of my chest.

"Either you work for me, or I'll let these monsters have their way with you. Aren't they wonderful? So unique, so special. They will make me millions when we can get the testing correct."

Rage has my fingers curling into my palms. My teeth tighten together until they hurt. Anger flushes my entire body with heat.

I can't stop myself. It's as if I'm having an out-of-body experience because I'm not a violent guy. I consider myself a lover, not a fighter.

I'll always choose to die fighting for who has never left me feeling lonely.

I wrap my hand around the gun, my father's clammy hand dampening my skin. We struggle for dominance, yanking and pulling on the gun. His elbow hits me in my nose, blood pouring from my nostrils and down my lips.

One of his monster bodyguards steps forward but Dad stops them.

"Don't. This is between me and my son."

"I am not your son," I growl, slamming my steel-toed boot down on his Italian-leather covered feet.

He shouts from the pain and yet it isn't enough for him to let go of the weapon.

Something sharp and quick snaps in the air, slicing the back of my knees. A growl echoes in the shop's chamber, and a long tail riddled with spikes drags across the floor. It scrapes deep divots into the concrete. The monster ignored the order from my father, and he is staring at me with the intent to kill.

Every single tooth he shows is sharp and pointed. He's ready to tear me limb from limb.

I drop to my knees from the pain. Blood drips down my legs, soaking my jeans. Even with the agony, I refuse to let go of the gun. Nothing will stop me except death.

"Stop doing this to yourself, Fitz. Stop fighting me."

"Listen to your father, Fitz!" Mom yells.

It's my turn. I slam my elbow against his groin and that causes him to crumble. Rearing my head back, I smash it against his nose. The bone crushes beneath my forehead. His blood spatters against my face. My ears ring and a violent electric pain zaps through my skull.

I'm dizzy. My vision is out of focus. I try to shake it off, kicking my dad in the stomach when the gun goes off.

If I thought my ears were ringing before, it's nothing compared to now. Even the monsters cover their ears. I groan, my hold weakening on the gun.

I refuse to relent.

The glass window that allows us to see into the office shatters. Holly flies through the space, her eyes glowing yellow, and her fangs drop to show her stance.

She's coming to save me.

Isn't that wild? I'm the damsel in distress and I don't mind one fucking bit.

Her tail wraps around one monster's neck, snapping it like a twig. He drops to the ground. His limp body is dead weight and his head smacks against the ground. The beasts' lifeless reptilian eyes view me in death.

Holly roars, ramming her horns through the skull of another. She yanks her head, the horns tearing through bone. Brain matter and blood fly through the air, landing on the ground next to me.

She's so damn sexy when she is protecting me. I'll need to put myself in these positions more often.

It leaves one beast left and my dad.

"You're fucking sick." I finally rip the gun away from him, aiming it at his chest, gasping for breath from our fight. My head is killing me. Warmth drips from my left ear and I wipe it away. Glancing down, I rub the liquid between my fingers.

Blood.

Holly screeches, her wings spread out in fury, and her talons rip through the last creature's eyes. She claws at his face, ripping it to shreds until it is unrecognized.

Black blood gurgles and sprays from his face. Grabbing his head with her hands, she twists it, tossing his body next to the others. She marches over to my mom next, drenched in the enemy's blood. Her blue hair is red, and the beautiful white of her feathers is splattered with it too.

There's never been a prettier sight.

Mom is lying on the ground, hands over her stomach. When the gun went off, she must have been shot.

"Do you even care that your mother is dying?" The man who used to be my father shouts at me, spit flying every-where.

"No. I stopped caring about the two of you a long time ago."

"She's already dead," Holly hisses, sauntering over to my side.

There's a small pain rippling through my heart. She was my mom. There will always be a part of me that will wish things were different.

"Do you care she's dead?"

His eyes swim with tears. "Of course. She was my part-ner. I loved her. And you took her from me!" He reaches for me, and I cock the gun.

"How many other facilities are there? How many?" I yell, shoving the gun against his forehead.

A serpentine grin spreads across his evil face. "So many I've lost count."

I don't think. I don't hesitate.

I pull the trigger.

His head jerks back, a river of blood rolling down the bridge of his broken nose.

And he falls.

I'm still trying to wrap my mind around what just happened as I look around. Blood is everywhere. There are five dead bodies. I'm sure the cops will be here soon.

"Are you okay?" Holly checks me all over for any wounds, snarling when she sees the cuts on the back of my legs. Her tongue licks the wounds, and they begin to heal.

"Oh, am I interrupting?" Lorcan stands in the middle of the massacre. He rubs his temples. "You two are keeping me busy and stressing me out. Come on. How dare you have a party without me? I thought we were friends. This is rude. You're rude." He points his fingers at us. "I'll be back for next time."

He snaps his fingers again, taking the bodies with him and leaving us to clean up our mess.

I stumble backward, the van catching me before I fall over. "I killed my dad."

"I can go to Purgatory to see if he is there and kill him again."

I tug Holly to me; uncaring how dirty we are with blood. "You'd do that? How would you even get there?"

"Lorcan is a friend. I know him from when I was in Purgatory. I'm sure I can hitch a ride. I'll find both of your parents and kill their souls, so they no longer exist in this universe."

"Would that take me and my sister from existence?" I wonder.

The wind is sucked from her sails. "I'm not willing to risk that."

"I love you Wild." I hold her close to me, needing her touch, her scent, and the way she holds me as if she never wants to let me go.

Like I'll never be alone again.

"I love you too, Doe Eyes."

She's my Wild.

EPILOGUE

HOLLY

The Four Horsemen are here, and they are bigger than I remember. Their wings are bigger than mine, and they have oddly stitched skin with bulging muscles. "Did your father say how many facilities there were?" Death asks, picking Storm up by his shirt collar to set him on the ground because the little feral animal is climbing all over him.

"No," Fitz answers. "He just said there were plenty." He stressfully runs his fingers through his hair. "I shouldn't have killed him. I should have talked to him more."

"Don't worry about it." Death sets Storm down again. "I can find his soul in Purgatory. I can get him to talk unless he is already in Hell. Either way, I can talk to him. We will find out where all these facilities are."

"That makes sense because when I met Holly, she said she was the only one at the facility."

"Do you think you could take us there?" Abaddon, the leader of the Hell's Harvesters asks, plucking Storm from Death's back. "Creed, get control of your kid."

"This is him under control. Take it or leave it." Creed taps his nails on the table, clearly bored.

"Demi's still annoyed with you, huh?" Rhett teases him.

"She's nesting. She needs her space."

"Whatever you have to tell yourself, man," Famine states, kicking up his legs on the coffee table in the living room.

"I can take you there. It isn't too far away. I'll be honest, I can't remember the exact spot. You'll have to follow me."

"This is a big problem." Conquest flips his blade over his fingers.

"No shit," War huffs. "There could be more of this fucking guy—" he points to Creed. "Out in the world doing who-knows-what."

"Hopefully killing all the people that annoy them," I mumble, staring at my nails.

Everyone falls silent and my sweet mate taps me on the shoulder.

"They are all looking at you, Wildflower."

I glance up from polishing my talons. "What?"

Creed points to me. "See? Someone who sees logic."

Abaddon stands from the chair. "No one can just kill whoever they want. We have an order for that. Humans can't know about the paranormal world. You need to be more careful. We can't keep cleaning up every mess because they are DNA experiments."

"That's hardly fair," Doe Eyes speaks up for me and others like me. "They aren't the same as a regular paranormal creature—I would think—they have creatures that clash. They are different and how they adjust to the world is different than me, a human, or you, whatever you are? Demons?"

"Close enough." War waves his hand in the air, uncaring.

"He is right, Abaddon."

"Rhett? You've been quiet." Creed leans forward, crossing his arms on the table.

"I'm tired. I have two newborns at home. I don't like leaving Mickey alone with all of the responsibility. Can we speed this up? What's the issue? Death, you find his parents and interrogate them for answers. Any other DNA experiments, we help if we can. It isn't Fitz's fault his parents were so terrible."

Fitz looks down, ashamed. "I should have known," he whispers.

"You should have."

"Creed," Rhett snarls.

"What? He should have."

I sneer at Creed. "I'll rip your tongue from your mouth if you ever speak about my mate like that again. He didn't know. His parents abused him his entire life. You don't know what they did to him and his sister when they were so young. Don't ever think Fitz wouldn't have done something if he had found out about his father spending the family fortune on monster DNA experiments. He is good. Inside and out. He. Is. Good. I'll fucking kill you the next time you imply that he is not." Smoke drifts from Creed's nostrils, his eyes burning with the color of his dragon.

"Okay, let's all calm down," Abaddon tries to interject. "I think the first order of business is going to the facility where you were kept, Holly. Death, you should search for his parents while we do that."

"That sounds like a plan to me," Death agrees.

"Great. That settles it. Tomorrow we will meet again to go over the details. I'm hungry and what I want to eat can't be found in this dimension." He pats his stomach. "Let's roll out, guys."

One by one, The Four Horsemen leave. Creed and I lock eyes, the urge to battle brewing between us.

"Okay, I think you two don't need to stay in the same room. Ever." Rhett shoves Creed out the door. "Fitz, I don't blame you, you know that, right?"

"I blame me," Fitz whispers. "All this time. Everything done to you, that was my family. How could you not be mad at me?"

"Because you aren't them. You never were. You're my best friend and if you need to hear it, then I forgive you."

Fitz's shoulders slump and he wipes away a tear, hugging Rhett so tight, the crocodile beast grunts.

"It's okay, Fitz. It's okay. Their thoughts and actions aren't your fault."

"I'm going to dissolve the company now that they are dead. I'm done with it. I don't want anything to do with it knowing that money was used to..."

I wipe a tear that falls down his cheek and lick it off my finger.

"I do that to Mickey too," Rhett says with a smirk. "I can't get enough."

"Me either."

"And congratulations, by the way." Rhett stops in the doorway. "It couldn't have happened to a better man."

"Congratulations on what?" Fitz sniffles, wiping his cheeks with his shirt sleeves.

"Holly's pregnancy." Rhett shuts the door, leaving us stunned and frozen in the house.

"You're pregnant. You're pregnant!" he shouts, picking me up and spinning me around. "Thank you, thank you, thank you. Holy shit, I'm going to be a dad. When were you going to tell me?" His hand is pressed against my stomach and his bottom lip trembles. "I can't believe it."

"I didn't know. Not yet. I thought maybe, but I wasn't sure."

Fitz kneels on the ground, pressing his cheek against my stomach. "I'm going to be the dad I never had. I promise."

"I know, Doe Eyes. You're already a better man than he ever was."

He glances up at me through dark, wet lashes, the moment ruined when his sister's ringtone blares from his phone.

"I'll call her back."

"Answer it," I demand. "You never know if something happened."

He digs his phone from his pocket and swipes the screen. "Hey, Sis. Oh, you guys are on yourway? You're almost here?"

Thunder booms followed by the heavy sheet of rain.

I don't have to worry about morphing into that woman I killed. Not since they will get caught in the storm.

"See you soon, then." Fitz hangs up the phone, takes my hand, and drags me upstairs.

"Going to bed already?"

"I need to feel you against me, Wildflower."

"I'll never say no to that."

"Oh, and I'm going to plant hollyhocks in the front yard," he says, opening the bedroom door.

"Why? Flowers die." I scrunch my nose in distaste. I would rather him find me someone to kill. Maybe he will warm up to the thought of me killing one of his exes someday.

He wraps his arms around my waist and those dimples show when that charming smile is directed towards me. "They do die but eventually, when the season is perfect–" he twists a strand of my hair around his finger "They come back to life and bloom, just like you did. Just like you'd always do. For me."

"I'd cross the pits of Hell and the unknown of Purgatory for you just to get a glimpse of your face if that's all I was allowed."

He gently closes the bedroom door, kissing me in slow tender motions.

"And then when I'm done with you, we are going to go swimming in the lake."

"Why?" I pout. "Because you need to start thinking about your siren. You have to take care of her needs. Your fins, your scales, they are dry. If I have to take care of you myself by holding you in the lake for your body to heal, then I will."

I tease him. "Well, if you care so much, we should do that now."

He tosses me on the bed and tugs his shirt over his head. "I'm a good man, but I'm not that good of a man."

This life with Fitz is all I have ever wanted.

But I wouldn't have it any other way since life is how it is because of me. He is my second chance at life and if I somehow die again, I'll escape Purgatory for a second time.

Nothing will stand between us. Not life. Not death.

And a love like that?

It's wild.

The End.

ABOUT THE AUTHOR

January Rayne is a paranormal fantasy romance author who lives in Buffalo, NY with her husband, son, two dogs, and two leopard geckos. Buffalo is freezing, but January loves when it snows as it gives her the perfect atmosphere to write a book for you to get lost in.

Scan here for easy access to follow me on social media:

ACKNOWLEDGEMENTS

I hope you enjoyed Holly and Fitz as much as I did! It was a fun and different dynamic to write since this was my first time writing an unhinged FMC. She challenged me and had me question my abilities from time to time, but I refused to let her win.

Thank you to everyone for the amount of patience it took for this book. I was slow writing it, pushed the released date, and struggled to get it done because of burn out. The support and love I received from my family, my teams, and my readers helped give me the motivation to finish this book.

I want to give a special shout out to Tiffani, Carolina, Bryckk, and my husband. There is no way I would have completed this book without you all supporting me, pushing me, and giving me those words of encouragement when my mind was being my enemy. The OCD was working hard to keep me down, but you all kept me standing. I love you guys so much. I don't know what I'd do without you.

Thank you to my alpha readers for once again reading a book quickly because I can't seem to make a deadline. You all rock.

And thank you to my ARC team. I appreciate everyone signing up for this book. I truly hope it didn't disappoint.

I am so lucky to be surrounded by such amazing people who are riding this ride with me.

Y'all are the best. I love you wild.

January